THE LAWYER'S TALE

THE LAWYER'S TALE

C. J. Miller

Copyright © 2002 Clive Hindle

Apart from any fair dealing for the purposes of research or private study, or criticism or review, as permitted under the Copyright, Designs and Patents Act 1988, this publication may only be reproduced, stored or transmitted, in any form or by any means, with the prior permission in writing of the publishers, or in the case of reprographic reproduction in accordance with the terms of licences issued by the Copyright Licensing Agency. Enquiries concerning reproduction outside those terms should be sent to the publishers.

> *Published by*
> **Matador**
> 12 Manor Walk, Coventry Road
> Market Harborough
> Leics LE16 9BP, UK
> Tel: (+44) 1858 468828 / 469898
> Fax: (+44) 1858 431649
> Email: matador@troubador.co.uk
> Web: www.troubador.co.uk/matador

ISBN 1 899293 973

Cover: © Corbis

The publisher makes no representation, express or implied, with regard to the accuracy of the information contained in this book and cannot accept any legal responsibility or liability for any errors or omissions that may be made.

Every effort has been made to trace the holders of copyright materials used in this publication. Should any omissions become apparent, the publishers will be happy to make the necessary arrangements at the first opportunity.

Typesetting: Troubador Publishing Ltd, Market Harborough, UK
Printed and bound by MFP Printing, Manchester, UK

Matador is an imprint of Troubador Publishing Ltd

PART ONE

CHAPTER 1

One thing was certain: a rollercoaster of a career in the law hadn't prepared Jack Lauder for Lorenza Kaliostri. On the face of it the meeting was overdue. Newcastle was a village and the names usually knew each other. Jack was a lawyer with an interesting history; Lorenza, a fiery beauty, born and bred on the banks of the Tyne, despite her assumption of an exotic name, was the wife of a celebrity who had not entirely forgotten his Tyneside roots.

"Who?" Jack asked innocently.

"You're kidding!" Lorenza exclaimed.

Sentenced long ago to exile by the Inland Revenue, the North East's rock music icon and self-styled satanic majesty, Max Kaliostri, had to make his visits home fleetingly, often in secrecy. Lorenza, therefore, came to Jack as a client tired of the long months and years of separation and seemingly bent on adding to the exponentially expanding statistics of the failure of twentieth century, marriage.

Divorce had never been Jack's favourite legal discipline. One of matrimony's most depressing features is the discovery that two people who have pledged their troth to each other throughout eternity haven't made it past the first bus stop. They'd always known they couldn't stand the sight of each other. The proof of that lay in the things they argued over when they broke up. Whose CD player is that? What would a woman want with a bag of tools? My mother gave us that vase. You can have the lounge carpet if I get the dining room.

The dog's mine, he wouldn't stay with you anyway. So you'd put me and the kids on the street just so you can move in your fancy woman?

So, when Jack saw the wasp-waisted brunette staring coolly at him from the other side of his desk and she explained her problem he knew he was in trouble. He tried to tell her he had a colleague who was good at this sort of thing but she wasn't having any. "It's you I want Jack," she said, "I'm told you're the only man with the bottle to take on these New York bastards." Jack blinked. "I'm serious," she said. "He uses Big Apple attorneys. They'll eat you alive if you're not careful."

Now that should have been warning enough. There were others in the North East legal fraternity better suited than Jack to handle a matrimonial case with international implications and he should have wondered why Lorenza had chosen him. For all his worldly wisdom he tended to be too trusting and willing to take others at face value. His professional colleagues saw him as a clever lawyer, particularly in trial situations – he had earned the dual qualification as an advocate – but one who somehow had missed the boat. Lack of ambition and a peculiar self-destructive tendency had not only seen him tread water whilst lesser talents hitched rides on rip tides but, on more than one occasion, had brought him into conflict with his profession's establishment.

So Jack didn't heed the warning of this meeting. Instead he bristled with indignation. Unfortunately, with that sudden rush of ego, he was hooked. So much for Feinstein Gluck Zimmerman Harper! He would sort this team out before lunch.

Satisfied with her impact, Lorenza sat down. Up to this time she'd addressed him standing. Her skirt was short and she was showing a lot of leg as it crept towards the thigh.

They were very shapely legs and Jack was not averse to the odd fantasy. He was also, surprisingly for his 40 years, very single, even eligible. Lorenza was a very sexy woman, about ten years his junior, and the expensive clothes only scantily hid a mine of opportunities. She took out a cigarette. "Do you mind?" she asked. "Unless you've got a line of coke?" She smiled quizzically at his horrified expression. "At Feinstein Gluck they keep it on the desk in a snuff box."

It transpired as she talked that her husband was the prime mover of a rock band called the Devil's Disciple. "Never heard of them," Jack said.

"Jack, you must be out of the ark!" she replied.

"No," Jack said, "can't say the name rings a bell." He listened as Lorenza painted an unsavoury picture of a man corrupted by wealth and licence, who had obviously begun to believe his own propaganda. Max had apparently started to hit the big time over a decade ago but his fame had increased when his music strayed from its heavy metal roots into something deeper and darker called 'black metal'. It was, seemingly, a natural progression. If his wife was to be believed, Max had, from an early age, become fascinated and then obsessed to the point of parody by the more arcane works of Alistair Crowley, then by the Manson cult in America and the series of horrific murders its members had carried out.

Lorenza seemed to be desperate to shock, even to frighten him. He didn't notice at first, thinking it perhaps her style and, anyway, she succeeded in drawing out his mordant sense of humour. "He drinks human blood," she said.

"No doubt suitably screened for all known viruses," Jack quipped cynically.

"He's sacrificed animals on stage!"

"Little ones, of course, in case they fight back," he responded.

Humour apart, the musician seemed deranged. Lorenza confided that he was secretly offering a large sum for someone to commit ritual suicide during one of his acts and, in case that wasn't enough, Max was even reputed, in one of his private magical rites, to have raised Pan or even Dionysus!

"Even Dionysus!" Jack exclaimed. "Fancy that!"

Lorenza didn't even soften the image by protesting that Max's bizarre behaviour was just an act and, if anything, she fostered the impression that the musician had succeeded in finding another level of existence in which angelic and demonic entities, supposedly the creation of human myth and imagination, were corporeal. She warmed to her theme and got into the tale of dirty doings in the rock world. It turned out that her real grouse was that hubby was not playing fair. He'd been knocking off every groupie he could get his hands on, usually to the accompaniment of some satanic rite or other to cloak his licentiousness with a quasi-religious or mystical significance. Apparently that was okay because Lorenza understood that a man like this needed to keep up his image as a total bastard but the problem was that Max had now revealed all-too-human frailties by falling head over heels with infatuation – she refused to use the word 'love' – for some "cheapskate actress". She wasn't even a name! "The little tart's not getting her hands on what's mine," Lorenza hissed with a venom which gave Jack a sense of sudden foreboding, rather as the male of the species must feel immediately after spectacular congress with a praying mantis, "so I figured I'd best put my claim in first."

Sound logic – not exactly the 'for better or worse' syndrome but there again the only straight bat Max knew was the one he purported to devour live for art's sake. Looking her straight in the eye though Jack asked if there might perhaps be a touch of hypocrisy here. Had she always kept the faith? "Jack Lauder!" she exclaimed saucily, "are you suggesting I like to get my leg over a toy boy or two?" Faced with such an explicit response his bottle went and he denied that such had been the force of the interrogation. She laughed and said, "liar! And anyway you're absolutely right, I screw who I want, when I want, where I want, how I want!" She looked at him archly. "My, that is a big desk you've got, Jack," and when his face turned crimson she burst into shrieks of laughter and uncrossed and then recrossed those gorgeous pins the opposite way. So it wasn't that she was bereft about the betrayal then, it was something else. Her face twisted malevolently as she replied, "I couldn't give a shit if he wants to screw the little bitch, we've lived apart four years now while he's been a tax exile. I've got my own scene here. I know he can't live like a monk, it doesn't go with the image for one thing, he has to screw everything that moves or people will start thinking he's just a pussy cat. He takes all that devil worship stuff very seriously Jack." She looked at the lawyer's captivated face and a malicious gleam came into her eyes. "You want to watch out for that, he can put curses on people." Jack shivered when she said that, a reaction she picked up. "That got to you," she added, making him look at her, one eyebrow raised. She was right. It had got to him for reasons of which she couldn't even dream. "He's always looking for more and more outrageous things to do, aren't we all?" she continued. "But no, there's a pride thing Jack. It's not against him, it's against the slag who thinks she can steal him from me. Usually he just puts the frighteners on any little bitch who tries to blackmail him and they hightail it back to the Mid-West before you can say you little slut. But this one he's not only banging, he's thinking of living over the shop with her! Over my dead body! She's going to get nothing, even if I have to take it all first. I'd strangle her with my own hands if I could. I'll find this one and she'll wish she was with all the rest – on the shitheap where no one can see them."

Jack was, once again, momentarily taken aback by her bile and had serious doubts about representing her. The seduced women in these situations can be excused more easily than the celebrities. They're usually single girls, and they're carried away with the idea of vicarious fame. Lorenza wasn't having the mitigating factors.

The more she told him the more Jack began to wonder why she should think he was the right guy to sort out this monster and it turned out she'd been recommended by Johnnie Hammer, a disc jockey on Radio Metro, whom Jack had succeeded in getting off a drugs rap.

His efforts to persuade her to consult an American attorney, as much out of disquiet with the case as out of the genuine belief that she might get a better deal with Californian laws of Community of Property, fell on deaf ears. For some reason Jack was the man and she wasn't having any of his trying to fob her off on to someone else.

Even so there was still something artificial about her show of anger. Jack was no stranger to the woman scorned bit. The anger towards the other woman, even if the wife has no real affection for her husband, is not unusual. The adultery is a two-fold insult: an implication that you are not up to the job and a betrayal by someone who should know better, another woman. Anyway, Lorenza was coming from the direction of the financial clout she'd lose if she didn't act. Jack didn't necessarily agree it was the best approach to think in terms of taking this sucker to the cleaners, as she put it, before the other bitch got in, but it was the approach she wanted to adopt and she was the client. Still, he couldn't fathom it entirely. Why the strength of the reaction if it was all right for him to screw around? The warning signs were there. He got locked in to the minutiae and lost the big picture. There were substantial financial holdings in this country, about £15,000,000 in total and the way she put it that would do nicely for now. Yes, Jack could freeze them stone cold, he could get a Mareva injunction against Kaliostri's worldwide assets, even his offshore banking shares. "Do it!" she said. She took out a cheque book and wrote one for five grand. Jack looked at it. It was more than his usual retainer after a first interview. "Will that do for starters?" she asked.

"Very nicely," he replied. "Might I mention," he remembered, returning to the mundane, "that if you want to go through with a divorce I'll need your marriage certificate for the petition. You have to give those details, date of marriage, place, maiden name etc."

"Okay," she said, "I'll see if I can root it out. You just get on with the other in the meantime." She laughed a throaty laugh. The business completed, she was about to leave when, as if as an afterthought, she turned back and asked Jack, "haven't I met you before?"

"Don't think so," he replied and added gallantly, "I'm sure I would have remembered."

Rather out of character as he had found her until that moment, she ignored the compliment as if she hadn't noticed and replied, "I thought I did. Maybe it wasn't this incarnation, eh?"

"Why?" he responded jocularly. "How many incarnations have you had?"

"Seven," she replied and it was so matter-of-fact that Jack blinked in a double take. After a few more pleasantries, Lorenza left her lawyer to spend her money.

CHAPTER 2

If Lorenza's visit had caused Jack something of a surprise, it was nothing compared to the one he got the next morning whilst opening the post in his firm's boardroom. Thirteen years before, Jack had acted in the murder trial of a client called Henry Herron. For one reason or another the case hadn't gone well and it would be putting it mildly to say that Henry blamed Jack for the wheel coming off. In fact, the convicted man had expressed such an undying hatred for his former lawyer that it now came as a bit of a shock to discover that he had apparently undergone sufficient of a change of heart to appoint Jack the executor of his will.

The bemused lawyer read the letter, which had been sent by one of the dead man's friends, and realized this was precisely the sort of practical joke Henry would play right at the very end. Was there anything to execute or was he just trying to give Jack a hard time *post mortem*?

The will listed a number of personal possessions. There was mention too of a journal but it wasn't in the packet enclosed with the letter and will. The author of the letter, one Mr. Pardoe, wondered if the journal could be turned into a book and promised to send it on as soon as possible. He didn't explain the impediment. Thinking about it, however, Jack reasoned that Henry would certainly have quite a story to tell. He might even tell the truth about the Langhorn murder.

Reflecting on those days now, in the comfort of his plush office and suddenly aware of the passing of the years, Jack realised just how many bad memories that time brought back – not only of the grisly circumstances of the case itself but also of something which had befallen him personally, something which had changed his life forever.

The re-emergence of even the deceased Henry Herron was a puzzle. Rack his brains he might but Jack could find no reason why the ageing villain should, in his final moments, want the assistance of a man whom he had claimed for the last few years to loathe. It warranted some explanation. None was to be found immediately in the documents detailing his meagre possessions. There was, however, an answer in the past.

PART TWO

CHAPTER 1

It would have been approaching the winter solstice of 1987 when this particular group of friends chose a bright and clear winter's day for a walk in the National Park of Langhorn Forest in the northern borders of England. The spruce and pine were covered in rime; the ground was as hard as iron. Leaving their car in a picnic spot the backpackers took the track signposted for the Billy Goat's Beard, a waterfall which cascades down from a crown of rocks known as Goat Head Tower.

They walked a quarter of a mile or so when one of the girls was caught short. Laughter from the rest of the group followed as she skittered off into the woods. At a sufficient distance she squatted down when an object in the bushes momentarily distracted her. At first she had the chilling thought that an intruder was observing her private moment; the object gave the impression of a face peeping round the bole of a tree but its inertia convinced her she was imagining things. Nearly finished, she heard her friends call from what sounded a tremendous distance. Wriggling into her tight jeans she returned their shout but, curiosity getting the better, she trod delicately over the broken branches to the object. Bending down, she turned it over gently. It was a severed, maggot-filled human head. Her scream echoed through the forest and brought her friends running.

☾

A few hours later, a group of serious looking people were

standing in a room lit by a fluorescent light. Two were policemen who stared down at the disembodied head while the pathologist worked swiftly, turning it over in her experienced hands. "The face has been partly devoured by wild animals," she said, "head severed, cause of death. The skull's caved in from the force of the blow."

"Weapon?" Superintendent Lowther, asked.

"I'd say it was something man-made. Any number of sharp, heavy objects could have caused it. It was wielded with great force. Either by a very strong person, which suggests a man, or, even more likely, it may have had a handle. A sword or an axe blade perhaps. It's a fairly clean cut. You see, jagged edge there and there." She pointed. "Otherwise, clean."

The Superintendent turned to his second-in-command, Inspector Barry Freer. No words were exchanged but the Inspector nodded. From a number tattoo on the otherwise bald head and a peculiar earring in a half-chewed ear, Freer had identified one of his informers, Tony Cooper, a scrap dealer from Tyneside. He recounted to his Superintendent the story Cooper had told him of his dealings with two local target criminals, Henry Herron and Blacklock Spiers. Shortly after the inspector had met him in a local pub the snout had gone missing. The question in the police officers' minds was, had these two notorious criminals discovered their fence was a police informer? The more pressing question was, what had happened to the remainder of the body? A search of the area had revealed nothing.

"Do we know if he died here even?" the Superintendent asked. Inspector Freer shook his head. The pathologist replied, "I would guess not." She pointed at the dried edges of the cut. "You see the spruce needles have been embedded in there, which suggests that the head has been catapulted, thrown or kicked even, quite violently into the ground. Was it found at the bottom of a bank, near a road?" Lowther nodded.

"My guess is," she continued, "it was hurled down the bank, which would suggest the death took place somewhere else. On the roadside perhaps." Lowther looked pensive. The death had happened so long before that the chances now of finding any evidence of where or how it occurred were remote.

The Inspector's hunch, however, turned out to be right. Surveillance of Tony Cooper's known associates resulted in some interesting observations. After a few weeks of cat and mouse Blacklock Spiers and Henry Herron were arrested and remanded in custody. Henry protested his innocence, whilst Blacklock, after initially saying nothing at all, had, the police alleged, made a half-confession The gist of this was to put Blacklock innocently at the scene of the killing in Langhorn Forest whilst casting the blame firmly on Henry for the act. A complication was that the confession was made not to the police but to a third party. The police were withholding the identity of the third party because of fear of reprisals from Henry. The result was that Henry had been accused of the murder by a person whose identity might never be revealed to him as the prosecution intended to apply for permission for him to give evidence behind a screen and under a false name. For anyone accused of serious crime, let alone murder, that was an unsatisfactory state of affairs but, try as they might, Henry's legal team could not break through the blanket of secrecy. At that point Henry decided to change horses midstream, jettison his under-performing team and see if he could get a better result by appointing a new legal team.

"You're kidding!" Superintendent Lowther said when his Inspector told him. "Jack Lauder? Are you sure?"

"I know it's a weird one that. He's not the full shilling, is he?" his second in command replied.

Lowther shook his head. "I think he's recovered from his accident well enough," he said. "Physically anyway. I don't know where his head is, though."

"He's been a right workiticket," Freer responded. "The lads down the Bridewell have locked him up twice that I know of for getting involved in bar room brawls. He's been mentioned in more than one report for drug abuse. And he's big mates with Joe Johnson. He's a wrong un."

Lowther's face was non-committal. Privately he had a lot of time for Jack, who had once worked for the Crown Prosecution Service. He had been sorry to see the young lawyer go so far downhill and nothing would have given him more pleasure than to see him rehabilitate himself after his dreadful injuries. "He never had much luck," that lad, Lowther said. "And I don't think it's changed if he's inherited Henry Herron."

It was true. Jack carried some baggage, more than even than these senior police officers knew. An orphan from before his teens, he had learned from a time when he was in and out of institutions, the memory of which, even now, could bring on the deepest depression, that ultimately you are on your own. The accident which the Superintendent had mentioned caused severe physical damage but that healed quickly enough. What took longer were the fits and longer term depressive tendencies. For some a near death experience centres the mind and makes them jealous of life; for others the effect is the opposite. They lose their self-respect and become afflicted by the notion that they should in truth be dead. Jack was one of those and for a time he was out of control, stumbling into a drink and drug abuse culture. His friend, Joe Johnson, mentioned so disparagingly by Inspector Freer and so notorious that he was known as the Border Bandido, served him well in those times. Jack was not one to forget past debts.

When he took on the Herron case Jack was in his twenties. He was getting over the accident and seemed to be piecing his life back together. He was of medium height, sparely but powerfully built and cheerful of look with piercing blue eyes. The rehabilitation process had left him for a time dependent on morphine and this was partly the cause of his experimentation with other pain-killing drugs, some of which could not be obtained by lawful means.

The murdered man's body had been found in or somewhere near a secluded glade of Langhorn Forest. By an odd twist of fate this was less than half a mile from the scene of Jack's accident. Among the depositions delivered to him with a 'Best of British' message from Henry's former representative was a photograph of a local landmark, the cliff known as the Goat Head Tower. Jack studied it dispassionately. Like everyone else he had to eat, to pay for the roof over his head, and appease the bank manager. Those needs also dimmed any appreciation he might have had that it was too early to take on this trial. Temporarily running on empty, Jack wasn't quite ready for a man as manipulative and paranoid as Henry Herron.

CHAPTER 2

Answering the call to visit his new client, Jack arrived at Langland Prison. "You've come to see the lifer?" the screw at the gatehouse enquired as the lawyer limped in. He had shed the crutches but the legacy of the accident was still there.

"Come on!" He replied, a mischievous sparkle in eyes as blue as alpine ice, "the guy's not even been tried yet!"

"I know a lifer when I see one," the screw replied.

After a few more jocular exchanges with the staff, Jack sat down and waited to be escorted to maximum-security. Struck suddenly by the thought of the compression of energy within the institution's walls, he shuddered with a presentiment of the evil which lurked in his future. The prison officer came for him and led the lawyer, slowly because of his continuing disability, through corridors of wire fences, past conning towers with vigilant guards until, after an elaborate use of intercoms and keys, they entered a building with no external windows whatsoever. The P.O explained, as he ushered Jack into one of the small cubicles provided by the prison for confidential interviews, that Henry, a Category A escape risk, was currently on the block in solitary confinement for some form of misbehaviour.

Jack was in the middle of a last check of a list of thirty questions when Henry bundled hurriedly into the room wearing sweatshirt and jeans, a vision of balding ginger hair and tanned, freckled skin. Scarred about the face, the result of an acid attack, Henry's muscular frame appeared wasted as if he had not eaten for some time. He later explained that he had become vegan as a means of guaranteeing decent food inside. The large bundle of depositions under his arm, when he came into the cubicle, testified to his intent. He shook Jack's hand with a dry, masculine grip. "Howay!" he said, "pleased to meet yous Jack. So what's the crack then? How are we going to fix these tosspots?"

Jack's predecessor had warned him that, although Henry might pretend to be thick when it suited him, he was in fact well educated. He liked to impersonate others and could do any accent; he could quote Shakespeare on piece. He might never have stayed very long at any school but he had used his various sojourns in the nick to good effect. "You sound confident," Jack said, a trifle nervous at this first meeting, although he couldn't quite understand why. It wasn't the first time he had met criminals with similar reputations for violence as that enjoyed, if that was the right word, by the man in front of him now. It was just that others, like his friend the Border Bandido, for instance, did not wear it quite like a badge of pride. To Henry it was his *raison d'etre*. He needed to be seen as tough and uncompromising in all circumstances.

"Sure, I'm as happy as a pollis in a park. Because I'm innocent," Henry replied. "You've read the deps, what do you think?"

"Henry, I don't have to believe you're innocent, I just have to know what your case is, so I can make sure it's put to the jury properly."

"No!" Henry thumped the table. "That's not good enough, don't you see? That's why I got you. I was told you always fight harder if you believe your client. I want to know, do you believe me?" Henry glared at his new lawyer with a ferocious, fanatical gleam in his eyes.

Jack was no stranger to this line but, even more, he was struck by the pent-up menace, which explained this man's atrocious criminal record. In and out of institutions from youth, Henry had been involved in weapons fights, armed robberies, assaults, grievous bodily harm. Reputed to have committed murders, including that of a police officer, he had escaped conviction. "I haven't been through everything," Jack hedged, "but there's a couple of things I need to know."

Superintendent Lowther had done a professional job, drawing the story out of a witness, whose identity had been protected but who was probably a fellow remand inmate of Spiers, of what Henry's co-accused had told him. This was to the effect that Henry had lured Cooper to a lonely spot in Langhorn Forest on the pretext of their doing a job together. Spiers had mentioned that it was near a graveyard of some sort, which seemed ridiculous when you read it, but the police had left it in. It was one of those details, which gave the statement the appearance of truth. The police were unlikely to have invented it. The place the witness described was somewhere within Langhorn forest. No one had lived in that wilderness for centuries so there was no need for a graveyard. It was one of those puzzles left hanging in the air. The witness went on to explain, still attributing the information to Spiers, how Henry had gone ballistic with Cooper, called him a grass and then struck him with a woodsman's axe. Spiers apparently denied the 'confession' and claimed that it was a fit up so Henry's explanation was the conspiracy theory. The police were out to get him because of his terrible past. "Yeah, okay," Jack responded, "but do you mean they want you so bad they'll let the real murderer go, just to stitch you up? I don't buy that but let's look at it from the point of view that Spiers did make this 'confession'. He doesn't incriminate himself, does he? He could walk on this but there's nothing more certain than that he was there. The logic of that is, either he did it or you did, so which is it? If it's him, why don't you just put it on his toes?"

"I'm nae grass," Henry replied venomously. "No way is Blacklock going to back that tosser up in the box! He's gannin to deny it. If we do it your way, that's what the cops want, a fucking cut-throat! That's why they've invented this lying bastard."

"Any idea who it is?"

"Nah, but it'll be someone Blackie was banged up with. I'm not dropping a mate in. They don't call me Cooper. I'm nae grass!" Jack blinked at the *faux pas*. Henry had just confirmed the truth of part at least of the second-hand Spiers story. Knowledge that Cooper was a police informer gave him a motive. Then the interview took another turn and became more and more infuriating as Henry revealed signs of a hidden agenda which Jack couldn't fathom. Acting as if he knew the truth but it wasn't time to tell it, Henry became aggressive. He called Jack's questions about discrepancies in his version of events "bullshit" and "fucking lawyer talk". Jack found himself hanging in to retain this client. Why? He didn't know. Pride maybe. Eventually it was Henry who called time. "Next visit," he said. He stood up and signalled to one of the guards. Jack looked at his notebook. Perhaps he had ten of his thirty questions answered. He could have kicked himself. His time was precious and yet he'd achieved little. Henry had simply taken the interview over.

In a complete change of attitude from his former snarling aggressiveness, Henry shouted after his lawyer as he walked down the corridor, "you'll do for me, Jack!"

Strangely, although gratified by Henry's confidence, the fresh air brought a sense of relief. This client was a driven man, used to persuading others to his will; he had a powerful intelligence, far greater than the usual petty criminals Jack encountered. His weakness, if there was one, lay in his underestimation of others.

The next time Jack saw Henry he'd studied the depositions. The evidence of Blacklock Spiers' confession to the unknown third party, who might, as Henry had opined, be nothing more than an old lag trying to get some advantage for himself inside or by way of early release from assisting the Feds, wasn't actually admissible as evidence against Henry. However, aired before a jury in a joint trial as evidence of some involvement of Blacklock Spiers, it would cause incalculable prejudice to the co-accused. The question was, therefore, what other evidence was there? What Jack had read was unnerving. Compelling circumstantial evidence included Cooper's girlfriend testifying to a grudge Henry held against her boyfriend; a lot of people believed Cooper was frightened of him; a lot more knew that Henry used Cooper as a fence. The police had suspected Herron and his accomplice Spiers of murder even before the body was found. This was the classic situation for a fit-up: a certainty in the policeman's mind of the identity of the culprit and a perception that a lack of evidence will ensure he beats the rap. Henry had beaten a few raps in his time.

Further adverse material lay in the bizarre way in which Henry had behaved after Cooper's disappearance but before the disembodied head was found. Going out of his way to antagonise the police, he'd led them on car chases, laying red herrings and creating false alibis. After the mutilated head was discovered, things became even stranger. Henry and Spiers went back to the scene of the murder. They were under covert surveillance. A search of the forest took place after they'd left. An axe was found, allegedly the murder weapon. The obvious implication was the murderers had returned to retrieve it. There was other evidence too. Impressions were taken from the tyre marks of a vehicle shown to have pulled into a clearing close to where the head had been found. The tyre marks coincided with those of a stolen vehicle. Independent evidence demonstrated that this car had been seen in Henry's possession and when, later, it was found abandoned in the Newcastle area, SoCOs discovered spruce needles in the boot. Spruce was the predominant tree of Langhorn forest. To put the lid on it, fibres found on the axe coincided with fibres on gloves seized from Henry's house.

"What about these fibres?" Jack asked.

"What about 'em? There's thousands of bloody gloves round like that. Howway! Every bloody fisherman on the fish quay has a pair!" Henry stabbed his stubby finger at the lawyer. "I don't want to start thinking you're in league with them!"

Jack didn't take offence at the insult. Paranoia wasn't unusual in this situation as the day of reckoning drew closer. He passed on to the next subject and discussed the tyre marks. Henry pointed out that they amounted to no evidence at all. Dozens of cars could have left tracks like that. It was just another piece of circumstantial. "That's the problem with circumstantial evidence," Jack said, "its effect is cumulative and the police are experts at building up coincidences until sooner or later there is one too many. We have to answer each one. We have to unload the camel, straw by straw."

"What's wrong with being frigging innocent until you're proved guilty?" Henry asked gruffly.

Jack smiled. "Another fallacy," he replied and turned the interview to the night Cooper was killed. "What night was that?" Henry asked. The circumstances of the discovery of Tony Cooper's death meant that only anecdotal evidence could be relied on to prove when he died. It was more a question of when he was last seen alive.

Jack had a stab at it. "Well, the last definite sighting was 2nd October."

"Piss off, I saw him after that." Henry went into a tirade about Lowther. He was a snide, a bent copper who framed people for the crimes of others. Jack made the mistake of looking at his watch.

"Story of my life, that," Henry added. "No one's got the friggin' time for Henry Herron, sod justice, Jack's got a business to run. Bollocks to Henry Herron. He's just shite!"

"Don't talk rubbish, Henry! It's not like the movies. You aren't my only client. What I put in for you I have to put in for a lot of others as well."

"Sod the others! Henry Herron is innocent!" He banged the table, then he grinned again. "Hey, if it's a bung you want, son," and he rubbed the thumb and forefinger of his right hand together, "I've got relations who're coming in the money." He sang the last few words.

"No," Jack replied, "that won't make any difference. Come on Henry. I need help on this. Look, the fibres evidence. There's fibres from your gloves ..."

" ... my gloves, oh my gloves is it?"

"There's fibres from the gloves on the axe," Jack said uncomfortably, thumbing through the depositions.

"Fancy that! Well there's an easy fit-up."

Irritated by the way he said this, Jack pointed out, "they were found by the forensic scientist, not by the police."

"Oh, they're not daft enough to find it themselves."

"Henry," Jack said, "where do you get this idea you're public enemy number one? You drive round with a daft van with 'The Wolf Pack' painted on the side; you once escaped a police hunt by driving to the Midlands with a bullet in your leg. No big deal. There's dozens of guys the cops want more than you." Henry's look said louder than words that Jack shouldn't belittle this client. He had a sudden flash of insight. Whatever else Henry wanted, he couldn't forfeit his street cred. The biggest, toughest bastard on the block was a reputation to be maintained at all costs, even if it meant a life stretch. Henry stared now at Jack with a look that chilled the lawyer's blood. Jack sighed again and carried on. "Fibres in the wound in Cooper's skull?"

"Cooper had gloves like that. They're in the forensic."

"Yes, but he hardly stuck his fingers in his own head wound, did he?" Jack couldn't resist the cynicism but he quickly tried to make amends. "Henry, this is getting us nowhere. We're going to carry on hitting a brick wall until we get some explanation for where you were that night?"

Henry said, "what night?" He wasn't going to let Jack in on this piece of the story yet.

"Sooner or later," Jack said, "you're going to have to tell me your alibi, if you've got one. Time's running out. Tony Cooper was killed in Langhorn Forest. The witness says you and Spiers were there. He says you did the killing and gives the impression Spiers had no prior knowledge of your plan. It doesn't matter what night it was. The question is, were you or weren't you there? Only when you answer that can we go on to deal with who did it."

"Who says Cooper was killed in Langhorn Forest?" Jack looked at his client, measuring this latest riposte. What was he playing at? Of course there was no evidence the killing happened there. It could have happened somewhere else. Henry leaned across and put his hand on Jack's arm. "Jack, you've read in the deps that Cooper's caravan went up in smoke on his allotment, right?"

"Yes, the night he seems to have gone missing."

"Handy, don't you think? Neat destruction of evidence?"

Jack looked back at him. "You mean bloodstains?"

"I mean a frigging bloodbath!"

"Right," Jack replied, "so you are telling me that Cooper was killed at his caravan. By whom?"

Henry tapped his nose. "I'm telling you nowt," he replied. "Speculation, that's what it is, speculation."

Although it was infuriating only getting a bit of the story, Henry was right in a way. If he gave that evidence, he stood a big chance of both accused going down. The police were probably banking on a cut-throat defence to cure the deficiencies of the circumstantial evidence. Henry had made it clear that he couldn't or wouldn't openly grass on his co-accused, even if he had any direct evidence to offer. The chance was he was pinning all his hopes on his legal team destroying the evidence of Blacklock's manufactured confidant and Blacklock, as part of some pre-arranged plan, going in the witness box and disowning the confession. He was between a rock and a hard place. "Do you think the police know you didn't do it?" Jack asked.

"Fucking right!" he snorted in reply. Seeing his lawyer's consternation, he added, "I'm just a thick gadgie, Jack. I'm not clever like ye, hinny. The only school I went to was Approved School. Borstal's where I did my degree. Yousis the brains, Jack, you figure it out." He had many voices and many faces, enough to have been on the stage. As if on cue, the guard appeared at the cubicle entrance and looked at his watch. "Tell him to fuck off," Henry added.

"I wouldn't be invited back if I did that."

"Well, I'll tell him for you." He turned round and put two fingers up at the guard. "Kiss my arse," he added.

"Okay Henry," Jack said, changing the subject, not realising then how momentous the change would prove to be. "Before I forget, what about the axe?"

"I know nowt about any frigging axe. All I know is I'm innocent. There must be thousands of bloody axes in the world."

"But only one murder weapon."

"Oh yeah? How do you know that?"

Jack sighed. "Body hair from the deceased makes it number one candidate for the murder weapon. I'm not sure where the hair was found. I suspect it was on the axe-head, though."

"What if there was no axe at the scene?" Immediately alert to Jack's suspicious look, he added truculently, "because it's a plant." He grinned again, the jackal grin. "It's bound to be. I've told you, I don't know anything about any axe." The problem with this client was not what he told you but what he held back. Like a guide who switches on his torch to show you the way, he let you see all sorts of phantasmagoric shapes in the torch beam before snapping it off and trying to convince you it was all in your imagination.

CHAPTER 3

It was the oddest trial Jack had experienced. The prosecution went easy on Spiers, whose QC continually whispered asides to Crown Counsel. Firm in his belief that Blacklock Spiers would do the right thing in the end and wary of saying anything which would provoke his co-accused into making damaging accusations of his own, Henry's performance in the witness box was so evasive that the jury smelled the proverbial rabbit off. Needing Spiers to bail him out, the big shock came when the co-accused's Q.C didn't call him to give evidence. Rules of court prevented Henry's team from calling him. The confession witness's allegations of what Spiers had told him stood uncontested by Spiers and limited the impact of any cross-examination by Henry's Q.C. It looked for all the world as if the allegations were true.

Blacklock Spiers sat in the dock, his head in his hands, unable to return Henry's stare. Whilst Henry was lifed off, Spiers got a manslaughter, the evidence of the witness portraying him as a dupe who had been at the scene, complicit in an assault on Cooper but without the necessary intention to justify a murder conviction. The jury never knew about a criminal record which proved him to be a psychopath until they'd acquitted him of the murder. Jack was inconsolable. Whether or not he believed Henry innocent or guilty, he hated to see justice meted out so disproportionately. The feeling that an unholy deal had been struck behind closed doors proved Henry right and his lawyer wrong: the Crime Squad did want him that badly. Jack had fallen for the fallacy that the police always want to get the right man. In truth he should have known from hard experience that they don't. In many cases, just about any criminal they want off the streets will do for a fall guy. At least Spiers didn't walk but, if the manslaughter verdict was bad enough, the sentence was worse. The man Jack thought to be at least as guilty as Henry ended up with three years. Halve that, deduct the time served on remand and it added up to 6 months on rule 43, after which a homicidal maniac would, once again, roam loose in the community.

Jack wasn't surprised either that Henry's appeal failed. He knew precisely how the system worked. The Appeal Court wasn't easily moved by pleas of miscarriages of justice against villains. The logic they usually applied was, he's got away with enough in the past, now it's payback time.

☾

About two years after the refusal of the appeal a document purporting to be Blacklock Spiers' confession to killing Tony Cooper arrived on Jack's desk. It exonerated Henry. Uncertain of the statement's provenance, Jack arranged to see Henry immediately. "I told you so," was the latter's comment when the lawyer showed him the document

"Have you seen this before?"

"Nah." Henry started rolling a cigarette one-handed, then he looked at Jack. He wore the characteristic grin he could turn on and off like clockwork. "Howay, that's champion, Jack. Some would say yous've got a second chance. About time and all 'cos you were nowt startling first time round. No more of these vain parleys eh? Let's have a bit more hoyin' about of brains!"

"Whoa!" Jack replied, "let's get that straight for a start. Your problems arose from the fact you weren't sufficiently forthcoming. You got it in your head that you couldn't trust anyone with the truth and you could have done a lot more for yourself in the witness box!"

Henry shrugged as if it was no fault of his. "Yousis the lawyer Jack. You should have advised me!"

His prodigious talent for moving back and forth between disguises, the pit yakker one minute and the frustrated professor the next, distracted Jack momentarily from the fact that the confession was no less puzzling. Why should Spiers write it? Jack wasn't much convinced by Henry's explanation that maybe Spiers had a conscience after all. "Oh, come on, Henry, pull the other one!" he responded. "You know as well as I do that Blacklock Spiers would sell his granny for an ounce of dope. People like him don't have consciences. What exactly are you doing back in bed with him? This guy sold you down the river, remember?"

"How do I know what his agenda is?" Henry answered. "As for me, I'm a free agent. I can mix with anyone I want. It so happens that Blacklock is useful to me, so mind your own on that score." Henry tapped his flattened nose.

"It's important!" Jack protested. "How do you expect to convince the Commission that the case should be referred back to the Court of Appeal if it looks as if it's been set up? Blacklock should make the running and provide an explanation why the confession is genuine."

"No way José," Henry replied, pointing a stubby forefinger at Jack. "I'm in here for a crime I didn't commit. I don't have to prove Jack shit. They can all kiss my arse. Looka, bonny lad, there's a lot of clever people in here looked at them deps and can prove the police are liars."

"Brilliant!" Jack exclaimed, "that's all we need! A posse of lifers to come and tell the Review Commission that all policemen are bent!"

Snarling at Jack's sarcasm, Henry pointed out facts in the dossier which provided some evidence of his thesis. "So why didn't you and the A team pick all this up in the trial, eh?" Jack could have pointed out the irrelevance of many of Henry's points, but he didn't. Deep down he had a conscience about the system he operated in. Its priority is not innocence or guilt but effective policing – law and order. The resources of the State are immense compared to the defence lawyer. He took the dossier from Henry – a little roughly perhaps, but that was the way he felt – and skipped through it. It looked impressive enough but with no way of checking its assertions, its 'proof' that Henry could not have committed the crime, that the police had known all along that Blacklock was the culprit, it was meaningless. "If they had the murderer, why protect him just to set you up?"

Henry studied Jack long and hard. At length he said, looking his lawyer straight in the eyes, "I've asked you this before, and you avoided the question then. Now I'm asking you again. Do you believe I'm innocent? I'm asking you man to man, not client to solicitor. Man to man."

The bluntness of Jack's reply took the hard-bitten criminal by surprise. "Well okay, no. I had big problems with a couple of things, Henry. Not only the evidence. That I can cope with. I can buy the 'plant' thing, the fabrication of interviews, for what it's worth. There's a couple of things which got to me. There was your change of story about the axe. This is the way you are Henry. You tell me what you think I need to know. Even now you're doing it."

"What about the axe?" Henry was tense now, his eyes narrow.

"You told me you'd never seen it in your life. Then, when it came to the trial, you gave evidence explaining how you'd seen it in Cooper's allotment and you might have handled it, and that's how the fibres could have got there. You changed your story. Then, at first when I saw you, you told me about all sorts of people who could have been responsible for the murder. You said Blacklock was with you on the 2nd October. No way did he do it. Now you're asking me to believe a confession from Blacklock that he did it on 2nd October. You've also told me you saw Cooper alive after that date."

Henry's face was livid as he looked at Jack. His mouth was moving but no words came out. Then, as if making a great effort to control himself, he said, "do you know there's a tape of the filth tapping up that wanker who gave the evidence of Spiers' confession?"

That was startling news. "No!" Jack sat back in his chair. "Do you mean a tape recording was taken in the prison of police officers suborning him to tell lies against you?"

"Aye, that's what I said."

"If there was such a thing, it would blow the case wide open. It would be more telling evidence than any after-the-event confession by a co-accused who can't be charged now with the murder because of double jeopardy."

"I've been told you knew about the tape all along, that you've had it." Henry's eyes narrowed as he looked straight into Jack's. The lawyer may have looked uncomfortable as he stared back because the villain added, "true is it?"

"Of course not," Jack replied. "Where did that notion come from?"

Henry's eyes misted over and he ignored the question. "I wish I'd known before the trial," he said. "I only found out from this lad I was in Long Lartin with. He was on dispersal too so it was the first prison we were in together."

"What did he tell you?"

"That they got wind of the fact this lad was gannin' to grass but they didn't know who on. Someone on the wing got a trustee to put the tape in the Cat A interview room, taped under a desk, then switch it on just before the cops came in."

"What happened to the tape?"

"The prison found it and they sent it to the filth." Henry was still staring fixedly at Jack.

He felt uncomfortable with those eyes boring into his brain. "They should have disclosed it to me," he replied.

"I told you. I heard they did," Henry continued, his gaze not wavering.

Jack was bewildered. "Who says I got it?"

"One of the lads was speaking to his solicitor, bloke called Kirby Potts, know him?" Jack nodded non-committally.

"He's mates with Barry Freer and Freer told him you got the tape. They, the filth that is, sent it to you."

"If they did, I never received it," Jack replied.

"Is that what you say?" Henry looked at him quizzically, giving nothing away.

"Of course it is. If I'd seen such a thing, I would have used it."

"Would you now?"

"Too bloody right!"

The P.O signaled Jack to leave. He was suddenly exhausted. The allegation about the tape had somehow unnerved him even though he didn't have the slightest idea what Henry was on about. He had the feeling, though, that he hadn't heard the last of it. Then, true to form, Henry simply switched subjects and hit Jack with another haymaker.

"There's a witness to Blacklock making the confession."

"Who?"

"Can't tell you that."

"Male or female?"

"Can't tell you that."

"Animal, vegetable or mineral? Give me the address and I'll contact the witness," Jack said.

"The witness will make contact with you. This person is taking a big risk. If this information gets into the hands of the police and Blacklock gets to know about it." He made a throat-cutting gesture.

There was no contact from the witness but Jack received a phone call from Henry. Having gained access to the Welfare Officer's telephone, he'd decided to ring to let his lawyer know the mysterious witness had alleged that Jack was refusing to interview him or her. Every time he or she telephoned, a member of Jack's staff would tell him or her that under no circumstances would Jack see him or her, nor should he or she make any statement which would assist Henry Herron, or he or she would get into big trouble. None of Jack's staff knew anything of these phone calls. Jack had also apparently refused to see Henry's wife. She'd never been in touch. Jack wrote to Henry that he'd left strict instructions that if anybody wanted to talk about Henry's case, they must be put through to him, even if he was engaged with someone else. Jack got nothing from Henry by way of response, then out of the blue he received a letter, which read as follows:

> Dear Mr Lauder,
> I have decided that I no longer wish you to represent me. I have transferred my instructions to Henry Solomon of Birmingham and I request that you forward all documents in your possession to this solicitor. I will not forgive you for how you have treated me. This is something that will haunt you for the rest of your life. You have let an innocent man rot in hell and you did not lift a finger to assist when you were the only one with the power to do something about it.
>
> Why you didn't I now understand. I used to trust you but I now know the police got to you. You suppressed the tape that proved my innocence. I have clear evidence of this.

Henry didn't choose to explain at this point what this evidence was and the reference to the tape baffled Jack as much on this occasion as it had earlier. Not only that but Henry then went on to tell Jack of others among the prison community who had little regard for him. No identification was made and, although it is an occupational hazard for a defence lawyer to be blamed for some of his clients failing to beat the rap, the revelation came as a mystery to him:

> There are people in here who know more about you than you think. You would have nightmares all your life if you knew how many people in here have it in for you and how many have sworn to get you when they get out. You are just another sheister on the make. What you couldn't get through your head is the truth. Henry Herron is innocent. Blacklock Spiers did the crime. Henry Herron did the time. You knew that all along. You are going to have reason to know it in the future. I promise you I will make you pay. No matter how long it takes, you will have reason to remember...

Effectively *functus officio* Jack was nonetheless sufficiently concerned about Henry's allegations to make enquiries of Lowther. What he discovered shocked him. There had been a tape recording and it had been seized by the police. "The prison authorities found out that someone had taped a mini-tape recorder under the desk in the interview room," Lowther told him in a matter-of-fact way. "They informed us and we seized it."

"Why was I not told about it?"

"Because there was nothing on it. Either the tape was faulty or it had run out by the time the officers got the informer into the room. It was just non-evidence. We didn't think any more about it."

"That's a very selective approach to evidence," Jack said stiffly. "Where is it now?"

"Destroyed. Shortly after the appeal."

"How convenient!"

"Jack, you can mount an appeal point on it but you know as well as I do, it will get short shrift. The Appeal Court isn't interested in might-have-beens." Lowther was absolutely right and Jack couldn't restrain the nagging doubt that something had been on that tape, something damaging which had been suppressed, only not, as his client now apparently thought, by him.

"Why should Barry Freer have told someone I had that tape?" he asked.

"Search me," Lowther replied. "What makes you think he has?"

"Henry told me."

"Oh, so it's gospel then!" Lowther laughed. "His word'll go a long way in a court of law!"

"The point is," Jack said. "I hadn't a clue it existed and now my client's been given the impression, for whatever malicious reason, that I've suppressed it.

"Tough!" the Superintendent replied. "My heart bleeds for you, Jack, and for your villain of a client. Just between you and me, Barry's got no love for you. He thinks you're as bad as some of your punters."

Jack wrote to Henry and explained what he had been told but received no reply. Now some time into his sentence, Henry had got it into his head that all sorts of evidence, which would prove his innocence, had been withheld and he was unlikely to be persuaded otherwise. The case became one of those bad memories. Everyone has them. Consigned to a locked and heavily strapped trunk in the attic, they don't let you sleep; they make noises in the night, forever begging to be released.

That was the last direct dealing Jack had with Henry. News reached him from time to time of the convict's exploits in prison, but everything came second hand and the stories were always apocryphal like the one about him walking round in a caftan, quoting Shakespeare to anyone who would listen. The impression was that the former hard man had gone stir crazy.

Jack heard Henry had been released only years later when, sitting at home some time shortly before the summer vacation, a knock on the door brought the news. It was the milkman, who stopped to chat for a moment. "I see they released Herron, that murderer!" he said. "You know, the forest man?" Jack remembered all too well but he contented himself with a remark on how time had passed. "That long?" the man retorted. "They should have thrown away the key. He should have died in jail. But he'll do no more murders like. I heard he's been released because he's not well. He's dying they say. His whole body is rotten inside. A bit like his mind. Strange isn't it, what he did to that other poor devil? He's paying now. Well, must get on. See you. Cheerio."

The milkman left Jack to digest his news. It refused to budge. In one sense was he happy that Herron was ill and dying? If so, why was he filled with this sensation of doom? That he felt relief at the imminent demise of another human being was a despicable thought but one he couldn't avoid. Then, in a flash, it was there, right before him, what he'd always hidden from, even though he'd never been able to escape it totally. Henry was right. Jack had done him a disservice by his honesty. He could have told a white lie, but he'd stated his disbelief. Brought up with an ethos of telling it like it is, it had taken him years to learn discretion. Henry had needed someone to believe in him and Jack had interpreted that to mean someone he could deceive. One of the deprived, Henry didn't see his downfall as his own fault. He placed the blame on others, and saw conspiracies everywhere. Jack's scepticism had led Henry to believe that his lawyer had attached himself to the conspiracy. Jack learned a lesson from that: not to be so cynical; give people the benefit of the doubt. There was a degree of irony in that self-assessment. Some of his critics, not all of them indisposed to him, would have said his problem was not too much but too little. Either way the realisation came too late to help Henry. Implicit in Jack's decision to accept his nomination as Henry's executor was the desire to make some kind of belated amends.

PART THREE

CHAPTER 1

It was a short time after getting the news of Henry's death that fate dealt Jack the hand of Lorenza Kaliostri and her self-destructive dispute with her rock star husband. Jack had made a good recovery from his injuries and was beginning to make something of his career. Life, though, lacked a dimension. He was still single and, whether as a result of the psychological damage caused by the fall or some other factors, he had found difficulty in sustaining relationships with women. Girlfriends came and went. Just as a prison regime results in odd and artificial relationships, difficult to sustain when the prisoner is released, Jack's ability to switch off when the going got tough was like a prisoner's, so that relationships, which might have blossomed in different climes would swiftly become stillborn. No one knew why he was so much the island apart from the main. In fact, no one knew much about Jack at all. He kept his roots a close secret. Although many who met him liked him instantly he had the reputation of a loner and he had a tendency once in a while to go off the rails and behave as if he was still a wild child instead of a lawyer approaching middle age. It was one reason why so many clients liked him. He was never judgmental, never less than understanding even about the worst human weaknesses. So, from inauspicious beginnings, his professional career flourished and he wasn't far off becoming a Geordie institution.

When Lorenza entered stage left he wasn't to know immediately how momentous this meeting would prove. For a start, he never got to the point of issuing the divorce petition because matters took an unexpected turn. He applied for and obtained an internationally effective Mareva injunction and only hours went by before he received his first transatlantic call. "Mr. Louder that, eh?" came the thick East Coast drawl.

"Lauder."

"Loader? What kind of name is that?"

From the voice Jack had a mental picture of a fat man with breathing problems. He ignored the taunt. "Who's speaking?"

"It's Kevin Kurtwangler."

"Hello Mr. Kurtwangler, what can I do for you?"

"OK, so you're the attorney for the Kaliostri lady?"

"Correct."

"You'll know we've been retained by the man?"

"The man? I presume you mean Mr. Max Kaliostri?"

"Mister Schmister," he replied, "don't fuck with me, pal."

Jack kept his temper. "I understood a Mr. Arnold Feinstein acts for Kaliostri."

"Arnie's a tax lawyer. He ain't the most switched on divorce attorney. But don't get your hopes up, buddy. That's why I'm on the case and I ain't taking no crap from you. The bottom line is the little lady's been fooling around. She gets the house, okay? She gets a million dollars okay? She gets to keep the car okay? She even gets to screw around with the disc jockey, okay?

"What if it's not okay?"

"We take the house, we take the million dollars, we take the car, and we cut the balls off the disc jockey."

"There doesn't seem much contest in those two deals."

"I thought you'd see it my way."

"Of course," Jack went on, "we could keep the house, keep the million dollars, keep the car, the disc jockey gets to keep his balls, and we get another ten million dollars?"

"Hey what kinda shit is this? You want we should start on you?"

"There's no need to take that sort of approach," Jack replied. "Why don't we get together and talk about this? I'm sure Mr. Kaliostri would be happy for you to fly over?"

"The man doesn't talk to motherfuckers like you! K Max could bankrupt your firm in no time. D'you know what kinda friends he's got over there?"

"You're full of threats," Jack said.

"And you're full of shit!" Jack's transatlantic colleague put the phone down, presumably as a negotiating tactic. The discussion had been robust to say the least. Jack was used to the tough tactics of city litigation lawyers but these Yanks took things to a whole new dimension with Mafioso tactics.

Jack had a dirty tricks department as well. The next week Max Kaliostri made a flying visit to England to discuss with his London accountants one of his company's merchandising deals for the next European tour. He was arrested as he got off the plane, the result of a complaint Jack had made about his lawyer's threats. These would have been harder to impute to Kaliostri if the airport police hadn't been up for arresting a celebrity on some pretext and if the musician hadn't compounded the problem by having in his possession enough cocaine to feed his habit for the few days he was in London. No sooner had he been arrested than a great hue and cry went out over the Atlantic airwaves. Mr. Arnold Feinstein and Mr. Kevin Kurtwangler arrived in London on the next Concorde flight. Mr. Feinstein was allowed through immigration. Mr. Kurtwangler was arrested for uttering threats over the public telephone and confined to a cell next door to his client. Jack wasn't at all surprised to receive a call from Mr. Feinstein at his London hotel. "Okay, okay" the American said, "call off the dogs."

"What dogs?" Jack replied innocently. It just so happened that Mrs. Kaliostri was sitting across the table from him at the time, her legs crossed but not so demurely. "I don't recall letting any dogs out." The remark made Lorenza mime a vigorous dance, using only her arms and magnificent torso.

"No need to fool around with me bud," Feinstein went on, "I know what this is about. I want my colleague out of jail and my client off the hook."

"That will cost a few dollars more."

Lorenza was ecstatic. She started to hum a movie theme.

"This sounds like a shakedown to me," the American said.

"It's not blackmail, it's called a divorce settlement, in full and final satisfaction of all claims inter partes."

"Don't give me any of that fancy Latin shit," the American attorney shouted, "I could buy and sell you ten times over bud."

"I'm sure you could Mr. Feinstein," Jack replied, "but that way your colleague and your client would still be charged with serious criminal offences."

"The Feds will back off if you tell them to." Feinstein said, "I've spoken to them."

"Ah, well, you're ahead of me," Jack replied, "in which event, I'm prepared to back off provided certain assurances are given for the safety of my client, and provided her friend gets to keep his balls." Lorenza laughed and shook a fist as if in victory.

"OK," Feinstein said, "you win. Let's not be ridiculous about this. The divorce settlement Kevin put forward was fine, you know that. You know this lousy jurisdiction of yours. The wife's not gonna get more than that from a judge in this country. There's no question of her getting access to everything the man's got. The court's gonna give her what it thinks is enough to keep up her lifestyle in the north east of fucking Britain for Chrissake! I've had input from top London alimony lawyers."

The American lawyer had touched a nerve there. He'd done his homework and, give or take a couple of million, he was on the right track. Lorenza's demands might be construed as excessive. "Get to the point," Jack replied crisply.

"So, okay, we fight it out, a lot of shit hits the fan, my client's in the crap, so's my colleague, but they'll ride it out. Heck, this is good publicity for Maxy baby! At the end of the day you'll have to take what's on the table."

"I'm still not following your drift," Jack replied.

"How much you getting paid for this?"

"Not enough."

"Okay, how does this sound? You take the deal on the table, and you get one hundred grand, cash, not dollars, sterling. How does that grab you?"

Jack looked across the table at Lorenza and winked. "You're offering me one hundred thousand pounds to compromise my client's claim on the terms already offered?"

"Yeah, it's a generous allowance. You have to withdraw the complaint against my client and my colleague at the same time."

"Maybe I haven't made myself clear," Jack said to him, "I told you I didn't like being threatened, but I also don't like being bribed."

Feinstein produced some sophisticated reasoning to demonstrate that his proposition did not amount to a bribe, merely an offer to pay Jack's reasonable costs. They must be on a different planet, these guys, Jack thought. Feinstein added: "The man can afford to be generous. Now let's get on with this shit."

There was a twinkle in Lorenza's eye. "You should take it," she said, "you may never see that much money again!"

Strangely, Jack was hurt by that. He continued to speak to the American lawyer. "I can't do deals with you on that basis. You must make an offer to my client. It must be more than the one already made."

"It's already in your client account, buddy," the American replied.

"What?" Jack exclaimed. Quickly he brought the bank account up on his computer screen and there it was, a telegraph transfer of £100,000, direct into the client account.

"How did you get the details?" he asked suspiciously.

"We asked another attorney near you, someone who deals with you regularly. A man called Kirby Potts. Know him?" the Yank drawled, reminding Jack of a similar conversation many years earlier concerning the same colleague.

Jack knew Potts all right. Reputedly the person who had put him in Henry Herron's bad books by repeating to one of his delinquent clients the lie that Jack suppressed a tape recording which would have proved Henry's innocence, Kirby Potts was the one in the local legal profession who deserved to wake up in the Kafkaesque nightmare of finding himself a cockroach. In fact, even that maligned creature would be justified in taking defamation proceedings after being compared publicly with this guy. Jack, however, said nothing about his local colleague, whom even the American did not respect sufficiently to protect his identity. "It'll have to go back," Jack replied, "I'll organise it now."

"Are you totally stupid?" Feinstein said. "You've never seen that much dough! The man is going to be seriously pissed if you don't take his offer." He then contradicted his earlier statement by adding, "do you realise he's getting some real bad shit thrown at him in there? I hold you responsible if anything happens to him. You are going to pay, pal. Big time! You'll be rat food by the time Maxy's finished with you. You are making serious enemies here, bud! I'm telling you, you are fucking history, you are a dead man!"

The venom with which the transatlantic lawyer spat out these threats, as if they were genuine and could be made real at any moment, was alarming but Jack kept his cool. "That's my lookout," he said. "I'm concerned only with my client's interests."

"Well take a bow Sir fucking Galahad! The Crusades rock on! Chivalry is not dead! Max's going to be really pleased with you. You're not a vegetarian too, are you?"

"No," Jack said, "why?"

"Because Maxy really likes eating vegetarians. He's not so crazy about meat-eaters. They don't taste as good. Capisce?" Jack said, "I can only give you two more minutes of my not very valuable time."

Mr. Feinstein sighed audibly. Bribery and corruption hadn't worked and he was running out of threats now. "Kev was right about you, you are a bag of shit. Okay, two mill, that's the deal."

"Sterling?"

"Dollars!"

"Make it sterling and I'll talk to my client." He winked at Lorenza, who hitched her skirt up a little more in response, then ran her tongue across shiny lips.

"Okay, you got it," the American replied with an air of resignation. Everyone kept slamming the phone down when Jack was trying to end things pleasantly.

A few days later Kaliostri's lawyers made an application for bail to the Court of Appeal. Jack was given notice to attend in case his evidence was required. The court was comprised of three High Court Judges, one of whom was Mr. Justice Parker. Jack had an interest in him: an alumni of the Royal Grammar School, it was rumoured that he was to be appointed the first Recorder of Northumberland. He looked also with considerable interest at the figure of Kaliostri as he sat in the dock. The musician looked down throughout the proceedings as his counsel outlined the many good reasons why he should be released. Among them was the suggestion that an inherent tendency towards claustrophobia had been exacerbated to the extent that the musician's sanity was in question as a result of his close confinement.

Jack was sufficiently moved to feel sure the Judges would relent and grant Kaliostri bail but Parker, who had obviously been delegated to play the lead role of the three judges, took up the cudgels. "The Court has the benefit of a report from the prison authorities," he told Kaliostri's barrister, who shifted uncomfortably on his feet, perhaps because there was something slightly unconstitutional, even if nowadays unsurprising, in the court having access to evidence which had not been conventionally proven. "I think you should read it." He handed the document across to the lawyer, who studied it impassively and then he turned and conferred with his client. "The document seems to suggest, if I read it correctly," the Judge continued, "that, quite contrary to the assertions you are making on his behalf, Mr. Kaliostri's needs are being catered for." He paused for effect. "It might even be said," he added with subtle acerbity, "that he and prison were made for each other." He looked quizzically at the now flummoxed counsel. "The implication is," the Judge added dryly, "that the whole thing is a cock and bull story."

"I hope it is not suggested," the barrister replied stiffly, "that my client invented a charade to deceive the court?"

"The court suggests nothing," Parker replied suavely. "It is merely another thread of a tapestry you have woven. If what you say is correct, Mr. Kennedy, your client should petition the Governor immediately to be placed in more amenable surroundings. This court is certain that he will be sympathetic."

"With the greatest of respect, that is unlikely," the barrister replied stiffly, his formal adherence to the rules of etiquette pierced for the first time, "as it is my client's contention that the Governor has some animosity towards him." Mr. Kennedy began to tread treacle. The three wise men looked askance at his attempts to promote Kaliostri's view that the Governor of the Scrubs had taken it upon himself to make the musician pay for the wrongs which he had inflicted upon English society. Like all conspiracy theories this one met with official intransigence and Mr. Kennedy was soon floundering like a beached whale. Parker put the stricken beast out of its misery. "Is that all you want to say, Mr. Kennedy?" he asked with a hypocritical smile and that was the end of Kaliostri's bail application. The musician had raised his head by now and he stared fixedly and, Jack could not help but feel, malevolently at the one among the Judges whom he perceived as his persecutor. A few moments later Jack stood up as the Court rose. Kaliostri caught the movement out of the corner of his eye. He leaned forward and whispered furtively to a tanned, sleek-haired man who turned in Jack's direction. He moved sideways across the bench and enquired who Jack was. The transatlantic tones led Jack to believe he was in the presence of one Kaliostri's American lawyers, perhaps Mr. Feinstein himself. When he made his identity known the American did a double-take but otherwise remained as suave as ever. He returned to Kaliostri and the whispering bout began again. The musician kept his head down, his face hidden behind a mass of flowing hair. It didn't escape Jack's attention how he clenched his fist and he heard words that Kaliostri clearly, in his anger, could not keep under his breath. "Come to gloat at me! I'll pay him back ten times over! I'll make him suffer. I'll get them all!" The venom in his voice made Jack shudder. He wanted to go over and say it wasn't true; he wasn't here to gloat; he wouldn't have come at all if the Court hadn't requested his presence and he had no desire to see Kaliostri remain in gaol. Discretion got the better of valour and he kept his own counsel. Kaliostri was led back down the stone steps by a prison officer who took him enthusiastically by the handcuffs and made his charge squeal in pain.

Back in Newcastle, Jack briefed Lorenza, trying not to express any opinion of her husband's plight but pointing out the facts and adding that the musician was obviously mentally disturbed by his incarceration, whether the case put forward by his barrister was fact or fiction. Lorenza looked on without batting an eyelid. She's a hard bitch, Jack thought, wondering uncomfortably what he'd got himself into. This wasn't what he'd become a lawyer for. He was about to say something when the phone rang. He was astonished when the receptionist told him Kaliostri was on the line from prison welfare. Alarmed, he asked, "how did he get this number?"

"He rang his home," the welfare officer replied and they told him his wife had come to see you. He's desperate to talk with her."

Jack repeated this to Lorenza, who looked suddenly more frightened than he'd ever seen her. "What am I going to do?" she asked wildly. "Am I allowed to talk to him?"

If she'd hoped he'd say no, he didn't oblige. "Of course you are," he replied without thinking that, one to one, her resolve might crack.

Lorenza cleared her throat and forced herself to say, "hi, how did you know I was here? Don't tell me. I know you're psychic." Her eyes grew gradually wider as she listened. She went pale and her legs seemed to wobble. Jack stood up, concerned, but she waved him away. "Yeah," she said, "I know. I really do.......I don't care about that.....I do care about you.....I just saw everything disappearing down the Swanee, that's all....okay, I believe you, thousands wouldn't." The call went on for ten minutes or so and, towards the end, something strange happened. Jack could hear bits and pieces of the caller's end too and they both began to speak in a foreign language. Jack had a modest facility with languages but this was not one he understood. It was a guttural, brutal language and, as Lorenza spoke, a look of intense concentration came over her face. Jack wondered if they believed the prison was listening in on the conversation. Kaliostri was still only a remand prisoner but they might still monitor his every movement.

Eventually Lorenza put the phone down and held up a hand in response to Jack's quizzical look. He watched her carefully as she sat weighing the pro's and con's. For all her objective beauty, a hardness emerged when she was deep in thought. Like a machine calculating, her features had no animation; the almost Egyptian cut of her hair hung like twin curtains over a face chiselled from marble. He shivered suddenly, as you do when someone treads on your grave. "I'm going to see him Jack," she said at length, "he wants a reconciliation."

Irrationally, Jack felt used. "If that's what you want, of course you've got the right, but aren't you acting in haste, on the strength of one phone call?"

Her voice was soothing as she replied. "I'll have this whole thing sorted out by the weekend. Otherwise, there'll be trouble. He's really got it in for you."

"Me?" Jack replied. "He's the one who broke the law."

"Don't do the crime if you can't do the time!" she responded brightly. "You don't really want to make an enemy of my husband, Jack."

He felt as if she was trying to deflect responsibility on to him and recalled his initial instinct not to get involved in this case. When Lorenza had first come to see him neither hell nor high water could have restrained her lust for vengeance. Now she had Kaliostri at her mercy, her pragmatism didn't ring true. If anyone could have gone fifteen rounds it was Lorenza Kaliostri. The whole episode had been a charade from the beginning. Maybe they'd been testing each other out, seeing who would blink first, two bored adults play-acting. It might have cost a few quid but lord knows what a night out in Paris would have set these two back! Maybe now it was getting a bit too close to the bone, too much like real life, so they'd called the crew off. Cut. "I don't want to be enemies with anyone," Jack replied. "It's a job. Nothing more, nothing less."

"He won't see it like that. He'll take it personally. Be careful! He has extraordinary powers."

Jack's scalp prickled as she said that and his whole frame gave an involuntary shudder, a movement she was quick to pick up. "What is it?" she asked. She was leaning forward as if she was concerned about him and, momentarily, that took him in. Once he had committed himself, it was like a challenge. He had to go on, assuming that Lorenza would notice if he dried up. "It's nothing much," he said. "When I was young I spent time in a home run by priests and nuns." She nodded, inviting him to confide further. "They used to scare the wits out of us. Dressing up as demons."

"Why?" she asked wide-eyed.

"I guess it was a Catholic thing. You ever heard of St. Peter's blowtorch?"

Lorenza shook her head.

"Well one of the nuns always came up with this image that if you sinned, really if you did anything bad, you grew a blemish on the soul which St. Peter burnt off with his blowtorch."

"Wow!" she replied.

"So, the way they made sure we behaved was to terrify us. As soon as the lights went down, you were just waiting for it. They come along the corridor outside the dormitory. They'd pretend to be all the fiends from hell and scare the living daylights out of you."

Jack had the vague feeling that Lorenza had homed in on his discomfort. Like a wolf which sniffs blood in the air or a shark, which can do so a mile away at sea, she focused on his weakness. He felt uncomfortable as she stared at him for what seemed an inordinately long time. "So you don't have any people, Jack?" He shook his head. "You're an orphan?"

Jack hated that word, hated the implication that it made him somehow inferior. Lorenza was on forbidden ground. "So?" he asked a trifle truculently.

"Something happened to you didn't it, back then?"

How did these people do it? How did they know so precisely where the jugular was? "No," he said but his face had coloured. His head was saying shut up but his mouth blathered on as if to cover over his confusion. "It's irrelevant, what's my past got to do with anything?"

It was obvious that she didn't believe him. "Come on," she said and it sounded gentle, "you can tell me?" Her attention was fixed now. Everything about her came to a point as she craned towards him, hanging on to his every word.

Jack's instinct was not to go into this but he had walked down this cul-de-sac and he couldn't get out. In any event it was a painful memory, one best left where it was. He shook his head. "Let's just say it wasn't a good time. People aren't always kind to children. I guess I had to learn early to look after myself."

"And this thing with Max brought something of that back?"

"Yes, I guess so, kind of like someone walking over your grave." He smiled. "Ah well," he added and shrugged. "Daft, isn't it?"

"No, it's cool. We like that."

"We?"

"You'll understand." She stood up to leave and made a victory v-sign from the door. As she was leaving she mentioned having a few friends round for a party. She wanted him to join the merry throng. Never much of a party animal, he tried to refuse but he gave in when she insisted.

CHAPTER 2

The musician and his American brief were released when Jack withdrew his complaint. That weekend, with some trepidation, he made his way up to Montagu Avenue. A video camera at the front door gazed at him blankly as he rang the doorbell. "Who is it?" a voice, distinctly female despite the robotic tone, said from inside.

"Jack Lauder," he replied.

"Jack who?"

He recognised Lorenza's voice despite the mechanical inflections. "Jack Lauder," he repeated gritting his teeth.

"Say again," and this time he heard metallic giggling.

"It's Jack! Your lawyer, Jack Lauder."

"Oh that Jack Lauder!" This was followed by guffaws. A whining noise invited a push at the door and it opened. Jack stood in a long marble tiled hall. Dressed in suit and tie – everyone else looked like a fugitive from the punk rock era – a bunch of flowers in one hand and a bottle of champagne in the other, he felt out of place. A group of young people regarded him coolly from their poses, draped over the furniture and the piano, glasses in their hands; Lorenza came down the hall, dressed in a black silk flowing thing. She fairly bounced along. Jack guessed she wasn't wearing a bra but she'd had enough plastic surgery to prevent landslides. Taking his presents without a word of thanks, she handed them to a waiter and then grabbed hold of him like a long lost friend. Her bosom heaved visibly below the low cut gown and she brought her leg forward out of the slit at the side. She had nothing on her feet except red painted toe nails. He had the impression of being slowly devoured. No, that wasn't quite right. It was more like the moment when the waiter delivers the meal to the table, lifts the silver lid with a cry of "voila!" and the diner appraises the plate rapaciously. "I have something to tell you," she whispered breathlessly, "but it'll have to wait." Her fingers were suddenly touching Jack's abdomen. He experienced a tremor below. It had been a long time and that cleavage was a cavern measureless to man.

"About the case?"

She nodded. "This is Steve," she said introducing him to a man who carried a camera and, from time to time, took pictures of the guests. He was wise enough not to try to capture Jack on film. "Champagne, Jack?" Lorenza said thrusting a glass into his hand.

"That's my name," he replied. He saluted her and quaffed from the glass. He wasn't the sort to take delicate sips.

Lorenza moved off and mingled with other guests, the cameraman's hand on her rear as if she needed to be steered by the rudder. The first person they spoke to was a man in a loud suit, whom Jack found vaguely familiar. The man made a bee-line for him and addressed the lawyer as if he was an old acquaintance. It became clear as he spoke that he hadn't the slightest inkling that Jack had not recognised him and the lawyer was too embarrassed by his forgetfulness to let on, so he let the other man do all the talking, simply nodding or shaking his head where it seemed appropriate. From the conversation Jack fathomed that he was a policeman and was struck by the incongruity of his appearance at a party where someone needing a favour at some later date might use the licentiousness of the occasion to try and compromise him. At least the realisation of his fellow guest's profession explained Jack's sense of familiarity but it was only moments before they parted, when they had apparently exhausted any meaningful conversation, that his identity became clear. "Bit of a turn up for the book, wasn't it, Henry passing away like that?"

"Henry?" Jack responded politely.

"Aye, Henry Herron. You know. You defended him?"

Of course, Jack realised, this was Inspector Barry Freer. Jack had had many dealings with Superintendent, now Chief Superintendent, Lowther in over a decade since that case but he hadn't come across Freer again. "Yes," he replied, "I heard he was ill. Then I found out he'd died. To be frank, I've had nothing to do with him for years."

"Nah. Blamed you, didn't he? Thought you hadn't done enough?"

"Actually," Jack replied stiffly, "he blamed the police for fitting him up. I was a minor cog in the machine."

"Not what I heard," the copper said. "I was told he had it in for you, big time."

"Who told you that?" Jack asked.

"Blacklock Spiers."

Jack sighed aloud. "Well," he said, "Blacklock and the truth are a bit like a couple of boxers trying to knock seven bells out of each other, aren't they?"

Freer's laughter seemed forced. There was strained silence for a few moments in which Jack first thought of and then dismissed as too antique the question of why Freer had misrepresented his knowledge of the Spiers tape. Then the policeman said, "any road up, what brings you here?"

"Oh, I know Lorenza," he replied airily.

"Oh aye, a few have been there," Freer said with a malicious wink and then added, "have you met the man himself?"

"Max? No, I can't say I have. Somehow I don't think it would be a good idea, either."

"Oh?" Freer's eyes glittered as he looked at Jack waiting for him to feel uncomfortable enough to continue.

Unfortunately, the lawyer fell for it. "Yeah," he added, "kind of a conflict of interest," he added. "I don't think I'd get on very well with him anyway. Seems a bit of a....." Then he remembered he wasn't at liberty to express opinions and he shut up.

"Tosspot? That what you were about to say?" the sneering copper replied.

"Well....." Jack said, truly embarrassed now. He had been about to use the word "megalomaniac" but it seemed better now to shrug and say no more.

"Good friend of mine is Max," Freer added. "I'll tell him you were asking after him. He clapped the lawyer on the back as each of them moved on. I bet you will, you snide bastard, Jack thought, He should have kept his mouth shut. He didn't want to prolong this hostility. Freer had wanted to get his dig in. That much was obvious. He'd tried with the Henry comment, then Kaliostri. Having got what he wanted, he could go off and misrepresent Jack even further to one of the richest men in the country and one who already bore a grudge against his wife's lawyer. This could be bad for business. Still, there was nothing Jack could do about it now, the damage was done.

At least his concentration could centre on a girl with blonde hair whom he had noticed glancing at him from time to time from the other side of the white, grand piano. The second time he noticed, he thought, hmm, quite delicious, and was beginning to have fantasies about those slender arms and legs, not to mention the white, provocative, bared midriff The third time he smiled at her, she smiled back. You're in here, son, he thought. He didn't have to do a thing because the girl moved on him. She was small, quite well made and vivacious, smiling as she walked towards him. "Hello," she said. "Josephine Jackson." She held out her hand and stared at his suit. "You must have thought this was the Oscars.

Obviously, you've never been to one of Lorenza's parties." It turned out she was a journalist and, once Jack had introduced himself and saw that his name rang a bell, he was a trifle disconcerted to find she too knew of the Henry Herron saga. Will I never be rid of that bastard, he thought. It turned out that Josephine was doing an item on well-known North East hard men. Henry's name had come up in that context and it was particularly topical because of his recent death. "You represented him, didn't you?" she asked. "How do you do that? How do you represent someone you know is guilty?"

"Who's guilty?" Jack responded wryly. "Do I decide?" Her question was innocent enough but Jack didn't want to dwell on the subject. He didn't ask why so many people remembered a case he would rather forget. Fortunately, he didn't have to struggle hard to change the subject because Lorenza came across and dragged Josephine away to meet someone. Jack, left to his own devices, thought, some you win and some you lose but, even though she had disappeared into the crowd, he could hear her laughing across the other side of the room. Attracted by the laughter, he turned in her direction. He was momentarily surprised to see a bevy of beautiful women staring across at him. Josephine caught his eye, winked slowly and deliberately, making him break into a grin. Her tongue curled slowly across her white, slightly protruding upper teeth, acknowledging the future promise.

Embarrassed by his excitement, Jack looked away. His eye was caught by an object on a shelf in an alcove lit by a concealed violet light. The ornaments on the shelf deserved a second glance. One was a lion with a human face, a sphinx-like creature. It wasn't without company: other erect statues of naked men and women with animal heads, and of animals, conversely, with human faces, adorned the shelf. They were curiously beautiful but in an unapproachable way. He didn't dare touch them and he noticed that no one else went near the alcove until he became aware of a tall man, dressed in dark clothes, who had moved silently beside him, Jack looked at him curiously. "Excellent workmanship, don't you think?" the man asked. The newcomer had heavily hooded eyes with long lashes. An abundance of greying, facial hair gave the impression of age and the dark eyes possessed their own depth of knowledge, perhaps wisdom. His voice had been soft, almost a whisper.

"Dangerous to leave them on show like that," Jack replied. "They should be worth a pretty penny." He looked round. Lorenza wasn't all that discerning about her party guests. There was someone here from each of her alleged seven incarnations.

"Ah, it matters not," the man said in a tone tinged with melancholy, "Max could recreate them at any time."

Jack asked: "you mean that Max Kaliostri did these?"

"Does that surprise you? That objects of great beauty should emanate from such a sewer of a mind?" The man looked at him with eyebrows raised.

Jack relaxed visibly. Not everyone here was a friend of the rock star. "No, perhaps my first thought was that these were precisely what I would expect," he replied.

"Oh?" The man seemed surprised.

"Yes, well, he's a bit of a dilettante, isn't he? These are good but they are essentially superficial. Like their maker." The man tugged on his beard. He seemed to be on the verge of saying something and then, without another word, he disappeared as suddenly and mysteriously as he had arrived. He just melted into the crowd and was gone.

Jack had been there about an hour and a half and was looking to make his excuses when the arrival of the obnoxious Kirby Potts put the cap on a pretty miserable evening. The florid-faced newcomer began immediately an obsequious, creeping deference to the minor celebrities he was rubbing shoulders with. He acknowledged Jack from across the room with a wave of a flowery handkerchief whilst ingratiating himself with a young girl, whose backside he pinched quite openly. The girl squealed and looked offended. Quite outraged, Jack stepped in. "Who is your friend, Kirby?" he asked politely. The girl seemed pleased with his intervention.

"Don't you know the Recorder's daughter?" the half-drunk Potts responded. He swayed on his feet and his words were slurred. "Jessica Parker, this is Jack the lad Lauder." Shaking hands solemnly with the young lady, Jack was surprised by her reaction. He had no idea she knew even his name. The daughter of one of the country's most prominent judges, the one indeed who had done most in the Court of Appeal to block her host's bail, although the incongruity of her presence at this party didn't strike him immediately, there was no earthly reason why she should know of him. Jessica seemed to seize the opportunity, however, to launch into an effusive paean of praise, as if Jack was the city's best known celebrity. With growing discomfort he noticed another group of Kaliostri sycophants, hanging on to her every word. His unease was compounded by the impression that the girl seemed to be acting, hamming it up terribly, as if she'd been put up to it. She reached towards him and put her hands on his waist. Her cheek touched his and she kissed him gently.

Extricating himself, Jack, aware of the grinning effigy of Kirby Potts in the long mirror, said, "whoa, young lady, hold on there. I'm not used to people making a fuss of me." Jack managed to persuade her to stop and, giggling with her cronies, she moved away to a safe distance from which she continually looked at Jack and smiled. He returned the smile in an embarrassed way and noticed the older man, who had spoken to him before, come over and talk with the girls. Jessica said something, which made the man look in Jack's direction. The lawyer returned the stare and the elderly man looked away as if he had a guilty secret. "Thought I was in there," Potts interrupted in his bluff way. "She might be the judge's daughter but she don't always do what she oughta." He laughed. "I've heard she's not that choosy. Looks like she wouldn't need much persuading to get 'em off for you! What is it you've got, Jack? Can I have some?"

Jack had no intention of indulging in vulgar talk with Kirby Potts but he was courteous enough to respond, even if it was only by changing the subject. "I doubt if her parents would be happy if they knew she was here."

"What! The old man would blow his top!" Potts responded. "She's a right little tart, though, Jack. All right for you bachelors, I'd say. Bit of a hippy. Always following Max around." He must have noticed Jack's surprise because he continued, "she goes to all his concerts. She's a groupie, man! Didn't you know? You're further back than the Chinese, you!" He laughed and clapped Jack on the back. "Aye, she's off to India with him, her and the rest of his harem. Sex on tap! Wish I could get some of that!" Kirby made a fist and pulled a lewd face. Jack looked across curiously at the young girl. He was thinking, I wonder if Parker knew anything of that when he heard his bail application. If so, he should have disqualified himself. The implications were, however, too big to grasp. Giving the Judge the benefit of the doubt he felt sorry for the Parkers suddenly, even if they were gigantic snobs. God, who would have kids, he thought. "Anyway," Potts went on, "wouldn't have thought Max would be very happy about you being here. He's here, you know."

"I was invited by Lorenza," Jack replied, "and I wish she hadn't bothered." He looked around, curiosity killing the cat.

"Where is he anyway?"

"He's in invisible mode," Potts replied.

Suddenly recognising that he shouldn't be here, and sensing that the champagne was beginning to go down a touch too easily, Jack sought out his hostess. "You wanted to talk to me?" he reminded her. "To be honest, I've got an early start tomorrow, and I was thinking of going home."

"Oh you can't go yet, Jack," she replied then added artfully, "you're right, I did want to talk to you." She opened the door of a room. Loud noises from the sofa led to a hasty retreat. "Oops, sorry," she said. She took him by the hand and led him up the semi-circular marble staircase into her room. "Don't be shy!" she exclaimed. A small sitting room with a bathroom off led through an arch to the bedroom, where a naked woman, as black as ebony and beautiful of proportion and face, reclined on a water bed. Liquid eyes examined Jack. Lorenza crossed to the bed and sat down. The bed rippled as she settled, causing the African girl to giggle. Lorenza began to stroke her thigh. "She's Ethiopian," she explained without looking at Jack, who had frozen where he stood, his breath held in a cage just beneath the windpipe.

Jack looked at the girl. She had an almost noble bearing. "A damsel with a dulcimer once in a vision I saw," he said when he had regained his composure. The words were lost on Lorenza but had the effect of putting her off balance. Her eyebrows arched. The girl looked up out of soft, brown eyes. He continued: "It was an Abyssinian maid and on her dulcimer she played Dreaming of Mount Abora..."

Time seemed to be suspended. The gorgeous girl sighed and stretched like a cat. "Wouldn't you like her, Jack?" Lorenza purred. "She won't mind, she's beautiful and bountiful." Jack felt like a voyeur as he watched them, unable to tear his eyes away. Lorenza arched her leg up so the whole of it was showing from the thigh down. What was on offer was tempting. Then, just after he'd thought about and rejected the idea, Lorenza seemed to tire of the girl and she shooed her out without giving her a moment to dress. The girl didn't seem to mind. It occurred to Jack that she was drugged to the eyeballs. He caught his breath again however as she brushed past him with a movement as liquid as the look in her eyes. Her hand reached out as if to shake his formally. He felt ridiculous as he took the slender hand with the long fingers and then as he tried to retract his he felt her clinging on. Another line of poetry occurred to him. "Her fingers were like the tissue of a Japanese paper napkin." Jack looked up into her eyes and saw something good and generous. Finally she took her fingers away and swayed out of the door, just as magnificent from the back.

Lorenza didn't stir from her provocative position but she had become altogether more businesslike and despite the incongruity of the moment Jack concentrated on what she was saying. She'd sorted out a deal with Max, one that meant she wouldn't have to worry about anything again, barring the end of the world that is, and now she wanted Jack to stop the divorce. He realised he'd been right – the whole thing had been playacting from the beginning. She stared at him, mouth slightly open, her tongue playing on the edges of her lips. "We want you, Jack."

There it was again. "We?" he echoed. She ignored his question. Her hands held his waist momentarily and her perfume overwhelmed him. Her voice low and gravelly, she added, "you know you want it? It's no big deal, just take it."

Momentarily, the temptation was great and multi-factored. The woman was a beauty, a great socialite, a catch as well as a notch on the gun; the idea of taking her here with her husband downstairs brought those echoes of more barbarous times when warriors took the spoils and humiliated their opponents, sowing their own seed in their women. The veneer of civilisation might have made men behave more responsibly but the atavism was still in the psyche. Still, the veneer overlay was not brittle in Jack and he quickly dismissed the urge to behave badly. Trying not to sound too flustered he replied, "no thanks, and think about it, it's hardly the way to celebrate the restating of your wedding vows, is it?"

She laughed and stood up. "You are so unhip it's unbelievable!" It was the work of a moment to remove the dress. She stood their naked. Jack caught his breath because she was one hell of a woman, but unfortunately she had this way of making the nape of his neck turn prickly.

"Well, I'm sorry Lorenza, but things aren't right. I don't want to, it's as simple as that, no offence to you." He wasn't lying. The presentiment of some unknown evil had dispelled whatever passion had made him ready to concede. She knew the game was lost because her tone became vicious.

"Don't patronise me you bastard!" she replied. "If we want you, we'll have you. What say do you have?" She picked up a silver hairbrush from the dressing table and threw it. It glanced off his raised hand. She flung open the walk-in wardrobe. Inside the structure, hanging on the side wall, was a series of faces – they looked like men with pained expressions. It took a few moments for him to appreciate that they were masks. Even then they looked like lost souls, tortured beyond belief, mortals suspended in their agony. Lorenza appeared not to give them a second thought as she pulled on a gown. It was black, covered in silver and golden shapes, like the planets.

"Oh come on!" Jack said.

"Do you know who I am?" she shouted venomously.

"Don't tell me," he replied, "the wicked witch of the west?" It was meant in jest but had the opposite effect.

Lorenza screamed. She took a stick from the wardrobe and pointed it at him, waving it like a wand. She began to chant. The door swung open and a number of men burst in. A flash popped as the man with the camera stumbled in the rush. The first man crossed himself, dropped to his knees and cowered. The others followed his example. Jack was shocked to see Potts among them. He could dine out richly on this one. Lorenza, naked except for the cloak over her shoulders, stood proud as a group of middle class males hit the deck. The next moment a rush of wind followed the congregation through the open door as if someone had left all the windows open. Jack could feel it against his back, as if it was pushing him over a precipice. Lorenza confronted it. It roared around her; her long black hair spread out horizontally behind her; her expression was ecstatic. The wind clutched her robe so it streamed out. Starlight appeared in a black void as if the roof had opened. Lorenza's body convulsed rhythmically. She turned towards him, pointed the wand and chanted. Josephine Jackson bowled in through the door like tumbleweed, as if she couldn't control her actions. She looked at Jack, white-faced, mouthing something. Lorenza screamed and pointed at Josephine with the wand. "I know you. I know what you want!" Jack had learned in a hard school that at times like this you show nothing, not a flicker of dread. He started to walk towards the door, leaning against the fury of that wind, one mother of a special effect. "Walk out on us Jack," Lorenza shouted, "and you'll regret it." The room seemed to be racing around her as if she stood in the middle of a twister. It was some trick of the lighting and the ventilation system. The lengths some people went to just to keep up appearances! "He won't rest until he gets you," she snarled. "You've made an enemy for life there. Bad move, what you did to him. You put him in danger and, worse, you made a fool of him. I tried to help you Jack. I did a deal with him because he threatened to kill you. But that's nothing compared to what I'll do to you now. You've screwed us once too often."

Now that was too much. Him screwed them! He hadn't charged her a penny more than she'd given him initially. Had she forgotten he could have got twenty times that for simply rowing along with Max's lawyer? Incensed, possessing a mental energy, which drove back the gale, he strode to the door, grabbing the petrified Josephine Jackson as he passed. They took the stairs two at a time, the blast trying to push them back up. They turned the corner into the hall and stopped in their tracks. The figure of the elderly man loomed up in front of them. Tall, his arms outstretched like wings, there seemed no way past him. Momentarily unnerved, clasping Josephine to him, Jack was surprised when the stranger smiled, bowed slightly and, striding down the corridor in front of them, opened the front door. It was flat calm outside. There wasn't a sound. "Jesus, I've never been so scared," Josephine exclaimed.

"Schizophrenia," Jack replied. "She's mentally ill."

"The guy with the camera," she said, "he was supposed to get a picture of you."

Jack stopped in his tracks but she locked arms and hurried him on. "You mean, like *in flagrante*?"

Josephine laughed. It was a shrill, weird, frightened laugh. "Of course," she replied, "of you screwing her. Don't be so naïve, Jack! What do you think they've got against you?"

"They?" Jack replied. Everyone talked in the plural.

The question seemed to disorientate Josephine. Momentarily, she was flustered. "She's a control freak! This witchcraft thing really scares me. Max is really big into it, you know? He's got incredible powers!"

"Don't you see that's what he wants you to believe? That's the point. Take it from me, it might be very clever but it's all conjuring and special effects, it's not real. You remember that guy at the door, the old guy? He wasn't fazed by it. What was she getting at with that abuse she directed at you?"

She seemed embarrassed. "She thinks Max and me had this thing. She's just got a suspicious mind."

"Has she got any justification?" he asked. Josephine didn't reply.

CHAPTER 3

On Grandstand Road they flagged down a taxi. "Come and have a coffee at my place," Josephine said. Jack didn't hesitate. The evening could end a score draw yet. He wasn't disappointed. Mutual desire dispensed with the foreplay and Josephine proved an energetic lover, her orgasms multiplying with each strangled sob, each short, sharp gasp of breath, as if she were asphyxiating.

The two of them must have dozed off after passionate lovemaking and Jack awoke to feel Josephine's back snuggling into his chest. The room was pitch black, punctuated by faraway light, like starlight. He couldn't see an inch in front of him but he could see the weird pinpricks of light in the distance. As he awakened he felt her stir against his loins. Her hair fell over her breasts as he reached for her. Vaguely, he remembered it as shorter but he took no notice as her moist and creamy body began to move rhythmically. Sighing, she pulled her knees forward on to all fours and uttered a deep-throated growl. The star dark room filled with the clamour of two ecstatic animals yelping in the throes of uncontrolled lust. He heard her grunted, incoherent words as if in a dream. Their intensity, as much as her movement, brought him to climax.

Savagely enjoyable, the experience left him dead to the world. He must have fallen into a deeper sleep this time because he awoke with a start. He was lathered. His head swam through thick mud as if he'd gone to sleep in a drunken state. Finding it difficult to move his limbs, his body drenched with sweat, he heaved his head towards Josephine's sleeping form and nuzzled her gently. Her body was wet; a strong stench pervaded his nostrils; he leapt back in shock. There was a gaping hole where her head should have been; her skin was cold; she had no head. His hand touched the frayed end of her neck. "My God!" he screamed. Pulling the bedclothes back, he leapt out of bed, struggling to find the light switch. His eyes became accustomed to the gloom and a form, the soft, sensuous shape of a woman, detached itself from the shadows and made for the bed. Was he dreaming? He could see the dim white shape of Josephine's body on the bed. The second female figure bestrode it and, staring in his direction, said, "Jack, it's you we want. Join us, come on!"

Lorenza reached one hand towards him; her body arched over the form in the bed. Struck dumb he couldn't speak. Was that blood he saw streaked across her back, in her long hair falling like a curtain over the prostrate form beneath her? Had she killed Josephine? She moved aside arching her back as she did so, stretching her thigh and leg like an animal, growling with lust. "Look," she whispered, "look at your lover now!" She pulled the bedclothes back and Jack found himself staring at the prostrate torso of a slaughtered pig. Lorenza's laugh shrieked at him.

Jack's mind raced. Grabbing enough clothes to make himself decent, he crashed down the stairs and into the street. Storm rivers gushed down the garden path. Pulling on his shirt and trousers on the move, he began to run the quarter mile or so to the Haymarket, imagining winged demons flying from the house in hot pursuit. He kicked up spray as he ran. A roaring behind him made him redouble his efforts, his breath coming in gasps, his lungs burning. The thing howled like a banshee as it came over his shoulder. He stumbled and fell to the ground, the water pouring over him. An ambulance passed by, its siren, the source of the awful shriek he had heard a few moments before. Deranged laughter seemed to echo on the wind but when he looked back up the street he could see nothing.

The cold water pulled him together and he jogged the remaining distance. When he stopped at a taxi queue, he looked at his hands. They seemed to glisten red. The moisture on his body felt sticky and uncomfortable and he had the awful thought that he was covered in the gruesome beast's blood. People in the queue looked at him strangely but his mind was in too much turmoil to care.

Eventually, he got a taxi and arrived home. It wasn't yet dawn. Fumbling with the keys of the door, he went into the hall. He stiffened immediately. Something was wrong. A black cloth was draped over the mirror. Ripping it off, he saw words scrawled on the mirror's surface in what looked like blood: "See you in Hell pig." He could hear the thumping of his heart as he began a thorough search of the house, checking all the downstairs rooms. Gingerly he moved upstairs, not knowing what to expect. He checked all the rooms and finally moved to the master bedroom. He put the light on. There was nothing to be seen. He went to the window, looking into the garden. Nothing. Puzzled, he picked up the telephone and rang the number of the local police station. "I want to report a break in," he told the Desk Sergeant.

"Oh?" The police Sergeant said as if he couldn't care less.

"Who's speaking?" When he found out who it was he treated Jack with a little more respect. "At home Mr. Lauder? My, my, you sound as if you've had a bad night." The Sergeant told him to wait there and someone would be straight round. Jack put the phone down and looked at the bed. Something was wrong. He hadn't noticed earlier a bulge underneath the duvet. Retreating slightly, as if scared to pull back the bedclothes, eventually he yanked them back. He yelled in shock. The bed was smeared in blood. At the top beneath the pillow was a white head severed at the neck. Gingerly, he turned it over. It was a pig's head.

Sitting in the kitchen he smoked a cigarette, a rare occurrence. He could barely hold a cup of tea; his fingers wouldn't lock together. The doorbell rang and he was gratified to see Lowther at the front door. "They've brought me in on this one Jack, you must be important," he said jocularly before the look on the lawyer's face made him realise something was fundamentally wrong. "Just kidding," he said. "I was in the front office when your call came through."

"I don't really know where to start," Jack said.

"Start right here," Lowther replied. "Anything stolen?"

"No," Jack said. "All they did was put that black velvet drape over the mirror. You can see what they wrote on it."

Lowther went up and examined it. "Looks like blood." They went up the stairs and Jack showed him the pig's head. "My God!" the hardened copper exclaimed. "Whoever put that there is giving you a message. That's how the villains warn grasses to leave town! What have you been up to, bonny lad?"

That wasn't an easy question, not if Jack wanted to miss out the more prurient details. "I was at a party at Lorenza Kaliostri's," he began.

"Oh, slumming it, I see?" the policeman responded. Jack felt like mentioning Barry Freer's presence but he bit his tongue. He didn't want to grass him up, even if he had no time for the detective. "I think this has got something to do with Max Kaliostri." Briefly he told Lowther what he could of his dealings with the rock star. "You know how to win friends and influence people," the policeman replied with more than a hint of sarcasm. "Right, let's see what we can find out!" They drove off in a marked police car to the Spital Tongues house.

When they got there, the lights were off, the place was deserted but the front door was unlocked. Lowther followed Jack up the bedroom, where his clothes were neatly stacked, as if housekeeping had cleared up after an untidy hotel guest. Jack stared round in disbelief. "Ah ha!" Lowther said, winking at the embarrassed lawyer, clearly aware now of the detail missing from the statement. The bed was made. There was no sign of its grotesque occupant. Just to check, Jack pulled the covers back. There was nothing there. Lowther looked at him. "You over doing it?" he asked. "Burning the candle at both ends?"

The next day Jack discovered that Kaliostri and Lorenza had left for America so they couldn't be questioned. His fears about Josephine's fate proved unfounded. She also turned up in the States with a new job as Kaliostri's media co-ordinator. Lowther managed to get in contact with her and she accused Jack of harassment, her recollection of events different from his. Jack got on his high horse. "Well, charge them and we'll bloody well see who the courts believe," he said. Lowther pointed out that the press would have a field day. "Prominent solicitor doesn't know if he knocked off the North's favourite television journalist or the rock star's wife! Or both! You couldn't win either way!" The policeman's broad smirk was justified. Jack had no choice other than to take the hit. God only knew what photos were being bandied around. "How do you do it, Stanley?" Lowther laughed.

CHAPTER 4

Jack's home was a rambling old Georgian house set in its own grounds not far from the North East Coast. It had originally served as the officers' quarters for the Spanish Battery and so lay within an easy horse ride of that ancient station, which was based on what is now Collingwood Hill at Tynemouth. The house had always been Jack's castle but around the time of these events there was a period when he felt so insecure that he perpetually laboured under the illusion that it was entered regularly by intruders – not burgled, just broken into. The thought forced him to take the practical step of changing the locks and he adopted a routine of checking the house every night. One weekend he had a lot of work on and was trying to catch up so he didn't go out on the town. When he'd finished he downed a couple of whiskeys and went to bed, falling almost immediately into a deep sleep.

He awoke suddenly from a deep and dreamless sleep into crystal clarity. Something had woken him. He lay there in the dark listening to the heating pipes cough and the old house creak. The fear, which had frozen him, was intensified by the darkness. Voices somewhere chanted a haunting melody in which his name was mentioned. Easing himself out of bed he crouched in the darkness, listening. The sound came from outside. He approached the window and, trying not to move the curtain, peered out through a chink. On the lawn round the sundial a group of people stood motionless, each holding a candle. Dressed like monks and nuns they sang and looked up at the house. Livid,

Jack picked up the telephone to call the police. The line was dead. It must have been cut. Jack moved back to the window. The group, now at the foot of the steps, stared up. Jack dressed quickly. It was five miles to the police station. He'd have to get out the back and run all the way. What would he say? He'd already acquired the reputation of a mild eccentric. Creeping down the stairs he listened at the front door. The chanting grew louder. His mind raced. Hands rattled the letter box; eyes peered through the slot. He pressed himself back against the wall, not wanting them to see him, and crept into the front room, where he crouched down below the double window. Suddenly a horrific face filled the windowpane and he started back in shock. The figure smashed the glass. Jack shouted out. The chanting got louder as if they smelled blood. The creature heaved itself in. Jack smashed his fist in its face. It lurched back. The chanting stopped. A shriek of laughter rent the air. The intruders darted away. They ran back and forth across the garden, jumping and shrieking like dancers in macabre ballet. They disappeared through the trees at the far boundary and were lost in the night. Jack wandered round for a few moments in a state of confusion and then he went down the cellar where he found a hammer, nails and enough wood to board up the broken window. Plucking up sufficient courage to go to the police station he checked up and down the drive when he came out of the front door then got in the car and drove away. A white plastic bag fluttered from a tree and made him jump out of his skin. A fox stared at him from a farm gate. In a state of nervous tension, he reached the police station. The uniformed Constable offered him a cup of hot sweet tea but the look on his face showed that he found the story incredible. Promising to send someone to look into it he shared his thought that it was probably a bunch of practical jokers, some former clients who might know Jack lived alone.

Secure in the knowledge the police were on their way, Jack was off guard when he walked up his front steps He took out his key, put it in the lock and turned it to find the door already open. Had he left it open? When he went into the hall he realised he hadn't. The house had been entered in his absence. Clothes and other belongings were strewn about the hall, wet as if they had been out in the rain. The mirror in the hall had been turned back so it faced the wall. Glancing up the stairwell he saw a white flash as something moved out of vision. He went up the stairs two at a time, shouting at the top of his voice. These hooligans weren't going to wreck his home. He'd caught them in the act and the police would soon be here. The Kaliostris weren't going to get away this time with their concocted alibis. He crashed through the bedroom door. It was pitch black and he was momentarily blinded because he'd come out of the light. In the pale gleam of the mirror stood a semi-naked, muscular man. He wore an oriental mask and held a wicked, long weapon, like a Samurai sword. Before Jack could react something was slipped over his head from behind. He put his hand up but too late. Garroted by a knotted rope and forced to kneel, he watched as the demonic, oriental face leaned over him. His eyes started to bulge as the rope tightened. The demon laughed. It pointed the knife. "Jack, it's you we want."

Sometime later he was shaken awake by two police officers whose eyes stood out on stalks.

It turned out there was only one police officer. "Who did this?" he asked.

Detained overnight at hospital for the neck wounds to be treated, Jack had pause for thought. This had to stop, even if it meant him swallowing his pride and asking for a truce. He knew what he'd like to do to the Kaliostris but escalation spelt disaster.

Duly discharged by the doctor, he rang Lorenza to ask for a meet. Unfortunately, he got the maid. Lorenza was out of town, had been for two days, and no, she hadn't left any forwarding address. Goodbye.

Anxiously, he waited for the next move but nothing further happened. Did Kaliostri feel he had paid him back sufficiently in kind for the one moment of genuine humiliation in his life? It seemed not entirely. In a malicious postscript, Jack received a summons to attend the Solicitor's Disciplinary Tribunal as a result of complaints made by his 'American colleagues' – the flattering description of Feinstein, Gluck, Zimmermann Harper. The charge had been tabled through the New York lawyers' local agent, once again the seedy, scheming Kirby Potts. It alleged that Jack had attempted to blackmail the American law firm into paying him £100,000 as a condition of dropping criminal charges against one of their partners and their client. Potts took up the cudgels with all the venom of one who had long harboured a grudge. Lorenza didn't answer her subpoena to appear and support Jack's case and, despite the entreaties of the Superintendent and others, the tribunal censured him without taking any draconian measures. They had to find something wrong. It was political. Jack had breached etiquette when, knowing that the American lawyer would be arrested, he had tacitly invited him to the country for a round table meeting to resolve the issues in the divorce. They might be colonials but they were entitled to a warning before being no-balled! "I knew you'd be all right," Potts told him afterwards in his sibilant voice, wary that his blows had been insufficient to knock out his adversary and now trying to curry favour and avoid any backlash.

"There was nothing personal. It was the clients. It was business, you understand?"

"Sure, let it lie" Jack replied, grimacing as he shook the man's limp, moist hand and looked into his tiny, currant bun eyes. The same went for the Kaliostris. Rather than perpetuate the feud, Jack hoped the deranged musician would let the dogs sleep.

PART FOUR

CHAPTER 1

Just as it had taken a simple twist of fate to put Jack in the hands of Max Kaliostri, another intervened now to put the lawyer firmly out of the madman's reach. Pressing commitments took him abroad for an extended stay and, if he was less excited these days than he had been in his prime about those occasions which forced him to travel out of the country, this trip had its highlights. He returned home reinvigorated, intent upon injecting the dynamism into his everyday life which he had experienced on his travels.

One thing he noticed on his return, when ploughing through the inevitable backlog of his post, was Henry Herron's manuscript journal. Mr. Pardoe had sent it in during his absence. He had so many things on his mind, including the need to earn a living to pay for the expensive trip he'd just undertaken, that he consigned the neatly written work to the back burner to dip into when he had more leisure time.

His renewed, positive outlook on life brought an immediate change of luck in the person of Rachel MacLean. He first noticed her in a small square in Newcastle City centre. She, like him, was gazing at the newly erected statue of Vulcan. It would have been impossible not to notice the girl's tall, hourglass figure, her long, straight, black hair and long legs. He wondered what her face was like. "Hmm!" he said as he took in the bronze figure of the lame god, cast in such a way that it looked like an astronaut. When he spoke aloud, Rachel turned and, noting the hint of sarcasm in his voice, said, "what?" Jack was momentarily struck dumb. She had the kind of face that would have kept the Tyne shipbuilders on the launch pad for a century. "Have you got a problem with it?" Her accent was lightly, liltingly Scottish.

Jack grinned. "I never saw the Romans as spacemen. I admit, though, it has its merits. Really, it's quite good."

"Oh, damn it with faint praise, why don't you?" she replied mischievously. "You can take my photo next to it, if you want?" She handed him her camera.

"Delighted," he replied. "I usually charge tourists but, okay, it's a freebie for you." As he looked through the lens at her snuggling up to the metal giant's limbs his light-heartedness rebounded on him. "Jesus, you are gorgeous!" he whispered. With her adopted pose of one knee slightly forward and her hips exaggerated, she was the sexiest thing he had ever seen. He had read somewhere that men think of sex some ridiculous number of times every day and he was proving it true in a few seconds. He took the photograph, attempting, by his leg movements, to conceal the effect of her presence, and tried to make small talk. "You're a visitor here, then?"

"I've just got a job at the university. Isn't that great?" Captivated by her enthusiasm, he quickly agreed. Desperate to keep her talking longer, he asked her if she knew anyone locally. "No," she said, "stranger in town."

"Could I buy you lunch? I mean, as you're a newcomer, just so you don't get the wrong idea about us all?" He looked at her hopefully. Could she discern his fear of rejection?

She gave no sign. "How do I know you're a nice guy?" she asked with a cute smile.

"You don't! Maybe I'm not. Nice guy isn't part of the deal!"

"Maybe I don't like nice guys. Always had terrible taste in men. If you qualify, you can buy me lunch." With that they introduced themselves and Jack learned his new acquaintance's name and that she hailed from Loch Carron. Their stroll down to the quayside by the old town walls provided him with the opportunity to discourse pompously, as if he was a person of great authority, on the city's history, something which, for some obscure reason, he thought might interest her. Rachel appeared at least to listen until, at the top of Dog Leap Stairs, he stopped. As he looked towards The Side fifty feet below he nearly passed out. It had happened once or twice – on bridges; in apartment blocks; even in aeroplanes.

"What's the matter?" Rachel asked anxiously.

The moment of *déjà vu* was gone as quickly as it came.

"Nothing," Jack replied brightly, "just remembered I had to do something, that's all. It's not important."

Eventually, they ended up in the Pitcher and Piano. Three bottles of wine later they lurched out, fast on the way to becoming soulmates. Jack had told this girl more about himself in a couple of hours than he could ever remember divulging previously.

Newcastle is built on a steep hill, which towers over the Tyne. They made three gallant attempts to get up Dean Street and then Grey Street but there always seemed to be a hostelry in the way. Finally, they capitulated and got a taxi.

"We could go to my place," Jack said, "if you're up to a snifter! I've got a great selection of malts."

"You see!" she exclaimed, "playing on the fact I'm a Highlander!"

"I thought you might find the offer too good to refuse," he replied.

"I may be one of those Highlanders who's immortal," she said. She fixed him with a bewitching look.

"Don't!" he groaned. "I've had my share of witches!" An arched eyebrow was her only response.

They took the taxi down the Coast Road until they came to Jack's house. "Very nice," Rachel said, appreciating, despite her inebriated state, the lines of the old Georgian house. Jack was in history mode so he tried vaguely to tell her some of the house's but his tongue seemed to tie itself up. He must have got some of it through, however, because she replied, "soldiers, eh? Must have seen some action and not necessarily of the warlike kind. But then all's fair in love and war, ain't it Jack?" For the first time he realised she was going to stay. In the taxi she'd been quite cuddly and hand-holdy but the lesson of Josephine was sufficiently proximate for him not to get carried away. It was sex, this, he kidded himself. None of that love entanglement. Being an incurable romantic hadn't helped him find the right woman up to now. He'd been trying to seduce Rachel from that first exchange but maybe he hadn't quite realised it. It was her perfume now which undid him as he helped remove her jacket and couldn't but lean in to the scent from the back of her neck. She felt his closeness and reached back over her shoulder to let him know the contact wasn't a breach of trust. He turned her round immediately and embraced her passionately. They kissed, open-mouthed, searching with the tongue and he let his hands stray. His brain, on the other hand, told him that this loose sort of sexual connection, an apology for a real relationship, had never done him any good in the past. His loins ignored his brain.

"The whisky can wait," he whispered between kisses.

"Chicken," she replied. He laughed as he propelled her upstairs. She shed one shoe on the lower stairs, another slightly higher, her top at the turn, her bra on the landing. He felt the urge to carry her giggling across the threshold of the bedroom.

After their first, heady encounter, Rachel uncoiled herself from the bed and padded naked across the floor to her bag while he watched, fascinated by the mannequin sway of her hips. "What are you doing?" he asked her as she searched in her bag.

"Just this, darling," she replied and returned to the bed, confident in her full frontal nudity, with a plastic bag.

"Is that what I think it is?" he asked suspiciously as she

spilled the white powder. "Whoa, sweetheart, you do drugs?"

"Don't be a spoilsport," she scolded as if she was in the right, "if you thought that was great sex, try it after this."

Here was a dilemma. Every instinct shrieked out at him to reject this, even throw her out, except one: the craving for adventure, for the illicit. No hypocrite, Jack had tried most of the soft drugs, and some a good deal harder, in his student days and, for a time, when he was getting over the trauma of his accident and still experiencing pain. His understanding of drugs and their effect had made him much more tolerant and imaginative in his later career when dealing with clients whose offending was drug-related. However, he took pride in having distanced himself from such things and it wasn't easy to succumb to temptation. What made him was partly the desire not to be thought sad or lacking in cool by this enchanting girl, partly the seduction of the experience she offered. Reluctant only momentarily, he sniffed the line she had measured like an expert. "Wow, you've done that before, babe!" Rachel exclaimed, kneeling to get her own fix. The drug's effect was immediate. A numb feeling in his head was followed by sudden euphoria and then raging passion. Having fallen into a drunken, drugged sleep shortly after the final exultant duet, Jack awoke with a start. His head throbbed; his tongue was parched; he had experienced a vision of the decapitated Josephine. He felt out frantically in the dark.

"Thank God!" he said as, dimly, he saw Rachel lying there.

"What is it?" she asked, awakening suddenly.

"Nothing sweetheart, just delighted to see you," he replied. He was thinking, how did I get this lucky? He fell asleep dreaming of next morning's possibilities.

He never discovered them. Waking up late on the Sunday morning, the sun shining through his window, the jackdaws clanking like farm machinery, Rachel had gone. He wandered through the rambling house, disconsolate. He hadn't even got her address and phone number. What if she didn't get in touch with him again? Why hadn't she at least left a note? He wouldn't dare go out all day in case she rang but he hadn't even given her his number. "Jesus!" he exclaimed rhetorically, realising he'd behaved badly. Just like any other human predator he'd only been concerned with getting her in bed. He was forty years old, Rachel was twenty-three. She'd been a baby when he was an adult and he'd just used her to gratify lust. That's all he'd ever done with any woman as far as he could recall but what a way to handle this young and unspoilt flower! He'd seduced her, led her astray, poured alcohol down her throat, invited her back to his place where, drunkenly, licentiously, he'd emptied the bag. That's all it had been about. He hadn't offered her love, just rampant sex. Rachel had probably woken up, wondered where she was, looked horrified at grandpa flat out and snoring in the bed next to her and done a runner as fast as those gorgeous legs could carry her. "If only I'd waited!" he remonstrated to the mirror, trying to tidy up the mess of the boat race. "If only I'd just shown her something different from what she probably gets from every bloke she meets! I've blown it totally! Just for one hot night!"

He was right. He didn't dare go out in case she rang. Sunday passed in an agony of waiting but no contact. Jack hardly slept that night. He decided to ring the university the following morning but he didn't have to because at 8 a.m, while he was wandering, bleary-eyed, around his kitchen, the phone rang. It was Rachel. "Thank God you rang!" he exclaimed, "I was worried about you. Why did you take off like that?"

She seemed relieved with his response. "I've been dreading ringing," she replied. "I wanted to yesterday but I couldn't pluck up the courage. I'm sorry, I just thought you'd think me such a slut. I panicked. I had to get out of there."

"Rachel I couldn't think that about you," Jack replied. "I thought I'd really blown it by just doing what every other bloke in the universe does."

"Oh," she replied in a slightly mocking tone now that she had regained her confidence, "so poor Jack Lauder is disappointed to find out he's as human as the rest of us? You're not the hero after all Jack!" After one night he could truly say that he loved the irreverent way she talked down to him; he loved her freshness and vitality and the way she made him feel – not whole perhaps, not yet, but more substantial. He loved the intoxicating experience she brought, the chance of life she gave him. Whatever it took, he didn't intend to blow it again.

CHAPTER 2

Getting to know his new lover meant an idyllic few days in which Jack lost all concept of time and, bowled over by her free spirit, some of his self-discipline. He had received an early warning of how devastating a drug habit can be for a professional career but here he was taking the same risks again. It had begun with the perception that Rachel's abuse of both alcohol and drugs was something he had to join to beat. She was not long out of her student days and mixed in circles in which drugs were fashionable.

Jack's strategy of sharing the experience reminded him that it was easier than he had perhaps believed to be seduced once again into that way of life. Ghosts of bad habits came back to haunt him. However, the fact that he wasn't a man of independent means meant he had to go back to work. The pressures that brought put an end to any renewed fear of addiction. One particularly busy day at court he had the misfortune to bump into Kirby Potts, whom he'd given a wide berth since the Disciplinary Tribunal days. Potts on the other hand went out of his way to talk. "Who's your Judge?" the creep asked.

"The Recorder," Jack replied tersely, not wishing to be impolite but at the same time wanting as little to do with Potts as possible. Even so, he couldn't miss the sneer which creased the latter's puffy, pasty features.

"Been in the wars a bit, hasn't he?" Potts smirked.

"How do you mean?"

Before the other man could reply the usher came out of the courtroom and took Jack's arm. "The jury's back, Mr. Lauder!"

"Got to go," he said relieved to get away.

"By the way, Max sends his regards," Potts called after him. Jack turned. The look on Potts' face affected innocence, as if the salutation was genuinely meant. So Kaliostri was still bearing a grudge and, with that reverse magnetism which seems to bind birds of a feather, he had succeeded in finding someone so capable of getting Jack's goat.

Jack didn't stick around after the verdict. He was due to meet Rachel and the summing up had already made the case drag into the evening. It was just as well it hadn't been a hung jury. His client pumped his hand as he tried to escape; Hans Heidemann Q.C, his leader in the case, gave him a wink; the police officer in charge of the case was choking in the bog; Potts had disappeared. Eventually Jack was trotting up towards Fenwicks. His old accident meant that he still felt the odd twinge in his knee when he ran long distances even though the limp had long since gone. On Northumberland Street he almost flattened Lady Parker, the Judge's wife. Jack's haste was the excuse for the collision but even so it took him moments to recognise his victim. He'd attended the odd socio/legal occasion at which the Parkers were guests of honour. As one of the newly-created solicitor-advocates who threatened the Bar's monopoly, Jack found himself treated with disdain at those gatherings so it was no surprise that Lady Parker feigned ignorance of his identity. He was of course aware of their daughter's penchant for low-lifes and, in particular, Lorenza Kaliostri's coven-like circle. Following Kirby Potts' revelations the night at Lorenza's party, he had heard – he wasn't sure from where – that Jessica was among the group of hangers-on who had accompanied Kaliostri on his latest jaunt overseas. That would give Lady Parker food for thought! Even so, he was shocked to find the Judge's wife changed almost beyond recognition. He remembered her as small and dark with a shock of black hair and a face pretty and youthful for her age, testifying to a life lived without pangs of conscience. Her hair was now white, her face was drawn, the crows' feet had forming a herringbone pattern beneath her eyes. Jack tried to act as if he hadn't noticed. "I'm so sorry, let me help you pick them up." Lady Parker was not so generous. "You clumsy idiot!" she hissed. Her face took on a twisted look and he found himself apologising when, in reality, he wanted to say, who the hell do you think you are? As he collected the fallen items he remembered Potts' words that the Judge had troubles of his own. Perhaps he was seeing some of that in the lack of charity confronting him. He bit his lip and restored the shopping bags, consoling himself that, with the trial going the wrong way, the Judge's wife wasn't likely to find her man a happy camper either. They deserved each other. He couldn't help, however, but feel some curiosity at Potts' words. His own detachment meant that he seldom kept abreast of the affairs of others; he was the last to know. He did know, however – it was a bit of an open secret in local legal circles – that the Judge had a bit of a thing going with a local female barrister called Shona MacDonald. Perhaps Lady Parker had found out? Either way, it wasn't his business. "Goodbye," he said somewhat formally as he took his leave of the disgruntled woman. She didn't respond.

Jack walked up to the Metro and rode it to the Coast. He took a taxi from the station to his door.

He had decided to take his new love to the George at Chollerford, a country inn on the upper reaches of the Tyne. Sprucing himself up he drove in his Mercedes to meet her at the Angel in the Haymarket – she didn't want him going to her house because she said it was a tip and she didn't much like the people she roomed with. Surprisingly unimpressed by the wheels, she seemed delighted, however, to see him. It was a bright summer's evening up by the Roman Wall. "What do you actually teach?" he asked as they drove.

"Languages."

"Which ones?"

"Well, Russian's the one I got the job for, but I know a few. Indian, Italian, Spanish. Then there's Mandarin and Japanese. It's not so hard. I've just got the ear. I know Arabic too. I moved around a lot when I was young. Lived in different countries."

"Because of your folks?"

"Yeah," she nodded but she was non-committal when pressed about her past. Neither did she seem interested in Jack's history, for which he was grateful because it was always painful to be reminded of how alone he truly was.

It was only during dinner, when he changed the subject to his meeting with the Judge's wife, that he got another shock. "Of course, I didn't know where to put myself," he said.

"No, of course not. And she didn't mention her daughter Jessica?"

"No, she didn't," he replied, puzzled that Rachel should even know the name of the Parkers' elder daughter. "Why should she have done? I scarcely know the girl, only met her once."

"It's just I know people at Uni who knew Jessica."

"Knew?"

"Yes. One of them told me Jessica had been killed. It's just as well you didn't say anything."

"What?" Jack exclaimed. "How? When was this?"

"I don't have the details," Rachel responded. "The official line is it was an accident but an investigation's going on in India. The truth is apparently a lot more sinister but there's a press embargo on it until the investigation's completed."

"Rachel, how do you know all this?"

"We've got...." Rachel paused and went pink, "*had* friends in common. I know someone who was out in India with her."

She paused again as if for emphasis, waiting for the reaction Jack gaped in astonishment.

"What!" he exclaimed, so staggered that all he could add was, "when?"

"Ages ago! I'm not sure!" Rachel snapped, fired by his show of impatience.

"I'm sorry, I'm so sorry," Jack said, bewildered, "I had no idea! How could I have missed that? I know I've been out of touch. It's not exactly been one party after another. I was abroad for months, then I met you. I didn't have eyes or ears for anyone else." If the final sentence was meant to move her it failed conspicuously. He finished forlornly: "And I've been stuck on this trial for weeks. I guess I've been a little incommunicado."

Rachel's reaction puzzled him. It was as if she felt she had given away a state secret. "Don't mention it to anyone that I told you," she said, "even I'm not supposed to know. The family is just getting over the grief and they won't thank me for bringing it up"

Jack wondered who on earth she thought he could mention it to. Hans Heidemann, whom he'd left at court a short time before, was the only person he knew who was closely acquainted with the Judge and, now their case was over, he wouldn't see him until the next blue moon. "I won't," he replied. "I don't know anyone who knows the Parkers and I agree, it's not a subject for gossip. I'll keep it to myself. But I'm allowed to know, aren't I? Come on, do you have the details of what happened?"

"I wasn't here either and I don't know any of these people. I only know what Janet Gillingham, told me but the way she described it, it was horrific."

"Hold it, hold it," Jack interrupted, the expression on his face showing that he was having difficulty in keeping up with all this, "who's Janet Gillingham when she's at home?"

"Just a girl I know from the University."

"Why should she mention Jessica?"

"She knew her," Rachel replied, "she's the local socialite, so maybe I've told her you're a lawyer and she thinks I know people in your world. I don't know. Do you want to hear this or not?"

She was suddenly and uncharacteristically flustered. He backed off. "Sure," he said, "sorry, I just wondered what the impetus was for the conversation. You're right, that's probably it. I knew Jessica. Not well, but I met her the once. It was quite memorable actually. What's Parker doing sitting though? He's a bloody callous bastard! I can't believe it. So what happened?"

"Well, I heard her body was found after a car accident. But there was some suggestion that was a cover up, that she actually died while taking part in some ritual thing."

"A ritual thing?" Jack responded. "That's an odd thing to say."

"That there was some kind of black magic connection, that's what I heard but you know what the rumour mill is like." She noticed his consternation and held out her hand to cover his. "That's all it is, Jack, a rumour."

"Then why mention it at all?" he snapped, unnerved. He hadn't appreciated that so many things had happened in his absence abroad but he knew now what had changed Lady Parker's appearance so radically. A funny churning began in his stomach and a shiver went the length of his backbone, picking out each vertebra on the way. When he'd finally found his tongue, he said, "what's been done about it? Has anyone been arrested?"

"The Indian police haven't a clue what happened," Rachel replied. "Think about it. If people as important as that can't do much about their inertia who could?" She then dropped a bombshell. "I gather her mother wishes she'd never met that man!"

"What man?" he asked.

"The musician. The guy who comes from here. It all started with him. She was besotted with him and his pseudo-religious quirks. She couldn't see she was just a plaything. She followed him everywhere, like a lap dog. He used her for these religious ceremonies. It's not the first time he's been implicated in murder, is it? There was that time in the States he was questioned about the death of one of his fans. They never got anything on him, though."

"Who are we talking about?" Jack asked, consumed by a peculiar sense of panic.

She snapped her fingers. "Stupid, isn't it? I must be going senile. You know the lead singer of that band that plays the Death Metal music? He comes from here originally." She screwed up her brow in concentration and then suddenly she had it. "Devil's Disciple, that's it!"

Jack's heart lurched. "Not Max Kaliostri?" he exclaimed.

"You know Max?" Rachel replied.

"Oh yes," Jack said, and he had a vision of Mr. Justice Parker refusing Kaliostri bail at the Court of Appeal. At the time, Jack had dubbed that inhuman. He hadn't of course known of the Judge's hidden agenda. Surely, surely, Kaliostri wouldn't have revenged himself on an innocent girl? It was the oddest feeling. There are occasions in your life when suddenly you sense that something has changed, that the earth has caught you up in its orbit, you're no longer in control. Jack shivered involuntarily, his whole spine seemingly loose and disconnected.

Hours later, whilst Rachel slept like a baby, the Devil's Disciple, who had put a pall on an otherwise brilliant night, still occupied Jack's thoughts. That was precisely who Kaliostri thought he was. Jack had learned a fair bit about his subject when Lorenza had seemed intent on divorcing the superstar. He wasn't only a musician of considerable, if perverted, talent but also a consummate artist. His stage-shows demonstrated a grasp of the art of the illusionist or magician, who could conjure the fantastic from other apparent dimensions to the extent that his audience lost touch with reality or began to believe in a different reality. The idea, however, that he had crossed the divide, which separated the money-spinning, macabre fantasies of his stage-shows from acts of bestial criminality, would have been almost too absurd to entertain if it hadn't been for the lawyer's own close encounter. Jack had rationalised those events, after the passage of time and the silence which had followed, with the dismissive thought that Kaliostri was merely barking mad. Now, however, his concern made him bite the bullet and telephone Kirby Potts at his office the next morning. "What were you trying to tell me yesterday about Justice Parker?" he asked his colleague who, in contrast with his apparent willingness to broadcast gossip on the previous evening, now affected the spirit of reticence. "I'm not sure I can tell you," he replied coyly.

"It's never stopped you before," Jack retorted. "I was told yesterday that the Judge's eldest daughter had died in India, that she'd possibly even been murdered."

Potts was silent for a moment and then he replied in his sly way, "possibly? I would put it higher than that. Ask me no questions, I'll tell you no lies."

Jack noted a certain glee in his voice. "Some people think that your client Mr. Kaliostri has something to do with it?"

"If anything of the sort is repeated on an unprivileged occasion, it will meet with a defamation suit," the reptile warned.

"Oh, I'm not the one to repeat it," Jack said, "but I can't understand why there's been no publicity."

"Wheels within wheels," Potts replied mysteriously. "Not really in the interests of anyone for something like that to get massive publicity, is it? The two governments got involved. That's all I can tell you."

Jack found himself suddenly trying to curry favour with his obnoxious colleague. "Kirby," he said, "do you have any reason to believe that Max still bears me a grudge?" He cursed himself as he said it but the truth was he was scared.

"Oh, no, my dear chap, of course not," Potts responded in a way which sounded less than sincere.

Jack left it there. He felt no confidence in Potts' reassurance. In addition, he was surprised that Jessica's death had been so well covered up. If a number of people in the city were privy to the secret, the Press should have made it a *cause celebre*. They wouldn't need much persuasion. Kaliostri had hit the headlines once or twice for his proximity to a couple of unexplained deaths of drug-crazed young women. The media usually seized every opportunity to mutter darkly about the Devil's Disciple, his following of devil worshippers and pseudo-vampires and the millennium cults his music spawned. They talked of a return to the Dark Ages, as if the eccentric musician could bring about such a catastrophe single-handedly. But it was all rumour and gossip. Kaliostri encouraged most of it. It helped foster his image of himself as Satan. The question was, had the nutter started to believe his own publicity?

CHAPTER 3

There comes a time in everyone's life when opportunity knocks. You get one shot only. Rachel was Jack's. She might be hanging round with him only because he was comparatively well off, a professional, unmarried with an uncomplicated lifestyle, but he didn't much care what her motives were. In the absence of the natural advantage of youthful good looks, he might as well make use of his other attributes. Even so, he didn't realise how badly he was smitten until he woke up one night having dreamt she was seeing someone else. Covered in perspiration, his heart pounding like a racehorse on the turf, this was bad! Losing her would be hell, like facing a black hole – if you were sucked in you would be smashed to smithereens. "I can't be falling in love," he said aloud to his darkened room, "I'm surely immune from that!"

Surprisingly, despite her preference for a Bohemian lifestyle. Rachel seemed to want to be with him. She was gorgeous. Her black hair fell the length of her willowy body, and – it hadn't been the effect of the alcohol – her eyes did alternate between green and grey according to how the mood took her. Her features were finely chiselled yet soft and her self-confidence and *joie de vivre* could have made a suicide on a bridge believe that hope springs eternal. Life without her would now be unthinkable. Jack hoped he could make her feel the same way but it wasn't going to be easy. Rachel stayed with him on the odd occasion but she refused to consider moving in and she wouldn't invite him back to her hovel, as she called it. One night they were together, he was getting ready for bed, she was halfway there already but had been interrupted by the need to look up a reference she needed. He gazed surreptitiously at her long black hair as it fell over her creamy shoulders and translucent slip. "Jack, do you believe in reincarnation?" she asked out of the blue. She was poring over some sacred text from the Dhammapada at the time, but that was Rachel, always searching. Not that Jack was disinterested, just that life had made other demands of him and he had ceased looking quite so deeply into the meaning of things.

"Don't know," he said reflectively, "but I always thought those Buddhists had a handle on the after-life in a way much less primitive than the rest of us. Why do you ask anyway?"

"I just wanted to know what you thought. I believe in it, you see."

"You believe in lots of weird things, so that's no recommendation," he replied with a mischievous grin. "You're taken in by all kinds of mumbo-jumbo! Is that a sort of inborn thing? Did your folks bring you up with all sorts of tales about synchronicity and the innate intelligence of natural things?"

"No!" she laughed.

"Chariots of the gods, monolithic black holes, alien abductions?" Expertly, he dodged the flying pillow. "I'll tell you the biggest mystery of all," he added.

"What?"

"You."

"Me?"

"Yeah, you. I mean where do you come from? I know you're a Scot but what's the crack?" He made vague gestures with his hands as if they added in some mysterious way to the meaning of his question. "You know? The s.p, the deal. What brings you here? To me?"

"Jack, what is this, the third degree?"

"No," he replied. "It's just me. I'm very forthcoming and up front. Sometimes I think I'd understand you better if I had...." He stopped in mid-sentence, searching for the words. The point was well enough made. Jack didn't have parents or siblings. He was used to being alone. Rachel never spoke of her family. He had enquired gently about them and other things too but she had always avoided the issue. "Hush," she'd say, "I don't want to talk about that. All right?" When they had decided they had a future together, he had naturally assumed that they would gradually get to know more about each other. Rachel was quite happy to talk to Jack about her hopes and fears, her everyday thoughts and dreams, but the past was a closed shop.

She nodded. "Jack, what's my name?" she asked.

"Rachel," he replied.

"You know the story of Rachel?" she asked in the tone a teacher might use to challenge children.

Jack hated to admit his ignorance but it was one of those Biblical stories, which didn't quite come to mind and he listened carefully as she explained the means by which Jacob had come to know his true love. "In the biblical sense?" he asked at length.

"You've got a one-track mind," she replied, simultaneously stepping out of her knickers. The action which followed meant that he never did quite catch her drift and once again she had side-stepped the issue.

Later, Jack fell into a deep sleep only to be awakened rudely by a call on the emergency number. It turned out to be from Tropical Tom. Jack had met some characters in his time, some good some bad. Most of the real characters he'd met were poor because the rich are only interested in money and the things it can buy. Tropical Tom was a character, if not a terribly attractive one. Long and skinny with thinning, curly, black hair tied in a ponytail at the back, sallow of complexion, almost always unshaven, sporting a thin moustache, he looked like a throwback to an unsuccessful Spanish Main pirate. He wandered round city and coast in the scruffy old clothes he kept in bags in his attic, all bought from Oxfam shops. He smoked tack and did heroin when he could afford it. He'd done time for pushing drugs and saw it as a way of life. His voice on the telephone sounded frantic. "You've got to come," he pleaded, "the witches are killing her!"

Jack was so used to being the fourth emergency service that bizarre requests from clients seldom struck him as unusual. "Who are killing whom?" he replied as soon as his befuddled brain was in some sort of order.

"The witches. I'm telling you, Jack," Tom shouted, "they've got Karen. You've got to get over here straightaway."

"Oh, howay Tom, I've had a couple of jars man. I can't drive in this state."

"I don't care. Do you want to be responsible for our Karen rotting in hell?"

Jack looked up at the ceiling. "No," he groaned, "I'll get a taxi." Used to being responsible for people being locked up, lifed off even – it's always the lawyer's fault – he'd never previously been threatened with having someone's eternal damnation on his conscience. Rachel smiled bleakly as he explained that one.

When he got to the house, Tom's brother Dekka was braying on the front door and he was the sane one of the family. He was as white as a sheet. "You look a bit off colour," Jack said.

"Have you met Lorenza?" Dekka countered.

"Lorenza? Now there's a name to conjure with!" Jack replied. "I'm thinking of the town's favourite daughter, Lorenza Kaliostri."

Dekka's next words blew him away. "Aye, that's her! The pop star's bit!"

When Jack had recovered sufficiently from the coincidence it turned out that she was also the bit in charge of a local coven. "Filthy rich!" Dekka added, which Jack didn't need to be told. He was still trying to come to grips with the revelation as Dekka prattled on. After all, it wasn't that odd. She did live here. The fact that, like Max, she dabbled in the occult was common knowledge. Jack had personal experience. "She's gorgeous to look at too," Dekka went on, "and pretty free with the coke. The downside is she's a sarky cow." Dekka explained that once, in party mood, he'd tried to get his leg over but Lorenza wasn't having any, and that had left him a touch disgruntled. Jack listened politely and didn't mention that he knew just about all there was to know about Lorenza Kaliostri.

Tom, who had disappeared round the back as Jack pulled up, now returned, followed by a police officer – one of those very young ones, new to the local force. He didn't appear to know who Jack was. Either that or he was intent on showing the lawyer no respect at all. "He can't get in," Dekka complained to the police officer whilst pointing at Tom.

"Is this your house, sir?" the policeman asked Tom, who was miles away, gazing wide-eyed at the door. So, after an uncomfortable silence, Jack nodded in response.

"Well, we'll see about that then," the officer said. He strode up to the door and bent down by the letterbox. "Come on, open up!" he shouted in best, stentorian style, as if that would send all the legions of hell packing. Jack pushed up behind him and tried the door. It opened. "It isn't locked!" the officer said to Tom accusingly.

"The witches were in there!" Tom said as if that explained everything.

The officer looked at Jack and Jack looked deadpan. "We'd better go in and have a look," he said.

The officer didn't push himself forward, so Jack went first. The light was on and the remnants of a meal lay on the kitchen table. They combed the house. No one was in.

"Gone!" Tom said. "Took off with Lorenza. They were sitting in the middle of the floor chanting spells. They put a curse on me."

The eyebrow of the law was raised. Jack smiled to himself. "Bit of a new one for you, then?" he asked the bewildered police officer. He stopped to examine a curious small sculpture of an animal with a human head. It was made of brass and heavier than it looked. The body and face were like the Sphinx's. He felt the ripples of its muscular, leonine body. Odd, but it felt warm and alive in his hand. He shuddered involuntarily and put it down, recalling that he'd seen similar artifacts at the Kaliostris'.

Tom was about to go berserk. "I'm telling you," he said, "she can do all sorts of things, that Lorenza. She contorts herself inside out, so you can see her belly. Do you know anyone who can do that? Just turn themselves inside out, arms and legs akimbo? She sat right there, doing that and grinning at me."

"That proves nothing." The officer replied, shaking his head with a scepticism, which took the hard-nosed approach to the nth degree.

"She can change shape at will. She can levitate. She can put her hands in boiling water and feel no pain. She's a witch." The police officer wandered round, sniffing things. "I haven't touched anything for weeks," Tom lied. "I'm shit-scared. Look, I found this." He pulled a wax doll from a pocket. It had a thin moustache, just like his, and was stuck full of pins. "Voodoo!" Dekka said knowingly.

"No," Jack interrupted, "not necessarily. The effigy of the victim is central to all forms of witchcraft." The assembly looked at him with a degree of respect. "I doubt it's voodoo," he continued. "Voodoo is just a corruption of an African word meaning the gods. Any form of western witchcraft would adopt this technique. No one has ever related the magical practices of western witchcraft to Polynesian and African practices. I think we're dealing with a bunch of lunatics here. Voodoo is a different thing. It's a clan thing."

"How come you know so much about it?" the policeman asked, looking at Jack suspiciously as if he thought he might be on something too. Little did he know.

"I've had reason to make a study of it," Jack replied, "because of something that happened to me once. Witchcraft cults generally are just an historical descendant of fertility religions. The Old Religion it's called. Red-hot pins through the organs of a waxen image are supposed to work in sympathy on the victim. It does work – on susceptible people."

"Well," the officer said, "most enlightening, I'm sure, sir. You would no doubt make a wonderful expert witness on the subject of witchcraft. When we need one we'll know where to look." Jack smiled indulgently. The policeman became officious, demanding to know whether Tom was going to report a missing person or not. Tom was equally insistent that Karen had been kidnapped. He explained that Lorenza was the head of the coven and they'd taken control of Karen's mind. They'd held meetings here in the house, dancing naked, except for the mask. "What mask?" the policeman asked, writing assiduously in his notebook.

"They wear masks. Sometimes it's like a devil's mask, African, Red Indian, Japanese. Sometimes they wear an animal mask. It depends on the mood he's in, or the things he wants to contact."

"Things?" the officer asked.

"He means elementals," Jack added helpfully.

That was almost too much information to compute and the police officer looked at Jack sideways and said, "what's an elemental?"

Jack ignored the question. His forensic training had picked up the other reference. "Who's he?" he asked quietly.

That seemed to get Tom flustered. "Did I say he?" he blustered. "I meant they."

Jack's eyebrows shot up. "Come and see me tomorrow, Tom," he said. "I know this is a police matter, there's not much I can do about it at the moment, but I need to talk to you."

"What about?" Tom asked suspiciously.

"Well, I'm not sure yet. I need to think it through. It's just something to do with Max Kaliostri. Maybe a pattern is emerging."

Tom looked as if he saw an appointment as a result on the night. Jack had no doubt that some drug had made him hallucinate – he had so many different chemical compounds inside him that he was a scientific miracle on two legs – but equally there might be some truth in what he'd witnessed. His wife might have joined a coven of witches. Many of these secret societies exist, often staffed with well-known respectable people, the sort whom you wouldn't suspect and who go about their working day like anyone else, then, for a comparatively small amount of time, turn into witches. Their disguises are often impenetrable but, once assumed, their wearers believe themselves to be the devil incarnate. Sometimes they are just charlatans and the true motive is sexual. Thus, Karen was probably bored. She hadn't been kidnapped; more likely she'd gone off on a frolic of her own. Sometimes, however, the explanation isn't quite that simple. Some of these people actually believe they have transubstantiated into demons or dark angels. Jack had a premonition about this one. Even human beings, too long subjected to the comfort and predictability of civilisation, retain a sense of the cosmic interrelation of things, and the events of this evening had awoken in Jack a ghost left to slumber but not yet put to rest.

CHAPTER 4

At court the next day Jack received news which brought back vividly the previous evening's events. A uniformed officer was waiting to give evidence on one of his cases and the defendant hadn't turned up so Jack engaged him in conversation.

"I could do without this," the officer complained. "I'm on the night shift at the moment. This is cutting into my sleeping time. It was a busy night last night."

"What, not routine you mean?" Jack replied.

"Not at all," the officer said. "We had this peculiar complaint about a missing person from one of the Bigg Market girls, the brass you know?" Jack smiled and he went on. "You know they use St. Nick's churchyard for a quickie with a punter?"

"No!" Jack grinned broadly. All the dignitaries of the eighteenth and nineteenth centuries were buried in the Cathedral churchyard and the idea of the Bigg Market prostitutes rollicking among the gravestones was almost too ridiculous to believe.

"Yeah, it's true. Anyway one of the lasses reported a girl went down there to do a trick with a bit of a mystery man and disappeared. We had half the force out looking for her."

"Did you find her?"

"No. It must have been a hoax, a ouple of lassies having a bit of a daft carry on! As if we haven't got enough genuine problems to deal with."

Jack quickly forgot about the conversation as he had another thing on his mind. He was at last to meet one of

Rachel's friends. Until now she had kept him away from them to the point that he had come to believe that she was either ashamed of them or of him, so this was a sign of advance in their relationship. Invited to the friend's house, they took a taxi because, Rachel assured him with a knowing look, it was bound to be a session.

Janet Gillingham turned out to be a single girl. It was obvious that she and Rachel were close friends. Jack hung back, slightly embarrassed by their effusive greeting until, as an afterthought, Rachel introduced him. Janet's initial reaction took him by surprise because it was as if she knew him well. "Oh yes," she said, "the legal beagle! I've read about you. You used to be a mountaineer." He wondered how someone like her, who had probably never even stood on an outcrop, knew of his past and said something in response but, in the way that awfully posh people have, she totally ignored him.

"I'll get us a drink," she said. "You make yourself comfortable, Jack." She made him feel like an old man. Bloody cheek! Jack thought, she'll be asking if I want my slippers next. Far too good-natured to say anything, he smiled bleakly. Rachel disappeared into the kitchen with her friend. The combination of the two young women, obviously at ease in each other's company to the extent that they seemed to share a great secret to which no one else in the world was privy, made Jack feel surplus to requirements. Not wanting to act so perfectly the role of the spare part, he didn't object when what was now becoming the inevitable line or two followed the alcohol. If he was uneasy about it, he didn't let on but he was more than dimly aware that he couldn't truly be fooling anyone with this pretence of being a Bohemian. It was all aimed at trying to hang on to Rachel and, if he had thought it through, he would have realized that pretending to be someone else would never do the trick. At the moment, however, he had to hang in there. The cocaine's effect, after his exertions of the previous night, was to fire him up then knock him cold. He had a brief recollection of the two young women laughing at him, presumably because he'd lived up to the retirement home image, but torpor overcame even that embarrassment. He woke up what seemed hours later feeling cold and stiff. He called out but got no reply. The voices were still audible but seemingly disembodied. He climbed carefully up the spiral staircase towards the attic. The door was half open. Peering in he saw them. Janet was on the telephone. Rachel was stretched out on the futon next to her. They seemed intimate, their limbs kind of loosely intertwined. Rachel seemed asleep but perhaps she was staring at the television. Jack did a double-take at the screen. It was a news item. Josephine Jackson was the reporter. Strange, he hadn't appreciated that she was back in the country. The volume was down low but he got the gist of the story. It brought back his discussion with the policeman at court that morning. The copper had been wrong. It was a murder. Janet seemed to be talking about it on the telephone. Feeling a little like a voyeur, Jack coughed and announced himself. "Hi," he said, "sorry about that. Fell asleep."

Janet covered the telephone receiver with her hand. She looked at him coolly. "Have you seen this?" she said, pointing at the screen.

Jack replied, "no, but it's funny, I was talking to a police officer about it this morning. Only he seemed to think it was a hoax. I had no idea it was a real murder!" He touched Rachel's shoulder – she had followed him to oblivion and stirred only slightly in response – and then saw Janet out of the corner of his eye. She was gazing at him open-mouthed. She began talking excitedly down the phone, speculating with her contact on the risk for all single girls. "Rachel's friend Jack is a lawyer and he says it's a murder," she said, emphasizing the last word as if the thought was scandalous.

Jack rubbed his eyes. "I gather she was a hooker," he said, his eyes fixed on Josephine as she described the m.o of the night girls and their penchant for the gravestones in the Cathedral – just as the policeman had said. "There's no risk for women generally."

"He says there's no risk for the rest of us," Janet repeated down the line, "he seems pretty confident."

"Who are you talking to?" Jack asked, suddenly irritated, but she ignored him and then his attention was attracted by Josephine's remark that other killings of a strikingly similar nature had happened. He hadn't appreciated that. Her next mention of a black magic cult blew him away. "You'd know something about that, lady," he said.

"What?" Rachel said, suddenly sitting up and stretching. Jack was suddenly aware of how gorgeous she was, so angular, from her long neck to her legs curled underneath her. She was like a mannequin.

"Nothing," Jack replied. The last thing he wanted to do was reveal anything of his embarrassing association with Josephine and her friends.

Rachel looked at the television then at Janet, who was still jabbering down the phone in excited fashion about the slaying as if it was the most exciting thing to happen in the city for years. "Haven't you got anything better than this to watch?" Rachel scolded her. It was obvious she was angry. Only the sad people of the world take a prurient delight in the manifestations of evil. Jack was proud of her. She got up, strode across the floor and switched the television off.

Janet looked at her open-mouthed, a smile forming in the corners of her lips. "Oooh, something's rattled your cage, madam," she replied.

Whether the result of the substance abuse or the unexpected doze, Rachel was in a tetchy mood and she rushed Jack out of there. He needed no second bidding. Something about Janet's over-indulgence in the macabre news item had filled him with a sense of revulsion. On the way home in the taxi, he mentioned this to Rachel but she wouldn't have anything said against her friend. "She's all right," she replied, "a bit scatty at times. A bit misguided. Particularly where men are concerned. But we can all ship some blame on that count, can't we?"

"I hope you're not referring to me," Jack responded light-heartedly, nuzzling into her and inhaling the rich perfume of her hair.

Strangely, she ignored his riposte. "Jack," she said, cuddling in to him, "can we go away somewhere for a couple of days, I really need to get out of here."

Great idea, he thought. He had a couple of lay days owing. Why not just take off for a week. The great thing about running your own show is, sometimes at least, you can just suit yourself. "Sure," he said. "Amsterdam, how would that suit?"

"Fantastic," she replied. "Ideal." Suddenly he couldn't wait to get her home and all other considerations fled from his mind. Later that night, though, wide-awake and as high as any kite, with Rachel sleeping gently by his side, either Jack was dreaming vividly or his imagination was running riot. Girls were being kidnapped down the coast; police officers were interviewing sardonic mafioso type individuals; Josephine Jackson and Max Kaliostri were trying to raise the dead in St. Nicholas's churchyard; Lorenza was taking her kit off whilst waving her magic wand at a prostrate Kirby Potts, who squealed like a stuck pig.

CHAPTER 5

Life slipped by without too much happening except that Rachel's work had begun to take her out of town. Not exactly ecstatic at the development, Jack was hoist on his own petard. Having explained how important work was in his own life, he had no choice other than to accept the payback. She was gone for a fortnight. Their usual method of contact was her mobile phone but it seemed to be permanently switched off. She didn't like him going to her home but, when he hadn't heard from her for a couple of days, he went round there one evening and knocked on the door. There was no response. The place just looked unlived in. The curtains were open but there were no signs of life. Puzzled, Jack retraced his steps and hoped she would call. She didn't, so at the end of the week he rang the university languages department. "Who?" the receptionist said. "I don't think we've got anyone of that name here."

"You must have," Jack replied patiently. "Please check again."

A pause followed and then, "no, 'fraid not. I think you must have the wrong name."

Jack put the phone down, mystified. His heart was pounding. Where was Rachel? She hadn't been in touch and now it looked as if she had lied to him when she'd told him she worked at the university. Why should she have done that? He tried her mobile once more but again it was dead. Work wouldn't let him fret for long. He had a lot of cases to clear up so he gave them the time he would have preferred to spend on Rachel. One night when he was in the office late the telephone interrupted his thoughts. It was well past closing time so there was no one in reception to answer it. He picked it up and said, "hello, Jack Lauder here."

"Hello, Jack Lauder there," Rachel's soft voice replied.

"Rachel!" he said. "Where on earth have you been? I've been sick with worry."

"I had to go away," she replied. Her voice faltered slightly. "Don't be too angry. I can explain everything."

"I'm not angry," he replied rather stiffly, although inside he was seething with resentment. "I've just been so concerned about you. I didn't know what had happened. It's great to hear you. You sound okay?"

"I am okay."

There followed a silence in which he expected her to provide some further details of her disappearance but she volunteered nothing. Eventually, he had to pick up the threads of the conversation and ask her, "where are you now?"

"At my flat," she replied.

"I went round there, hoping to find you," he said. "The whole place was deserted. I thought you had flatmates?"

"I do," she replied, and again he detected the hint of nervousness in her voice as if she didn't like being interrogated, "but they've been away too."

He felt like saying, how convenient, but he resisted the temptation and turned the screw a different way. "I even rang your department." He let it hang there.

"Oh yes," she said, after a pause.

"Yes," he replied, "and strangely enough they had no record of you."

"I know," she responded, seemingly nonchalant enough, "I left there some time ago."

"You didn't tell me," he said.

"What are you? My keeper?"

He was staggered by that response. Suddenly he realised this could be the elbow. Jesus, he didn't want that! He'd take her this way rather than no way at all. "I didn't mean that," he replied, back-tracking. "Look, perhaps we should get together. There's some things I want to say to you."

"There's some things I need to say to you too," she replied. That didn't sound good. It did not sound good.

"Like what?" he tried.

"Not tonight. I'm just back. I'm exhausted. I'll meet you tomorrow, no Saturday."

"What's wrong with tomorrow?"

"Leave it out, Jack. I'll meet you Saturday."

"Where? What time?"

"The Greek. Lunchtime. One o'clock." There were no pleasant valedictories. He was left with the dialling tone.

That put the cap on the evening and just as he was leaving a Fourtrak pulled up outside the office. Joe Johnson, the Border Bandido, athletic of build but as broad as a brick house from his days as an SAS operative, climbed out and walked towards Jack's car as he wound the window down. "Figured you'd be burning the midnight oil. I've got some information for you, Jack," the big man said.

"Yeah," Jack replied. "I'm up to here, mate. Too much bad news for one day. Do you fancy a pint?"

They stopped off at the Tynemouth Lodge. Joe checked the clientele first. "Heard this was a busies' pub," he said. "No one obvious, though."

"Well, what's the news?" Jack asked wearily.

"Do you know a gadgie by the name of Tom Spencer?" Joe asked.

"Tropical Tom?" Jack responded. "What about him?"

"Is he supposed to be a friend of yours?"

"No!" Jack laughed. "He's just a client, that's all."

"Aye, well, he's not to be trusted, believe me, marra! He's

been gannin' round like a loose cannon. Reckons he's had you over. Something to do with their lass? He was put up to playing a trick on you."

"Who told you this?"

"Wey, the grapevine, y' nah!"

After Joe left, Jack took a stroll round the park to clear his head. From a bright, new beginning, both in his career and his personal life, things had become murky again. Next to the statue of the Old Wooden Dolly, once the figurehead of an ancient sailing ship, he saw an elderly woman feeding the gulls. She had with her an even more elderly, black dog, which showed no interest in the bird life as it flocked in. Young seagulls, looking like prehistoric creatures, strutted round squawking as the stronger adults pushed them aside. A rook sat on Dolly's head, staring at the competition. Jack smiled. The birds looked like a bunch of lawyers down the courthouse with the judge presiding over them. Eventually the woman, whom he recognised as one of the homeless people of the borough, a regular beggar in the thoroughfare near where he worked, began to wend her way towards him. "Got any change, Mr.?" she asked. Jack smiled and took his pound coins from his pocket and handed them to her. "God bless you!" she added and walked on. The rook turned and stared after her with anthropomorphic interest. As soon as the old woman had gone, it dropped down, its wings spread like an umbrella, to share in the spoils. Even as it fed, it glanced maliciously around. Jack suffered from the odd notion that he was in its sights.

CHAPTER 6

Rachel was late arriving on the Saturday. She came through the door laden with shopping, her face shining, a healthy tan revealing that she had been somewhere in the sun. When she saw Jack, she couldn't look him straight in the eye. They had agreed to meet at a little Greek restaurant called Rosa Lena's on Westgate Road. The restaurant was bright, modern and cheerful. Greek music played in the background. It wasn't the kind of place where you could easily disguise a lover's tiff. Jack stood up in an old-fashioned, formal way when Rachel appeared, immediately realising that she was already making him behave out of character. She chatted on gaily for a few moments about her trip to the Eldon Shopping Mall, prattling to avoid the serious business. They ordered food and a glass of white wine. Rachel made hers a spritzer so it was obvious she wasn't expecting a session. After she'd gone on for some time, Jack said, "Rachel!"

She stopped, her eyes lowered. He had the feeling this was bad news. If she had anything good to say she'd have looked straight at him. Her whole body language spelled out things he was sure he didn't want to hear. "Yes," she replied quietly.

"I think you've got something to tell me."

"What? Like where I was this last two weeks?"

"No," he said, "maybe that's entirely your own affair. What I'm more concerned about is why you felt it was okay just to go off and leave me worried like that."

"Don't stifle me, Jack," Rachel replied.

"I don't want to stifle you," he said. He felt desperate. This was the Dear John talk, the concrete shoe walk. He gambled everything. "Look, you don't have to tell me anything. It's entirely your business what you do. Perhaps I was getting too serious. Is that what you're saying?"

"I felt we needed to cool it, that's part of it."

Jack nodded. It was what he had dreaded hearing but at least it didn't come with the final put down. Maybe, though, he wasn't reading between the lines. It might just be her style. "Okay," he said, "perhaps I have been coming on a bit strong. I don't know why. I'm not used to this." Rachel leaned across and tenderly stroked his face. He held her hand there, rubbing up against it like a cat. When he looked at her downcast eyes she seemed about to cry.

"No, no, go not to Lethe,
neither twist wolf's bane tight-rooted for its poisonous wine,
nor let your pale forehead be kissed by nightshade,
ruby grape of Proserpine."

Oddly, in that it was so old-fashioned, his words, spoken without solemnity, cheered her visibly. "You know how to get to me, Jack," she said. "You really do." He looked at her quizzically. "No, I really mean that," she added.

"Oh no, I get it," he laughed. "I've heard this one before. I'm great but the problem's with you, right?"

"I don't blame you for being so cynical," she replied, "but it doesn't do you justice. It's not you. You'll have to accept that I'm not ready for any big commitments."

"Hey, who said I was? I just want to have fun!"

"Yeah, yeah, all right," she replied.

"Is it the age thing?"

"Partly, I suppose."

She was honest at least. "I could get plastic surgery, a face lift," he joked.

"They'd need a twenty ton crane," she replied.

Jack burst into laughter. It was good. It relieved the tension. "And pneumatic drills," he added, "a team of navvies and a couple of dray horses."

"Jack, you're not supposed to be a nice guy, you're not supposed to be romantic," she laughed, "you're a lawyer for God's sake, the repository for all the world's ills. You're supposed to be a bastard!"

Something about the way she said that felt odd but he ignored it. "Yeah, no one's got any time for us as a breed, have they? Anyway, that's it, that's me, warts and all. So, even allowing for the fact I'm a lawyer, do I still get to see you sometimes?"

"Of course," she said.

"What? Just as friends?"

"No," she replied. "Just like before, only with a different emphasis."

The difference would be that she would be in charge now. It was to be what Rachel wanted. Should I agree to this, he asked himself. It was demeaning for someone of his years and experience. But he'd already compromised big-time for this girl. He'd changed his lifestyle, dropped his old friends, skived off work, binged on booze and shattered the drugs laws! Stop being so pompous, the demons said. Do you want to keep on seeing her or don't you? There was no argument. His heart ached at the thought of losing her totally and, yet, he knew it must happen sooner or later. This was only the prelude. She would soon be seeing someone else. She already was. That's where she'd been. Jack struggled to hold back any questions or cutting comments because he knew that such a show of possessiveness would be the coup-de-grace. Instead he changed the subject. "I've got this really strange thing going on at the moment," he said.

She leaned forward as if for confidentiality. "Tell me," she prompted. She looked at him, one quizzical eyebrow raised. Jack had been referring to the history of his connection with

Mr. Herron and of his surprise at being entrusted with the stewardship of the dead villain's estate. "It had to wait while I was abroad. Nothing's spoiling. It's not as if there's masses to leave to anyone, but it's the surprise that after all that blaming me for his conviction, he thinks highly enough of me to take care of his last wishes. I don't get it." He paused momentarily. "The problem is," he added at the end, "I have a feeling that he did it on purpose. To let me know that he was right. He was innocent after all."

"Ah, but was he innocent of the act or innocent of the heart?" Rachel replied.

"Come again," he responded, "what do you mean? Is this another of those peculiar verdicts you have in Scotland?"

Rachel sighed as if Jack had exceeded the bounds of any reasonable person's patience. "Another of your characteristics," she said, "is your ability to grasp the last lesson of life, you know the one it's usually too late to profit by. What you have to try and do is anticipate the next lesson rather than getting to grips with things too late."

Jesus! Obviously she'd observed him very closely over the last few weeks. Not that he'd ever thought she was an airhead. "I thought I was quite good at that," he replied in a wounded tone.

"The problem is," she went on. "You should share these misgivings of yours more and I'd sharp put you straight. You can't just walk away from problems. You've got to grasp the nettle and deal with them. You're dead meat if you don't. They'll get you in a dark room, dive-bomb you and reproach you for all the wrong you've done. They'll make you believe you're evil!"

Why did he get the impression she was talking about herself rather than him? "Great!" Jack said. "I really feel better now. So what's the cure then or is it all doom and gloom?"

"The cure's in your own head. You come to terms with it! You start by learning, for the next time this happens, as it probably will, that you are only human, you can only do so much."

"Come to terms with a guy doing life because of my mistake? A few years ago he could have been hanged by the neck until he was dead!"

Rachel regarded Jack with the sort of look a nurse might reserve for a terminally ill patient. "Sometimes things happen which are unfair. You can't say I never do any wrong. And you can't keep on punishing yourself when you make a mistake, you are only human after all. You're not infallible."

It occurred to him that she was actually saying something about them, that there was a deeper meaning in her words.

"I'm merely facing up to facts. I was found wanting and there's not a damned thing I can do about it. I feel like a surgeon who's just buried the evidence."

"Remember what I said. There's a difference between innocence of the act and innocence of the heart."

Long after they had parted Jack had reason to remember those words. Wasting time on those unworthy of their efforts is a trap some lawyers fall into. Mere mortals, sometimes they get it badly wrong but, usually, they give it their best shot because they are often the last resort for a lot of people. It isn't easy always to decide who is worthy of the effort so a lot of lawyers, Jack included, resolved the dilemma by trying to help everyone and often paid for their pain. If they jettisoned those people, they ended up on a scrap heap of lost causes piled high enough to rival Everest. The fateful words Henry had uttered to him were, "I'm giving you a second chance. Not everyone gets that do they?" He was right, but Jack had no more got it right the second time than the first. Why was that? It still puzzled him. Rachel was saying, let it go. More than ever before his heart felt as if it would burst if he couldn't see her. Could he accept just being friends? It was better than nothing. Could he worship her from the sidelines? Could he stand and watch her in the arms of another man? God, he had it bad. He'd never felt like this before. No wonder she said to cool it. I must be like a furnace when she's near me. She must get singed just coming through the door. Of course, he hadn't found out a thing. She hadn't even hinted at where she'd been or with whom. She'd simply taken control of the conversation, steered it in the direction she wanted to go, dropped a bombshell on him so he would know precisely where the no-go areas were and he'd ended up accepting any scraps he could get from the table. Alone that night, Jack almost allowed his jealousy and resentment to spill over into anger. It was all very well for her to tell him how to think. Like she had everything worked out! Still he had to admit she had a point. Yes, it would be a wonderful thing to be always one step ahead of life, to have already in the ledger the next lesson it is going to teach you, so that when it thinks it's going to dump you on your backside you can say, "wrong one, chum! Grasped that particular nettle a long time ago." Chance would be a fine thing.

The reason for all this self-flagellation was that, far from being able to just let it go, it was hard to face up to the fact that he might have been responsible for an innocent man's conviction of a capital crime. Doctors quite often bury their mistakes whereas lawyers merely condemn theirs to a lifetime of despair. Rachel had hit the nail on the head. "It is the expectations of other members of society which are too high. Those who assume that, because you have a degree of forensic training, you have somehow forfeited the basic privileges of humanity, one of which is the right, once in a while, to be wrong, are of course themselves never found wanting." Wise words. Even so, for a man with a conscience, the law is no place to hide.

Aware that its apparent lack of priority had made him neglect the dead villain's wishes, particularly as he had spent so much time abroad shortly after getting the instructions, Jack had brought the Henry Herron letter and other documents home so that he could study them at his leisure. The letter was written in the small, neat, but barely decipherable handwriting of a gentleman called John Pardoe, once a fellow inmate of Henry's. Jack presumed from this that, some time towards the latter part of his sentence, Henry had been considered safe enough to be allowed a cellmate, having spent the early years in solitary. Mr. Pardoe promised to call on Jack. The letter gave no clue to his whereabouts. Three other points made it remarkable. The first was an allusion at the end of the text to the fact that, although Jack was to be the executor of Henry's wishes after death, it was Mr. Pardoe himself to whom "has been entrusted the task of carrying out Henry's last wishes during his lifetime. I am his spiritual heir." Jack raised his eyebrows at the hyperbole. The second point was the document which accompanied the letter. Wrapped in a plastic envelope of the sort used to protect valuable documents, it proved to be the will. It had been prepared meticulously in the knowledge of imminent death. Henry had studied law during his imprisonment and had crafted his own testament. It was apparent from a brief check that he had no financial worth. The will set out bequests of every item of property he owned. He wanted to give something to everyone. Even Jack was mentioned. He got Henry's latterly delivered journal "with the hope that he will seek a publisher for it, so that others may know how to avoid the pitfalls I fell into." An admirable if, knowing the author, unexpected sentiment. Henry's fishing tackle and huntsman's knives went to his 'adopted son', Douglas Thornton. God, Jack thought, he must be a grown man now. Henry couldn't resist a little joke. To Blacklock Spiers, the one whom he claimed truly to be responsible for the Langhorn Forest murder, he left his mother's bible, "to help him tell the truth in the future." It was a litany of names from the past. Henry was living years behind the times. It is unnecessary to prove wills in the event of the estate being too small to justify a grant of Probate, but any executor has the right to prove if he wishes. Jack resolved to do the decent thing and prove the will.

Now that he had a little more time, he flicked briefly through the journal but soon lost interest. He wanted to see if Henry had anything more to add on the Langhorn murder. It was true that the journal started with this topic but it turned out to be merely an introductory explanation of why Henry found himself behind bars with the time to jot down his life story. He quickly dropped it in favour of reciting every event which had happened to him in his life from early childhood. His recollections were of living in the country, hunting and fishing and camping out in the wilds of Northumberland. A cursory glance through revealed nothing further of the Langhorn murder and, vaguely disappointed, Jack put the journal away. He didn't really want to spend his leisure time reading the life history of Henry Herron, no matter what pangs of conscience still consumed him about their dealings. The third point of interest seemed at first a non-point. A document appeared to have been mistakenly included with the will. It was a letter from a Leicester solicitor addressed to Mr. Pardoe at Long Lartin prison, presumably where he'd met Henry. It read simply:

> Dear Mr. Pardoe,
> Re: Goat's Head Cottage, Northumberland
> I am writing to confirm in accordance with your request that I hold the deeds to the above property on your behalf. I enclose herewith a receipted schedule for your safe keeping.
> Yours sincerely,

A schedule of deeds was pinned to the page. Jack made a mental note to hand this to Mr. Pardoe when he met him.

Still puzzled by this assignment, he was on the verge of going to bed when his doorbell rang. It was a blustery night and he wondered who could be abroad at this hour. He went to open the door and was astonished to see Rachel. "Hi!" he said and for a moment he was so taken aback that he simply kept her there.

"Well, can I come in?" she asked him wide-eyed.

"Of course, I'm sorry," he said. "I was just surprised to see you."

Rachel took off her coat. She wore a tiny dress beneath. He guessed she'd been out – with someone else. She was dressed to kill. It was tasteful enough, provided you had the body to carry it off, which she did, but no one dressed like that unless they wanted to impress. Jack bit his tongue. He wouldn't say a word. No sign of his burning jealousy would pass his lips. Rachel had indicated that she intended to take control. She did so now. "I wanted...." she said and hesitated. "To see me?" Jack prompted her.

For a moment she seemed to be on the verge of saying something. Then she just kissed him. Oh Jesus, he thought as he squeezed her. It was a roller coaster ride, this one. He didn't know whether he was coming or going. Was this a consolation prize? This was the dilemma: stand up against it, tell her it's not on, she can't treat you like this? Or just go with the flow? The problem was the current was a rip tide.

CHAPTER 7

A few days later Rachel had gone off on a jaunt again and Jack was back to working late. About eight-thirty he was tired but he'd broken the back of the logjam. It was a wet and windy night. The firm's offices were a large, unruly rabbit warren and a noise, which sounded like a door slamming upstairs, made him stop what he was doing and listen hard. Had the cleaners left the front door open? That wouldn't be like them. He went to investigate up the staircase immediately outside his door. Arriving on the top flight, he moved from room to room, putting the lights on as he went, when suddenly the electricity failed. He cursed aloud and then heard what sounded like a snicker of laughter from the stairwell. He peered over the banister into the depths and recoiled in horror. On the ground floor, looking up, stood a skeletal figure. Jack shouted out and the face disappeared but not before he had time to take in its ghostly pallor and thin, cruel lips. Jack wondered if his mind was playing tricks on him. Plucking up the courage to go downstairs he missed his footing in the darkness and crashed to the middle landing. A queer sound like laughter could be heard mingling with gusts of wind, which slammed against the building and rattled the windows. Jack had sprained his ankle and he hobbled into his room. The moon shone white through the windows overlooking the deserted square. Torch, he thought. There was one in his car. Feeling his way downstairs, he fiddled with a bunch of keys for the right Chubb and gazed fearfully over his shoulder in case the intruder appeared. Finally he let himself out. The wind was blowing a gale, whipping loose newspapers up and down the street. They circled and somersaulted with a ghostly slowness like figures in a dance; they stuck in the railings of the park opposite and flapped like birds trying to escape. He opened the tailgate of the Mercedes and felt in the toolbox until he found the torch, then, feeling a little braver, he glanced up at the office. From the landing window next to his room the ghoul stared down, its eyes fixed upon him with a look of such malevolence that his muscles froze. He got no more than a glimpse before, once again, the disembodied face disappeared. Getting a grip on himself he limped up to the door and crossed to the stairwell. Nothing was visible. He carried out a search of the first floor and found nothing. The second floor was equally empty. He walked back downstairs, wondering if his mind really was playing tricks. The initial pain in his ankle had subsided. He went down to the basement and shone the torch around and noticed the grill window was open. He reached up and shut it. If the cleaners had left it like that someone might have climbed in. He studied the fuse box. A lever was down indicating that the lighting fuse had been overloaded. He reset it and the lights flooded on. Breathing a sigh of relief, he made his way back upstairs. The papers were precisely as he'd left them. He no longer had the stomach for work and decided to finish the letters the next morning.

Before leaving, he stood a moment at the stairwell, where the ghostly apparition had first appeared, and listened hard. Nothing stirred except the wind. It had ceased attempting to batter its way into the building like the advance artillery of some ghastly army and had been reduced to a soft soughing sound. It occurred to him that it sounded like something he had once read: the hopeless torment of all Dante's souls in the faraway circles of the Inferno.

He had left the car unlocked and he started it up and drove away, resisting the urge to speed. The way home took him through a succession of country lanes. The moon had disappeared and it was pitch black, the obscurity exacerbated by rain driving against the windscreen. He craned forward as he drove into the torrent. The road ran with water. It came up to the sills of the vehicle in a sudden flash flood. The purple sky cracked with forked lightning. The deafening crash of thunder overhead nearly made him lose his grip on the steering wheel. He turned the fog beams on and they reflected against the swirling rain, whilst, inside, the instrument panel produced a ghostly glow. He looked in the mirror. A reflection in the windscreen stared back at him, the apparition from the office! Another rose behind it – a face of such cunning ferocity, which, though human, seemed to have more in common with an animal's. Its lupine leer said, "I have cornered you. There is no escape." Before he could react a hand reached out and grasped his throat. Something went over his mouth; he was suddenly fighting for air; his right foot pushed down on the brake; the car shot across the road, aquaplaning in the flood.

Jack didn't know how long he'd been unconscious. He came to with a torch shining in his face. It was held by a police officer, who beckoned to him to wind the window down. "All right, are you, sir?" he asked suspiciously, "I saw you go past a few minutes ago. What's happened here? I know you. You're Mr. Lauder, aren't you?" He leaned over to see if he could smell alcohol. Jack opened the door and got out to see how the vehicle had come to rest. It had slewed into the kerbside and was parked halfway into the road. The floodwater had receded and a stream ran down the tarmac about three inches deep. He looked at his watch. It was 9.20pm. Accompanying the policeman to his car, he felt relieved when the green light came on the Alcotest device.

The officer looked at him, surprised, and shook his head. He'd counted the kudos already, thinking he had the scalp of Jack Lauder. "You passed out?" he asked. "Do you suffer an illness of some sort?"

"No, I don't," Jack said.

"Are you on any drugs or medication?"

"No. I had the distinct feeling someone was in the car with me."

The policeman grimaced as if he found that off the wall. "I didn't see any passengers when you went by. How did you pass out?"

"I don't know," Jack said. "I thought something was put over my mouth. I was driving along perfectly normally, given the conditions, that is. I saw what looked like a face reflected in the windscreen."

"Who was it, sir?"

"Oh, I don't know officer," Jack replied. "I didn't get a clear view." He was about to go on to recount the earlier incident at the office but thought better of it. It wouldn't have made sense to a road traffic policeman , one of those officers accustomed to dealing with real-life horror, picking up the debris of accidents, the dead bodies, the bits of severed limbs, and to dealing with grieving relatives. He wasn't the sort to take Jack's story without a fairly large pinch of salt. His expression showed that he thought the lawyer had a screw loose.

"I think you've been overdoing it a bit, sir," he said, "if I were you I'd see a doctor."

When Jack got home he rang Rachel's mobile. There was no reply. He sat by the phone in the dark, no one even to share this unusual moment with. When he thought of it, maybe it was a good thing. If he'd told her he'd misled the officer, that the second face he'd seen had reminded him of Henry Herron, she probably would have realised a wire was loose. He put the lights out before closing the curtains. He stood there looking into the garden. Was someone standing in the shadow of the willow tree? He couldn't see anything but he imagined that death-mask of a face glimpsed in the office. A mighty howl on the wind, like a large wolf, made him shudder. "My God!" he said. He threw the window open and looked out but the wind chose that moment to get up and he was drowned in a flurry of rain.

The next morning, before going to Court, he made some enquiries into Henry's death. It didn't take long to locate the doctor who'd signed the certificate. He was from Newton St. Abbs, a small town in the Borders. "Oh yes," the doctor said, "I do remember him." Silent for a few moments, he added, "he was a funny kind of chap, just released from prison, I think." Jack assured him that would be correct. "Typical terminal illness case. He was pretty well wasted when I saw him. He was very emaciated. I remember the tattoos. He was a distinctive looking chap. Very bright eyes."

"Did he have a history of illness from prison?"

"Yes. He brought his own notes. He'd been released because of terminal illness and of course he didn't last much longer. There was a post-mortem to confirm the diagnosis. Advanced cancer of the spleen. Just about incurable."

CHAPTER 8

Tropical Tom had never taken up the offer of an appointment after Jack's weird night in Whitley Bay, nor had Jack forgotten Joe's revelation of Tom's duplicity. It was time to put a theory to the test. Jack knew where he'd find this particular dreg of society and took up a position on the Cullercoats Metro Station. Tom would arrive sooner or later, on his way to town to do a few deals. There was no point in going to his house. He wouldn't answer the door.

About 1.30pm Tom came swinging over the bridge looking as if he'd already had his first snort. His head up in the air, his coat swinging behind him, he walked with a jaunty stride as if there was a cushion of air between his boots and the ground. Jack kept out of the way, waited for him to get on the Metro, followed him and sat down next to him. "Hello Tom!" he said. Listening to his Walkman, his eyes closed, the drug dealer jumped in fear when he saw Jack. "Found your lass yet?" the lawyer continued affably.

"Aye," Tom replied, trying to get over the shock, "thanks, Jack."

"Fancy that. How did that come about? Did you get some supernatural assistance?"

"I divn't know what you're talking about," Tom said suspiciously.

"Well, your lass disappears, kidnapped by witches. Now she's turned up, but you've not said a word to all of us who were worried about her. No more contact?" Jack let it hang there and watched the petty crook lick his lips nervously.

"Those people .." Tom started to say.

Jack craned forward. "Yes?"

"Well," he went on, "I got them wrong, didn't I?"

"Did you?"

"Yeah, I think so, Jack. I mean I thought they were bad people but they're not really. They're New Age people. They know lots of things I didn't even think about before."

"Try some of these things on me," Jack said.

"Oh no," Tom began to laugh, "I couldn't do that Jack, you'd never understand."

Jack decided to get to the point. "I have some very reliable information that you have been playing tricks on me."

"I don't know what you mean," Tom blurted out.

"A certain little night call out about a lass who's done a runner, kidnapped by aliens?"

"Never in the world! That was true, Jack. I swear it!"

"You're an asshole," Jack said, "and I'll tell you what I'm going to do. I'm going to get you well and truly busted. If you don't tell me who put you up to these mind games, I'll make sure they throw away the key."

"How can you do that Jack? Everything I've told you is privileged." They always know their rights these people! Obligations they're backward on but they know what they're due. Tom looked at his lawyer nervously. .

"Try me." Jack took out his mobile phone. "I make one call to Lowther and I tell him that yesterday Snowy Abdullah delivered you enough tack to get an army stoned. You know where it's stashed? It's underneath that floorboard where you keep your cash. You know how I know this? Snowy's a grass. He's very frightened of a good mate of mine, no names, no pack drill."

"I divn't know what you're talking about!" Tom's face was puce and his lower lip quivered.

"Don't you," Jack sneered, and tapped out the Divisional police Station number. "Chief Superintendent Lowther please?"

Tom's eyes rolled frantically. "Okay, okay, Jack, don't do that, I'll go away for a long time. I'm on a bender now, you know that."

"Who's the man behind this little joke of yours, Tom?"

"He's the head honcho," Tom replied. "Look, it's hard to talk about him Jack. He's a scary bloke."

"Is that it?" Jack put his ear back to the mobile.

"You don't understand Jack. He's a real warlock. Do you know what one of them is?"

"Yes, a piss artist, like you," Jack replied.

"No, no," Tom replied frantically. "You're wrong, Jack! He can make you do things. He can make you see things. He can make you feel pain and he's nowhere near you. Jack, this guy can do for you."

"Who is he?"

Tom licked his lips nervously again. "Max Kaliostri."

Jack sat back in the seat. Lowther's voice, saying, "hello, hello," was on the telephone but he switched it off. Of course he had already suspected the answer but its confirmation had increased the weight of the burden. He had secretly hoped that it wasn't something personal. Not for the first time he wished he had never taken on that case against Kaliostri. He'd had the chance of turning it down but ego had overcome judgment. In many ways that was the story of his life. Still, ruminating on what might have been would avail him nothing now. The chips were down. One of the wealthiest men in the world, armed with a battery of apparent super powers, had decided to intervene personally in his life and exact retribution for a perceived wrong. "Super powers!" he exclaimed. Tom gaped at him and he looked at the drug dealer with utter disdain. "I'll wrap them round his neck," Jack threatened with perhaps more bravado than he felt.

Tom, recovering his composure, smirked back. "I'll tell him you said that," he rejoined.

The Monument stop was coming up. Jack stood up and flicked his Metro ticket at Tom's face, catching him square in the eye. Acknowledging the drug dealer's discomfort with one finger, he got off the train. Seething inside, he took a taxi back to the office. He threw himself into his work with a furious energy. It was five o'clock when the receptionist called and said a woman wanted to speak to him on the phone. She hadn't given a name, it was apparently personal. The receptionist knew Rachel's voice and it wasn't her. Mystified, he took the call.

"How are things there?" a female voice asked him coyly. The voice was familiar. Surely not..."Hello. Jack, it's Josephine, I've got to speak to you."

"Josephine ... I don't know what..." He paused and then he ended lamely. "Long time no see?"

"I know I should have got in touch. I had to go away. It was wrong taking off like that without saying anything to you after ...well."

Not just that, pet! he wanted to say. Why did you accuse me of harassing you? But he held his tongue. "You're quite well?" he continued.

"Yes, only ..." She sounded puzzled. "There's a problem Jack?" She wouldn't say any more on the telephone. She insisted on meeting him the next evening and suggested the Egypt Cottage, a little pub close to the television studios where she worked. Curiosity got the better of judgment and he agreed to meet her. The coincidence of his meeting with Tom was still fresh in his mind. The jungle tom-toms had started beating and this might be the riposte. Josephine's business was likely to have something to do with Max Kaliostri.

CHAPTER 9

Josephine's call had caught Jack at a low point. Among other things, Rachel was among the missing again. He was almost used to it now. She'd turn up out of the blue; he wouldn't be able to ask where she'd been, what had happened to her, for fear of frightening her off; she'd be as passionate as ever when they were together but it wouldn't be enough – for either of them. It couldn't go on like this. Obviously, he wasn't exactly what she wanted because she seemed happy enough with their infrequent if highly charged meetings. It wasn't only self-pity that made Jack miss so much this young woman, who had strolled into his life out of the great blue yonder. He appreciated as much as any physical attribute her cool head, her lateral thinking and an intuition, which, in the short time he had known her, had proved at times to be simply startling. Years of forensic training had taught him not to jump to conclusions and sometimes a different kind of mind sees things in another perspective. That was one of the reasons why, when she was away, he'd begun to feel really lonely, more so than he could ever remember feeling in his life. He'd got used to being alone and then someone had turned up and shown him the other side of the street, one he'd never known existed. Unfortunately, the street was her element and she crossed and re-crossed at will, often leaving him behind. No one needed to tell him the difficulty a free spirit such as Rachel would have fitting into his daily routine. Sometimes, though, it doesn't matter if you know exactly how to avert a crisis. You still can't do it. He had got on with life, hoping in a micawberish way that things would sort themselves out as if by magic but, in his heart of hearts, he knew it was a crime against humanity to expect a gorgeous creature like her to spend her life with him. Like a falconer but possessed of a conscience he was trying to remove something proud and breathtakingly beautiful from its proper environment, clip its wings and put it on a pedestal for his friends to admire.

It was dark when he turned the car down by the quayside. The streets were wet. It had rained incessantly for days. The damp came up through his shoes and made him shiver. He pulled up close to the pub and was about to put some money in the meter when he remembered it wasn't necessary after 6 o'clock. A tramp shuffled towards him, wearing a pair of battered old trainers and a coat which reached down to his ankles. His shirt lay open at the neck, covered by a long, shaggy beard, and his long hair was streaked with grey as he stood under the street light and looked at Jack with a baleful eye. He was tall and straight even if he'd fallen on hard times. Something about him stirred Jack's memory but he couldn't place it. An arrogance in his bearing made Jack think wryly that he didn't have the right demeanour for a street person. The tramp seemed to anticipate his thoughts. "Got any spare change, guv?" he asked. The question was a cocky one. Jack looked in his eyes. He had seen before the hollow emptiness in a beggar's eyes, that look of being lost in a vast universe with nowhere to go. The eyes of a beggar remind you what it is to be unloved and alone. Jack didn't see that here. This beggar's eyes were fiery and determined and strangely compelling. Just my luck, Jack thought, a Trotskyite tramp. "What's the matter guv, cat got your tongue?" A satyr-like leer suffused his face. Almost without thinking and as if he felt duty-bound to do so Jack passed him the coins he'd intended feeding into the meter. The tramp didn't speak. He looked at the coins in his hand. "Fuck you!" he cursed and he flicked them at Jack disdainfully.

"What's the matter," it was Jack's turn to ask, "has the price gone up?"

"Aye," the beggar said, spitting once on the pavement, "in line with inflation." He tramped off down the street towards the Mens' Palace, his shoulders hunched into his coat. As he walked he chuntered on like one who has lost his marbles and, when he was a safe distance away, he turned and pointed, shouting incoherent remarks apparently into the night air but Jack had the distinct and uncomfortable impression that they were aimed at him. The only clear remark he caught from the tirade was, "they're never the same, you know, not when the devil's bent their minds!"

A young couple came along the pavement in the opposite direction. Still in earshot of Jack he stopped them and, in a loud voice, regaled the shocked pair. The young couple, protecting themselves beneath raised umbrellas, stepped off the pavement into the torrents running down the culverts to avoid his ranting. Long after the passers by had scuttled off and the street had fallen silent and the drains ceased to run, the man stood on the City walls and raved at a river dressed in a silver train by the rising moon.

Jack turned into the pub. Life seemed to be getting more peculiar by the moment. Things weren't happening in the predictable way that one brought up with a background of practical and rational thought felt entitled to expect. He wondered if the earth had shifted slightly on its axis. Was it yet another of these millennial phenomena? He struggled to recall the prophesies of Nostradamus. Was it some time about now the world would end? He pushed open the pub door. Hopefully, he'd manage to get a pint first. The Egypt Cottage was garishly lit and full of arty types from the television studio, talking in loud plummy voices, some of them dressed not much differently from the tramp outside. Jack made enquiries of one or two whether Josephine had been in yet. A couple of blokes knew her; they shook their heads. "Haven't seen her mate," one of them said in a Cockney accent. "She's a great one for standing blokes up."

"You've had that experience have you?" Jack asked with a smile.

"You can say that again. I've arranged to meet her twice and she didn't show. I mean she's worth waiting for once, but no woman's worth waiting for twice." His friend laughed. "You on a good thing with her?" the Cockney went on.

"No," he said, "we have a little mystery to clear up between us, that's about it." He took a sip of his Guinness.

"Ah, well Josie's a mystery in herself isn't she? Great lass, great looker, great body but..."

"You mean she's a tease?" Jack prompted him because he'd stopped in mid-flight.

"Hey, not just that, she's got some weirdo ways man. Really strange. Some of the people she hangs around with. Wow!"

Try as he might he couldn't wheedle any more information out of the man. He continued shaking his head and added, "you'll find out if you hang around her long enough."

Meanwhile the cockney's colleague had been looking at Jack as if he recognised him. When the pressure of the eyes became too much to bear, Jack looked at the man and said, "I'm not sure I've had the pleasure." He held out his hand, which the other man took with a firm grip. Jack noticed his athletic build. The man had a dark, sunburnt skin and a beard.

"Bob Lindsay. I met you years ago," the man said. "Aiguille du Midi. You came up from the Plan. Frendo was it?"

Jack smiled and relaxed. "Yeah," he replied, "I remember it well." He recognised the other man's name at least. He was the editor of a number of local crag guides and a sometime television pundit on mountaineering generally, usually rolled out when a major Himalayan expedition had somehow caught the public imagination. Obviously, this pub was where it was at, at least in the media circles.

"You don't do any now, do you?" Bob went on.

Jack returned his steady gaze, slightly surprised that he should know that, even more that he cared. "No," he replied quietly. "I kind of fell out of love with it."

Bob's next remark was surprisingly blunt and revealed that he had become as much journalist as climber. "Someone told me you lost your nerve after your accident. I was sorry to hear that."

The statement had a ring of familiarity. Each time he'd met former mountaineering friends, he'd come up against that attitude of well-meant pity tinged with contempt, more or less as if his erstwhile colleagues felt that he had cheated somehow; that he was duty bound to go on until he succumbed to their game of ghosts. Slightly irritated that someone whom he didn't even know should presume to enquire into his innermost psyche, Jack responded with apparent equanimity: "lost my nerve? Is that what they say? Well, I guess I don't know because I've never put it to the test."

"That's the problem," Bob replied with an air of omniscience, "you've got to get straight back on the hill after something like that or you'll never be the same again."

"Maybe," Jack replied. "Anyway, nice meeting you." He took his drink and sat at a table some distance away from the men at the bar. After about half an hour the two men got up to go. "Looks like you're in the same boat as me," the Cockney said. Jack gave Josephine another half-hour and then he left. It was getting late and he was anxious to get a night's sleep before his case the next day. On an impulse he decided to stroll the couple of hundred yards along the road to the television studio. The walk was fruitless because the doorman wouldn't allow him past the foyer. "I'm sorry," he said in response to Jack's question, "I'm under strict instructions not to give out information about Miss

Jackson. We get a lot of funny types hanging around here waiting for her. There was a scruffy guy a few minutes ago." Jack felt like saying, "do I look like a funny type?" But long exposure to the law had led him to appreciate that it is dangerous to ask a question if you're not sure of the answer. Gloom unlifted he trudged the rainswept street back to the car. From a few yards away he noticed a long score down the passenger side and sighed in exasperation. The paintwork on a Mercedes costs a fortune. "Sod it," he said aloud, but he was lucky it wasn't paint stripper. He looked along the road. "That bloody tramp!" In an even fouler mood, he drove up to Spital Tongues to see if Josephine's light was on. It wasn't. He got out of the car and knocked on the door. There was no reply. Dejected, he drove home. As soon as he entered his house he knew immediately something was wrong. It's started again, he thought. He made an inspection of the downstairs rooms. Venturing upstairs he could smell a sweet cloying fragrance pervading the house. It emanated from his bedroom. He pushed open the door. The mirror had been covered over. The sweet smell was so strong he had to throw open all the windows in an attempt to get rid of it. He checked outside through the open window, but there was nothing in the garden. Then he noticed an object over the mantelpiece. He had an abhorrence of crucifixes, not because he was anti-Christian, but because he found the depiction of the passion of Christ so sadistic. The crucifix had been nailed to the wall upside down. He picked it off and stood it up correctly. There was nothing else out of place. He looked carefully at the twisted form of the Saviour. It occurred to him as he took in that tortured figure that it is odd how this graphic and apocryphal scene is re-enacted year after year in human society – the stakes not quite so high perhaps but the method essentially the same: the torture of the scapegoat. For some reason, though, one look at that figure, one moment's appreciation of that agony, and he no longer feared his intruders. It was fortunate for them that they had quit the scene.

CHAPTER 10

The next day Jack received a phone call. He wasn't sure if he was surprised or if he had half expected it. "Josephine," he said with feigned affability when the identity of the caller had been made known to him, "I spent a very pleasant hour in The Egypt Cottage waiting for Godot. He or rather she didn't show."

Her voice in response sounded guarded. "Something came up. Couldn't get, Jack, sorry about that."

"How is it I find there to be a distinct lack of sincerity in that apology?"

"It's just the cynical lawyer in you," she replied. Still, there was something distant about her voice.

"Oh yeah? Like the guys who came to see me last night. Not that you could have had anything to do with that of course."

"What are you talking about?" she replied.

"Oh, come on! Pull the other one! It was just like the old days. A bunch of tossers breaking into my house."

"Jack, I had no idea! That means they know I tried to speak to you...."

He snapped. "Look, don't give me that. If your friends break in my frigging house again, I'll hang the bastards out to dry."

"Jack, a reaction like that might be just what they wanted....." Her voice broke off.

"What do you mean?"

"Precisely what I said," she replied, "they're not my friends. Not any more. Joking aside, the reason I didn't come yesterday was..." and her voice dropped to a whisper, "I'm being watched. I wanted to warn you."

"Like you did last time when..." He couldn't finish the sentence. If not exactly a conversation of meaningful silences this one had its retentive moments.

She seemed almost wounded. "Okay Jack, I'll tell you what I'll do, I'm on location tomorrow, and I'll meet you straight afterwards."

"Hey," he replied, "I'm not making any more dates with you. You don't keep them. I'm told you've got a reputation for standing blokes up!"

"Why don't you come to where I'm working, then you know I'll be there? I will feel safer then too."

"Where's that?"

"Gibside Chapel. Believe it or not, I'm doing a series on spooks." She laughed that same attractive laugh.

"You'd know a lot about that subject," he replied unkindly. However, with less reluctance than he'd imagined, he agreed to meet her.

For the miserable weather of that autumn, the following evening turned out fair. There was a rainbow to the east over Blaydon and the last rays of the sun were streaming through the leaves as Jack took the footpath down to the chapel. Crewmembers with cameras and equipment were making their way up so he was bang on time. The chapel was an attractive monument, sandstone coloured with large windows, cupola-shaped, in a tranquil spot; the Collingwood Monument stood about a mile down the parkway; actors strolled in the evening sunshine in Elizabethan costume. A coach with four black horses stood on the road outside the chapel. The horses were fractious, the lead one pawing the ground.

He stepped across the threshold. A warm amber light filtered through the windows and cast shadows on to the interior walls. Something moved in the shadows beneath the image of a cross cast by one of the windows. The refraction of light inverted the cross. He shivered involuntarily and then the movement came alive. Something black erupted, with a sharp cry, from beneath the cross and aimed straight at his head. He ducked as it parted his hair. Swinging round he heard a loud squawking. A raven sat on the lintel above the window. It strutted there, almost human with a bright-eyed, affronted expression. Jack laughed nervously at his reaction to a trapped bird. Quickly he retraced his footsteps out into the setting sun. The bird watched him, beady-eyed. As the light flooded in through the door it saw its escape route and followed Jack out. It flapped up into the sky with loud, bloodcurdling screams.

Jack saw Josephine's blond hair in the shadow of one of the doorways. She was looking over some papers held by a crewmember, a black man who was talking to her intimately, obviously making some suggestions for the programme. She was dressed in tight fitting jeans and a cashmere sweater, which rolled up tantalisingly over her exposed tummy. He noticed that since he'd last seen her she'd had some piercing done. A gold ring gleamed from her belly button. Attached to it was a chain in the form of an emerald and ruby snake. Jack approached the duo and the producer turned and looked at him suspiciously as if he were an intruder. Jack ignored him and moved towards Josephine. "Hold it, man," the black man said and he reached out and grabbed Jack's wrist. Jack stared back at him uncomprehendingly, then he looked at Josephine. Her face was blank. He was conscious of the man's fingers, digging into his arm, restraining him

"Josephine?" Jack said.

She did an affected double take, put her hand to her mouth and replied, "Jack!" as if she was astonished to see him. The man's grip dug into his arm and he grew angrier. "Ben, it's okay," Josephine said at last and, with one final, mistrustful look, the man released his arm.

Jack rubbed it. The man's fingernails had drawn blood, so intense had his grip been.

"Who's the gorilla? Part of your private army?" he asked with a trace of bitterness. He looked down at the red weal on his wrist, slightly darkening as the clot formed.

"Hey, cool it man!" Ben exclaimed.

"Cool it!" Jack replied. "Like you did? Whoa! I need to go back to school to learn your kind of tolerance!"

"Hey, you never know what's going down, man. I've got to be on my guard. Get it?"

Jack's manner softened, although his arm itched like crazy. "Yes, sorry. I appreciate you get some oddballs hanging around."

"Okay man," Ben said, and he knocked his fist against Jack's. "Respect," he said and walked off. It was strange because Jack watched him go but, nevertheless, he was there one moment, the next he was gone. It was as if Jack had blacked out momentarily. He became dimly aware of Josephine talking.

"Sorry!" she said. "You're right, though. You've got to be aware of stalkers! We do sometimes get some weird people hanging round."

"That's what the doorman at the studio said too," Jack replied. He cut short her apologies for what had happened in the past. "Josie, it's simple," he replied, "we went home to your place, we both fell asleep, I woke up with Lorenza Kaliostri. I dreamt you'd lost your head and turned into a pig, Alice in Wonderland style. I wonder what gave me that impression? I got back home. I found a pig's head in my bed. A bunch of clowns ransacked my house. For all I know the same bunch came back last night! You pissed off. Told the police I'd been harassing you. What is there to explain? Just tell me what you want from me now!"

She returned his look with something approaching sadness. "You're right, I'm sorry, it seemed like a good joke at the time, but those were different days. We were all out of our heads most of the time. Both Max and Lorenza wanted to bring you down. Lorenza said you needed your ego pricked."

"Great!" Jack said. "I just tried to help her, that's all. That's what I do. It's a job. I didn't ask you lot to interfere in my life."

She sighed. "It's no use digging up the past. I want to help you."

"Well, if that's true, try this one. Does the name Jessica Parker mean anything?" The mention of Jessica's name seemed to blow her head away. She was rattled. "The bigger question is," Jack went on icily, "was she murdered?"

"Wow, hold on Jack, just go steady now. I think you've got hold of something you don't understand here. I don't want to get into any finger-pointing shit. I've got a career to think of." Jack was puzzled. "So why did you want to see me? Just to blow hot and cold?"

"Okay, okay," she went on, holding up her hands, "calm down, just let me get a hold of this. I can't handle this kind of shit Jack. It's been on my mind for a long time. I've got a confession to make. Okay, so someone wanted to play a prank on you, right? Someone thought you are a jumped-up pompous twat who'd done them a bad turn, okay? So they say let's play a trick on Jack, yeah? Let's say I'm recruited to help with that, okay? So we play a trick, in bad taste maybe but still just a harmless trick. Let's say the person who's the centre of the trick, i.e me, doesn't know the details. I'm just supposed to slip you a Micky Finn and then get out of there, right? Well, I had a bit of discretion. I could hang around and enjoy the premier cru, as it were." She smiled at him artfully and let her hand drift across his arm. He noticed, suddenly, his wrist was burning where the man had grabbed him. Josephine didn't notice his discomfort and carried on prattling. "After that, I just wait to hear from people what's happened. That's it.

Okay. That's me. That's my bit. Now here I am and...." Suddenly, her voice began to crack and she looked round her fearfully.... "there's all these frightening people come out of nowhere...."

"People coming out of nowhere?" Jack replied, puzzled.

"Yeah, real scary people. Madmen, real scary freaks... suddenly .... suddenly there's a girl dead and I'm scared..."

So that was it. She was worried it might happen to her. Jack pressed home the advantage. "What was that news report you did? The one about the girl in St. Nicholas' churchyard?" She looked round wildly. Jack's eyes followed hers and he saw what looked like a movement in the bushes to his right. "Who's that?" he asked.

She shook her head. "Nothing, it's all right, just one of the crew." Then she seemed to compose herself.

"Why can't you tell me outright? Is it the Kaliostris?"

She looked around frantically. She put her hands to her head and screeched. "Piss off Jack," she said. "You haven't got a clue how serious this is. It's not just them. There's others involved now. I can't grass on these bastards. You don't know what they're like. It started out as a joke but it's out of control. It's out of control."

"You don't believe this mumbo-jumbo do you?" Jack's tone softened at the genuineness of her fear.

"If you saw the kind of things they can do, you'd believe it."

He went up to her and put his arm round her. Momentarily she snuggled in. "Look, you can't get out of a nightmare unless you wake up. To wake up you have to make a concession to real life. You have to accept it. If you know these people carried out these atrocities, you've got to tell me. Come on, wake up." He scratched his arm, noticing with brief concern that the wound still hadn't congealed.

Josephine looked at him out of tear-filled eyes. "I daren't say anything, I just daren't. These people could make me do or say anything they want. Do you realise what a risk I'm taking meeting you? Do you know what could happen to me if I lose his protection? If he throws me to the wolves!" She had worked herself up into a frenzied state so Jack tried to soothe her. "Well what are you doing here if you don't think I can help you?" She pulled away and backed off. "Who is this he?" he called after her, "who else is involved?" She started to walk away. Jack thought she was just trying to put some distance between them to get her head straight so he let her walk, and then he realised she was going to walk out of the clearing. "Josephine, come back!" he shouted after her. "Where are you going?" She disappeared into the gloom. "Christ!" he thought. He had to follow her. She was his link with sanity. He started to run, calling her name. When he got to the edge of the wood she'd disappeared into thin air. He looked round. All the other crewmen had left while they'd been talking. The sombre chapel gazed at him unblinkingly. He began to feel a sudden chill of fear. Something wasn't right. A young woman doesn't simply walk off into the wood and disappear. He stepped through the trees calling her name. The floor was a carpet of bark and cones and leaves. The only sound was of a noisy parliament of rooks, circling the wood like a black cloud, shouting their raucous goodnights. Penetrating deeper and deeper into the forest, his voice becoming more plaintive with every call. Emerging from the trees, he pulled up short. His throat dry, his head suddenly full of a kind of night, he stood on a precipice, looking down fifty feet or so into a canyon. "Wow!" The exclamation escaped from his mouth and he strove to control his swimming senses. He must have been staring for a long time before he realised that a shadowy figure, dressed in black and hooded as if by a monk's cowl, had emerged from the trees on the opposite side of the dene. The figure had its back to him. The point of the hood and spread cloak gave the impression of a giant bird. Jack's mind raced. He wondered if there was a Benedictine or Dominican community here, then he remembered they were doing a historical documentary, a dramatic reconstruction, using actors. Reassured, he hailed the figure in a friendly way, but it didn't acknowledge his call. A sudden sound made him cast a glance behind but no one else was there. Even so he sensed something and felt his scalp prickle. The hooded figure turned and started speaking in a loud voice. "Throw yourself down! He will put his angels in charge of you!" it said with a laughing lilt to a tenor voice. Jack was too shocked to respond. "Or perhaps I should give to you all that you see?"

Jack had recovered his composure. "So what do you want in return, Mr. Kaliostri?"

The hooded man didn't respond to Jack's educated guess but continued levelly. "I think you should have left well alone but you can decide now if it is enough or if it goes on." He started to walk sideways across Jack's line of vision, disappearing behind and reappearing from, the tree trunks, waving his hands about. Each time he reappeared he fixed Jack with a stare. The lawyer found his eyes, even from this distance, strangely hypnotic and had the distinct impression that he had looked into them before. "But people do sometimes make foolish mistakes, it's almost impossible to watch everyone all the time." The man spoke as if it was all too tiresome, as if he was resigned to being surrounded by idiots. "Then someone has to come along and pick up all the loose ends and atone for all the mistakes and put things back together again." He paused, smiled and added brightly, "just like Jesus!" He clapped his hands together.

"Jack, it's given to some to make fools of themselves. You're on the verge of that. You think you're a hero, but you're not. You're one step away from being an idiot. You have it in your power....*you* have it in your power to end this." Jack smiled. "Power, is it?" he replied What powers do you have that make everyone so frightened?"

The hooded man had placed himself on the bole of a felled tree and he stared in Jack's direction. "The power of persuasion. To make people become themselves, sometimes with unexpected consequences. I say things have gone far enough and offer you a truce."

"Forget it," Jack replied scornfully, "I don't have any right to forgive the kind of wrongs you've done. That's why you're going down for murder, Kaliostri." He suddenly realised that he was looking in the other man's eyes and they seemed to burn. I shouldn't do this, he thought and he averted his gaze, at least he thought he had.

The other man remained as suave and cool as ever. "You really don't understand, do you? Watch my lips! It's not as it seems. The lesson I am teaching you has nothing to do with madness. For a start, you have the wrong idea about people. You think of them as Homo sapiens, the pinnacle of evolution. Have you watched them emerge from the Underground or in a crowded street, at a concert, in a shopping mall, at a football match? Their stupid faces, their ignorant, inane comments? Black, white, pink, yellow, what does it matter? They are nothing more than cells, nothing more than flotsam and jetsam, leaves on a gnarled, old tree.

"Thanks for the philosophy lesson," Jack said, "People aren't perfect. In many ways they're no different from the rest of the animal kingdom, but that doesn't mean they have to be victims of sadists like you."

Kaliostri laughed. "Victims are born, Jack. Prey is put there for predators. It is the way of creation. Think about it. Do you have Christian values? Your God nonetheless allows you to slaughter the creatures of the earth in their millions, even for waste. There is no Christian piety there. Think of the thousands of slaughterhouses up and down the country and the millions of carcasses hanging in them and tell me we are all God's creatures." He smiled and in the same matter-of-fact voice added, "you think you are on the side of right and I am in some way evil. I have always been fascinated by the angels and the demons of the earth, Jack. It is astonishing, is it not, that one man's hero is another's villain? No more so than the ancient religions where the victors earn the right to exalt their gods. You question my powers? Let me give you a little demonstration and perhaps then you will realise why you should walk away."

Jack nearly jumped out of his skin as he heard a trumpeting sound like a herd of elephants. "Yes, Hannibal for instance, striding over the Alps and descending on Rome. To Carthaginians a deity, to the Romans, the embodiment of evil. Think of it. We were talking of Christ and he is of course the Messiah, the Saviour. But is he? To the Jews he must be a demon." A movement in the bushes to Jack's right made him look across. A dark-skinned man, wearing a white Arabian *burnous*, peered out and grinned. His eyes rolled as if he was in a trance. He ran a curved knife across his throat then melted back into the trees. "Wasn't he one of the *sicarii*? Yet, in his name the Jews have been persecuted since the Dark Ages and no more so than in the civilised Europe of this century. Read the Koran. You will understand why. They were condemned from the moment they worshiped the golden calf." Another frond of leaves parted and Jack stared at the beautiful Ethiopian girl from Lorenza's party. She stood tall and statuesque, her neck elongated by bands of gold. A rustle to his left made Jack turn and this time a figure dressed in black with an oriental, skull-like face leapt out. A sweep of a sword cropped the bushes in front of him. He fixed Jack with a stare and then he too disappeared. The next moment a bloodcurdling roar rent the air and the wood parted. Jack jumped aside as a wild boar crashed through the undergrowth. Kaliostri lectured on: "Mithras, Orpheus, both visited the underworld and were resurrected again." A clamour started as if the wood had suddenly come alive with creatures. Jack felt like the grouse must feel as the beaters invade their space. Voices began to chant: "I am the servant of the one God. I beseech and constrain thee forthwith to appear in thy proper shape, that I may have thy glorious assistance."

Jack's scalp prickled as he saw the hooded man's lips move. A lightning flash rent the sky and a thunder crack made Jack's eardrums ring. Kaliostri cast his gaze on the sky. Disembodied faces parted branches. "They're actors!" he called out. "You don't fool me." Suddenly the chanting stopped, the figures disappeared. An eerie, pregnant silence hung over the wood. Kaliostri smiled as he crossed Jack's field of vision. He had something up his sleeve, something awful. Cobwebs brushed Jack's hair. A rustle behind him made him jump and turn on guard. Nothing was there and yet the air crackled. Something brushed his face. He flailed his arms as if warding off insects. A great weight seemed to press down on him. Feeling as if he was being pushed to the ground, he turned and crashed through the undergrowth, running deep into the woods. To his wild, scared eyes, beneath every bush was a peculiar creature: a hedgehog with a human face; a wildcat whose eyes opened and shut like a semaphore lamp; rabbits with grins like sharks; birds with leathery wings. He ran this way and that, exhaustion bringing the resignation deadly to survival. He rushed out of the trees to find himself on the path. He heard a loud howling like the wind in a funnel and then a coach, driven by the four furious horses, rattled round the bend, bearing down on him. Sitting on top, cracking the whip, was a nightmarish figure cloaked in black. The horses hooves thundered and the air shrieked. Jack flung himself into the trees as the coach thundered by. He stood up and ran deep into the undergrowth and then pulled up sharply as the ground disappeared in front of him. Teetering momentarily on the brink of the cliff, he fell flat on his face in fear. He had a vision of somersaulting over the cliff like the Gadarene swine. He almost wanted to as if something external was compelling him. It might be the only escape route. Then he heard the noises. They sounded like hundreds of lost souls creeping stealthily through the undergrowth, hunting for him, calling his name. His eyes scanned the ground frantically. At first he could see nothing, then the ground beneath his feet began to ripple. Long lines of earth crept towards him as if silent creatures burrowed beneath it. He watched in horror as the lines reached his feet, living cables pulsing rhythmically. The leaves of the trees rustled. His heart threatened to fight its way out of his rib cage, sounding like the beat of ominous tom-toms. Creatures moaned and sighed all around as if circling him, closing in for the kill. Voices cajoled him to jump. He would be safe. *He will put his angels in charge of you.* He looked up. The trees leaned over him as if examining a prize. Eyeing him from one of the branches was a rook. The same as the one he had first seen in the chapel? The malevolent look in its eye made his blood freeze. *They will support you in their arms.* He tried to stand but, with a squawk, the bird flew at him, knocking him backwards. He grabbed a root as he fell over the precipice. His mind racing with all kinds of images, he hung there with one hand, expecting the huge bird to strike again. Nothing happened. The wood was filled with a funereal silence. He pulled himself back to the top of the cliff. When nothing disturbed the silence he clambered over and began to make his way back through the wood. He didn't go to the car. That's where they might wait for him, whoever they were. An hour's walking brought him to the main road. After another mile of constantly diving into the bushes to avoid each passing vehicle, which, he imagined in his fevered state, to be a black coach full of weird, murderous creatures, he found a pub. Its occupants looked at him strangely. Were they all in on the conspiracy? He rang Lowther. He wasn't in. Jack banged his head on the box. When and how would this nightmare end?

CHAPTER 11

It was the next day when he finally got hold of Lowther the policeman listened to his story. He made enquiries which revealed that a film crew had been filming scenes in the parkway. The movie's theme centred round a series of historical mysteries, which might explain some of the things Jack had witnessed. On the crucial question of identity, however, enquiries showed Kaliostri was abroad on a musical tour of European capitals. Nonetheless, Jack was convinced that somehow Kaliostri had worked another illusion. "Josephine Jackson's played a trick on me once before," he reminded Lowther. "I got the impression she was frightened. She knows something about these murders. Also she did a piece on the St. Nicholas' murder."

"The what?" Lowther asked.

Jack told Lowther the story he'd got from the police officer and how it had coincided with the news item. "Does it ring any bells?" he asked.

Lowther looked mystified. "I don't know of it," he said. "but the east end's my bailiwick, not the City. I'll look into it." The policeman looked slightly crestfallen. For all the fancy attributes of the Holmes computer, the collation system had apparently fallen down badly. He had an interesting angle, however, on Jack's experience of the previous evening. "Tell me more about the producer laddie, the one you met with Josephine?"

"About 6 foot, slim build, thirty odd. Black, African I think, rather than Caribbean. Why?"

Lowther looked at Jack knowingly. "He scratched you," he said and waited for his words to sink in. "Unfortunately, it's probably too late to get any evidence from a medical." The Superintendent set off to make enquiries.

Not a fan of black metal music, nevertheless Jack thought it worth a shot to listen to the Devil's Disciple CDs he could get his hands on. The music was disturbing, it wasn't simply about dropping out of society, or even anarchy, it was about chaos, the advent of the devil. One song was about an ancient Viking ritual of revenge. Called 'The Blood Red Eagle' it depicted a slaying in which the victim's rib cage was opened and the heart and lungs torn out and devoured. 'Nosferatu' told of the sexual charge of drinking a bride's blood in the act of lovemaking. Another song, 'The Wolf's Cry' had lyrics, which Jack found vaguely familiar but he couldn't catch all the words. He heard enough, however, to know that it was the description of a murder. Evil is a psychic force existing in all humanity, it can be tapped into by people with special powers, just as much as any other force. Listening to those depraved recordings, which had made their creator such a wealthy man, Jack was unnerved by their powerful, destructive force.

Intuition made Jack root out the file of the Kaliostri divorce. He came across Max's photo, which Lorenza had left with him for proof of service. He was younger then but it didn't matter. The man in the photograph was familiar enough. Kaliostri's cleverness might have caught him out this time. The musician wasn't out of the country. The mystery tramp of the Egypt Cottage stared at Jack. "Good God," he muttered, "his disguises are good." Kaliostri might not know Jack had that photo. Lowther would have to listen now. Something else in the photograph caught his attention. Behind Kaliostri stood a group of people. Jack found a magnifying glass and studied one of the group carefully. He could have sworn it was Rachel's friend, Janet Gillingham.

He was about to pick up the phone to ring the Superintendent when Tropical Tom arrived in reception. Jack wasn't minded to be friendly but, as soon as Tom walked in, it was obvious he was distraught. "Not Karen again, is it?" Jack asked cynically. Tom nodded. He was trembling. "They came to the house and took her away, Jack. This bloke, built like a brick shithouse he was, made me kneel down, tied my hands behind my back. They stripped Karen with me looking on, they put this gown on her, said she was reborn. I thought they were going to have me but they weren't bothered."

"You've pulled this particular leg before," Jack reminded him.

"Jack, I put my hands up to that. But I'm serious this time."

Jack could see from the look on Tom's face that he wasn't acting. "Was Kaliostri there?"

"Nah. You must be joking. He doesn't get involved at that level."

"What level does he get involved at?"

"I divn't nah. I've never been in the circle."

"What happened the last time they took her away?"

"She didn't say but she came home a couple of days later with her pockets stuffed with tenners. She's been getting plenty since. Cash that is, not the other, not with me anyway."

"What makes you think it'll be any different this time?" Jack asked.

"Jack, she's been gone over a week!"

"Do you mind if I ring the police about this?" Jack asked him.

"I don't want trouble with the pollises," Tom said, panic in his voice, "I don't want them sniffing round down by."

"That's sometimes the price you've got to pay Tom," Jack replied. "Do you want me to help you or don't you?"

Resignedly, Tom nodded. Jack telephoned Lowther. He mentioned the photograph and his encounter with the tramp when Kaliostri was supposed to be out of the country. Lowther suddenly became animated. Jack glanced across at Tom. The disappearance of Karen gave real cause for concern. It looked odds on she was the next victim.

PART FIVE

CHAPTER 1

Jack spent the next couple of weeks strutting about like a bear with a sore head. The reason wasn't only the seemingly dead slow pace of the enquiry into Kaliostri; it was also the rather faster pace of his love life seeping down the drain. More than once he'd wanted to call it a day but every time he plucked up the courage to tell Rachel she came up with something that made him bite his lip and hang in a little longer. For instance, this time he hadn't seen her for a month but he knew she'd been back in town at least once in that period because a mutual acquaintance had mentioned bumping into her on Northumberland Street in mid-October. She hadn't bothered to make contact. The worst bit was she'd been with a bloke younger, better looking than Jack and pretty well heeled to boot. He saw the 'game over' sign flashing but still he couldn't let go and the main reason was she wouldn't let him. More than once, in the depths of despair, he'd looked in the mirror and not liked what he saw – a middle-aged man losing his head over a beautiful young woman. It was an old story. He wasn't the first to become so deeply infatuated that he would have changed his whole way of life just for a word of encouragement. The true description was that he was an idiot. The arrangement just couldn't work but still he persevered, more in hope than anticipation.

Rachel's frequent disappearing acts were explained by her new job in Paris, although she was as opaque about that as about her past. Fortunately there was a direct flight between

Newcastle and the French capital so it could have been worse but it meant whole weeks without seeing her. He couldn't understand why she bothered keeping a home in Newcastle. "A good excuse to see you," she told him pretty unconvincingly. Jack knew all about difficult decisions. The Gordian Knots he had cut for clients had led him to understand that there are seldom any truly wrong decisions. It is better to make a decision and live with the consequences than it is to vacillate and do nothing. One night towards the back end of October Rachel got in touch. She didn't act like there was any problem between them or apologise for leaving the contact so long. She even suggested she come round and stay with him. Shortly after she arrived he said, "I know what I meant to tell you," and he mentioned the photograph of her friend, Janet Gillingham. "I think she's big mates with the Kaliostris."

She didn't bat an eyelid. "So what?" she replied, "I found out very quickly that she's always in with the in-crowd. She's a very frivolous person."

"Yeah, but the Kaliostris?" he ventured.

"Well, who else is a celebrity in this town?" she replied. Yes. She had a point. Who else was? Newcastle was a village. There was nowhere north until Edinburgh, nowhere east, west or south. It was kind of its own little island and everyone knew everyone else's business. "You're a celebrity," she added with a mischievous smile.

"Me?"

"Yes, you! Don't act as if you don't know it! Everyone knows you. Everyone's got a Jack Lauder story." He was almost sucked in by this. Rachel knew a lot of people who either knew him vaguely or had heard of some of his exploits. He had handled some very high profile cases – the public interest law matters were the ones people remembered, and of course the big criminal cases. "Like that forest murder," Rachel said. "That was a *cause celebre*."

Immediately on guard, he asked, "why do you mention that?"

"Just everyone remembers it," she replied with another of her big-teeth, big-hitting smiles. "He was the one who bore a grudge against you?"

"Yeah? Who told you that?"

"Janet Gillingham," they said in unison. Both of them grinned but Jack didn't feel humourous.

"Your friend takes an unhealthy interest in me," he said. "I'm not sure I like it. Particularly with her connections with the Kaliostris."

"Now you mention it, she does know a lot about you. You remember she knew you used to be a famous mountaineer?"

"I was never famous," he replied.

"No? Not what I heard. What happened? Why did you give it up?"

Jack shrugged. It was no longer difficult to talk about. "Just took a flier," he replied. "I wasn't roped. I was lucky enough to hit a ridge after forty feet or so and I stuck. The pain was waking up afterwards. I'm not sure I had any bone unbroken."

"Jesus!" Rachel exclaimed, "I never realised!"

"Yes," Jack smiled ruefully, "so I doubt if I'll ever climb again. What I can't understand though is why Janet Gillingham would know any of that. She must have been a child when it happened.

Rachel's reply shook him rigid. "I suspect she gets most of her information from Max."

Max? His eyebrows shot up because she had used the musician's given name.

"Janet says he's got a bit of a thing about you. Sort of this town ain't big enough for both of us." She looked at him expectantly and seemed on the verge of adding something but ultimately she looked down at the floor. She looked embarrassed, her cheeks scarlet. Jack eyed her narrowly. What was going on? It wasn't so much the thought that

Kaliostri had something against him – a lot of people might know that – but the familiar use of his given name? Perhaps he was mistaken. "Rachel?" he said eventually.

"Yes?"

He detected a degree of nervousness in the response but took the plunge anyway. "What about me and you?" he asked.

"What about us?" she replied brightly, playing for time.

"Well, we've done quite a lot of downsizing lately, since you've become Britain's gift to the EEC, so what about taking it up a level?"

"What do you mean?"

"I mean one little word...."

"Commitment?" The green eyes were grey again.

"Right in one!" Jack replied.

Rachel sighed and leaned back on the sofa, revealing an expanse of gorgeous thigh but Jack wasn't going to be sidetracked this time. This conversation had to take place. "Can't we just carry on like we are?" she asked.

"Rachel, I love you." There it was. Right up front. She looked at him askance. "You don't even know me," she replied. "Except of course in the biblical sense." Her half-hearted attempt at levity met with silence and she found herself forced to add weakly, "what's wrong with just going on the way we are?"

"What way's that? I don't see any direction here. And, yes, you have raised a good point, sweetheart. Why don't I know anything about you? You appeared in my life in the present with no apparent past. Why is that?"

"Jack, don't go there. You'll regret it," Rachel replied.

"Why not?" Jack said, "what's the big mystery? Do you think I care what you've done in your past?"

She held up both hands. "I don't need to hear this," she said. "I'm telling you, that is the one subject that will break us apart. I can't hang round here and listen to this. I'm going."

That was it. Her face was set so firmly that he knew it was curtains as he kissed her goodbye on the doorstep with a taxi doing the motorised equivalent of champing at the bit outside, not even knowing if or when he'd ever see her again. Then after she'd got in the taxi, she opened the window and said, "hard as it may be for you to believe, I love you too. That's why I'm doing this. I've done everything wrong and now I'm trying to do the right thing. Goodbye Jack!" She shut the window and the taxi drove off leaving him in turmoil. Love him? She had a funny way of showing it. In two sentences he'd had his hopes raised to the skies and then dashed on the rocks.

☾

It was now early November and the autumn winds had bared the trees and brought the mists in from the North Sea. Rachel had disappeared back to her Paris bolt-hole, possibly never to surface again. At this low point in his life Jack had another shot of *déjà vu*. He heard once again, after a deafening silence, from the mysterious Mr. Pardoe, the self-appointed spiritual heir of Henry Herron. Surprisingly the communication was by letter, written in the same small neat hand as his first. It read as follows:

> Dear Mr. Lauder,
> Sorry not to have been in touch. I need to speak to you about Henry's will. I have information on some extra property, which I think is quite valuable! The problem is I can't arrange to call in and see you. I've just got a job (not easy when you're fresh out of the nick!) And I wouldn't like to jeopardise it. I'm working 8.00am to 6.30pm (long hours, eh?). Could you call and see me next Tuesday at 6.30pm at my place of work, Burkey's Scrap Yard on Middle Engine Lane? I look forward to seeing you then.

The letter had a Newcastle postmark. Strange things had happened to Jack, but he'd never met a client in a scrap yard before. He drove there about 6.15pm the following Tuesday. It was a dark, desolate night with fog hanging above the ground. Winter was well and truly in and the ground was iced over, a blessing in disguise as it was muddy and his shoes would otherwise have been caked as he stepped out of the car. The skeletal pulleys of the ruined lift shaft, which had once led down to long-abandoned mine workings, loomed up, disembodied, out of the mist. In the blanket of fog, it was as if he could hear the muffled, ghostly voices of the thousands of miners who, over the generations, had trodden this path into the bowels of the earth. He had hoped that Mr. Pardoe would be waiting for him at the gate but no such luck. He would have to go in search of Henry's mysterious trustee. It was cold, his breath froze as soon as it hit the air, and he turned up his coat collar. His footsteps echoed hollowly behind him. He had no idea what job Mr. Pardoe did, nor where the office was. Ahead of him was a long avenue of rusting automobiles piled on top of each other. The silence was eerie. In the fog the line seemed interminable. He turned right, down another lane piled high with the rotting hulks of cars in a graveyard of modern inventions and ingenuities. A sudden noise made him jump out of his skin. He turned to see a flotilla of rats disappear under a rusting shell. "Hello!" he shouted cupping his hands.

"Hello!" the echo came back.

He walked on a little. "Hello!" he shouted again. The echo returned, playing off the walls of metal, then there was another echo, a fainter one. Was that a voice? He called again. The echo returned, followed by another shout, as if in mimicry. He began to feel concerned. No one was there. The workmen had gone home. He wondered about turning back when the voice came again, nearer this time. "Hello!" he shouted in reply.

"Hello!" the sound was nothing like an echo this time. He walked towards it. Ahead of him, standing between two cars and looking as if he was working, stood a man. He looked elderly. He was wearing a flat cap and a blue garment like a boiler suit. Jack quickened his step. The man appeared to stop and listen but he didn't look at Jack, then he disappeared behind the cars.

"Hey!" Jack shouted and increased his pace to a run. Reaching the cars, he looked round. No one was there. He stepped round the car. About twenty-five yards away a figure slipped between two more wrecks. Angry now, he followed.

"Hello!" he called and again the voice replied on top of the echo. The shadows moved and, bizarrely, the man climbed over the bonnet of a car on to a wrecked lorry. Jack climbed up after him, cursing, knowing now something was wrong but determined to get to the bottom of it. The man jumped down the other side and went across Jack's line of vision. Jack followed him in and out of the ruined wrecks until he found him standing in the middle of a muddy track, holding a torch, apparently searching for something. Jack tried stealth. He bent down, crept around the back of a lorry and peered at the man from beneath the tailgate. He hadn't moved. Jack tiptoed across the frozen mud until he could put a hand on the man's shoulder and spin him around. He fell back shocked at a dreadful mask of scars. The man's mouth was open and his three or four teeth were like tombstones. He mouthed something Jack couldn't hear, pointing at something in his hand. He shone the torch on it. It was an old fashioned hearing box. He had wires protruding from both ears. He began to laugh, a gurgling, awful laugh, then he turned and pointed up a row of old bangers. A vehicle, its headlights on full beam, turned the corner at the end and drove slowly towards them. Jack turned to question the old man. He'd gone. The car moved steadily towards him. Beside it, distorted in the glare of the lights, strode a tall, dark figure. Shrouded in a shining mist it looked satanic in flowing cape, its face as pale as the moon. Jack turned and ran down the aisle. The car gunned into life; the tyres screeched; it raced like a stock car towards him, the back end skidding. Jack turned into another aisle. The vehicle followed. Jack leapt over a collapsed car. His pursuer slammed into the pile and demolished it, wrecks tumbling everywhere. Disentangling itself from the wreckage the vehicle came after him. Turning another corner he found himself in a cul-de-sac. The car rushed up, its full beam on, until it had him up against a wall of rotting machinery. It pinned him there, its engine roaring like a wild animal; it revved and reared, held on the footbrake. Jack leapt upon the bonnet and threw himself against the windscreen; the ghoulish face from his office stared out at him. It didn't flicker; it wore the same cruel expression, the eyes dead. Suddenly the vehicle went into reverse. Jack was thrown off the bonnet onto the ground. Loud laughter echoed in the fog as it did a hand brake turn and disappeared round the corner.

Jack lay there listening until all trace of the vehicle had gone, then he stood up. The place was like a maze. He stumbled round like a drunk trying to find an exit. He'd given up hope, afraid he'd have to spend the night in the cab of some motorway wreck, when, unexpectedly, he came upon the gate with the Mercedes still parked up. He walked round the car, checking it out and, on the nearside, at the kerb edge down by the back wheel, lay a bundle of rags. He nudged it with his foot and it rolled over on its side. He gagged as he recognised human flesh. It was a woman's naked abdomen. He fell on his knees in shock. "Jesus Christ!" he said. The scrapyard was as silent as a tomb. A crane loomed out of the mist like a dinosaur's skeleton. Slowly, deliberately, he turned the corpse's head towards him. A knife stuck out of her neck. "Josephine!" he whispered, utterly distraught. He bent down and kissed her cold and lifeless lips. It wasn't love he felt – another had long since stolen his heart – but it was more than affection. Without thinking, he drew out the knife, releasing a squirt of blood. He jumped back in horror and then, his sense of duty getting the better of the desire for self-preservation, he got on the mobile to the police, reporting what he'd found. He stood there a while until at last he heard a car engine. The Feds arrive mob-handed like silent ghosts out of the mist. "What's going on, sir?" one asked lightly, a mood which didn't last long when his colleagues discovered the body. Another officer jumped immediately to the wrong conclusion. "You filthy bastard!" he shouted and it took immense self-restraint for him not to strike the defenceless lawyer. "I'm the one who called you," Jack said but it cut no ice. He handed his keys over to the policeman and was taken to the station in a police car. He tried to keep his cool as he gave a statement to another suspicious officer. "Is that how it happened?" the officer interrogated. "She wouldn't let you have your end away so you did for her?" Nice to know you're loved and respected, Jack thought. He was put in a cell. No V.I.P treatment, it was the bog standard four breezeblock walls, plastered white, a cot without blankets and a seatless toilet.

He had just fallen into a doze when he heard the key in the lock. For a moment he had the queer feeling he was buried in the rock, beneath a landslide; the noise was the angel of death, sliding back the bolt to release him into the underworld. Only it wasn't. It was his earthly gaoler and release wasn't on the agenda. Bundled unceremoniously along the corridor to the interview room he passed a number of bleary-eyed coppers, all of whom seemed to leer at him like creatures from the underworld. He was booked through the custody record and then manhandled into an interview room. Chief Inspector Barry Freer gazed at him smugly. "Sit down, Jack," he said in his sibilant tone. The interrogation began.

"You knew this girl?" Freer asked him.

"So did you," Jack replied. "We met her at Lorenza Kaliostri's party. Remember? Like we met Jessica Parker?"

Freer flinched visibly. "Those things aren't connected," he replied.

"No? Are you sure? Have you checked that one out?"

"I'm asking the questions," Freer snapped, visibly put out and seemingly eager to change the subject. "Have you had sexual relations with Josephine Jackson?"

"When?"

"Answer the question."

"Not recently."

"Are you prepared to give a DNA swab?"

"If I have to. Why?"

"The girl was raped before she was killed. What were you doing down there?"

"A chap called John Pardoe asked me to meet him there."

The Inspector laughed dryly. "At a scrapyard. You always conduct your practice at a scrapyard? Come on, let's not beat about the bush! You went down to shag the girl and she changed her mind!"

"Why should I take her to a scrapyard?"

"Because you're a pervert, that's why."

Jack's anger began to rise but he controlled it. "Pervert?" he asked, "what do you mean?"

"You married?"

"No."

"How old are you?"

"Forty."

Freer looked at the D.C. "Forty and not married, what do you think, Tom?" The Detective looked at the lawyer and said, "maybe he swings both ways?"

"Knock it off," Jack replied, "do you realise how pathetic you sound?"

"For the tape, note there was no denial," Freer sneered. Then he added, "will we find your fingerprints on the knife?"

"Yes," Jack said, "because –"

Freer shouted, not letting him finish, "because you stabbed her with it!"

"No!" Jack protested, "because I removed it from her neck."

"Why didn't you tell the officers that at the scene?"

"They never asked."

"What kind of cold-hearted bastard are you?" Freer sneered.

"The sort who could rape a young woman and then kill her to keep her quiet," the D.C added.

"No," Jack said, "I'm just pointing out how quickly you people jump to conclusions."

"Put him back in the cell," Freer said. "I'm requesting authorisation for further questioning. Will you give that DNA swab?"

"Yes," Jack replied.

"If we get a match, it's porridge for you, bonny lad."

Jack knew exactly how they'd play it. They'd get a match from her mouth where he'd kissed her after death and they wouldn't let on. They'd call it positive and it would justify holding him longer, seventy-two hours maybe. Could it justify a charge? Even the accusation would ruin him. He had the feeling that a few scores were being settled here.

The interview began again later. By this time Lowther had found out what was going on and now he was present. It was obvious that he'd been fed enough poison to treat his erstwhile friend with suspicion. Even so, he was sceptical enough to give Jack a chance to explain himself. "It would help me greatly if you could produce some evidence of what you were doing down there when you found the body?" he said.

"I've told your colleagues all that. I went to visit someone."

The Superintendent looked at him as if to say, a likely story. "Get this man a cup of tea," he barked at his accompanying constable.

"Okay, don't believe me," Jack said. "I'll prove it to you, if you take me back to the office."

A hot mug of tea later, Jack was signed out in Lowther's custody. They went to Jack's office where he retrieved Henry Herron's probate file and handed to the Chief

Superintendent the letter he had received from John Pardoe. "It's technically a breach of client confidentiality but someone's taking the piss anyway."

Lowther relaxed visibly. "Well, that does put a different complexion on things," he said. "Who do you think's behind it?"

"Kaliostri," Jack replied.

"Jack, this guy is a very important person in this city. He's the kind of person you check your facts about."

"Facts? You mean he's not here? He never is."

"I mean precisely that."

"Like the night I met the tramp?"

"I only have your word for that."

"And now you have the death of Josephine. That's going to go down well publicly, isn't it?"

"There'll be a media circus," Lowther admitted. "What I have to work out is what you've got to do with all this, Jack."

☾

Jack got home to his mausoleum and crashed into bed. On such a night, he could have done with Rachel to go home to but he'd got used to the fact that she was never there. "It's really getting me down, this," he told himself drowsily as he slipped off to sleep knowing he'd wake at exactly four o'clock in the morning, problems buzzing round his head and shouting "groundhog day!" It's amazing how, at that time of the night, every twinge in the body feels like the symptom of an incurable illness and every external problem feels like the one that's finally going to send you to the wall. Rachel, where are you, he thought. But it was no use. She still wasn't there.

CHAPTER 2

Back at the office the next day, none the worse physically at least for his ordeal, Lowther came to see him. The message he brought was short and surprising. "Jack," he said, "I've drawn a blank on the murder in the city."

"The St. Nicholas' one?" Jack replied, looking surprised. "You mean there's no record?"

"Nothing. Zilch. There's no evidence of any murder! Where did you get it from?"

"Off the telly. I watched the programme. It was a news programme."

"Okay," the policeman replied, "I'll do some more digging."

"It was Josephine Jackson, the reporter," Jack added and, when he saw the policeman's face he mistook his look for one of surprise and continued, "yes, the very same! I've told you, check out Kaliostri. Josephine was a friend of his. He'll be in this up to his neck!"

Something seemed to be troubling Lowther and, sure enough, it came out. "We found another body," he said.

Jack's breath caught in his throat. "Where?" he asked.

"A house in the Spring Garden Estate. Just recently tenanted."

"Who was it?"

"Karen Spencer," the officer said. "Tom identified the body. He needed to because she'd been there a long time." Jack sat shaking his head. "The thing is," the Chief

Superintendent went on, "when we ran DNA tests, you wouldn't believe what we found."

"Try me," Jack replied, steeling himself for another revelation. "The same DNA as turned up in Josephine Jackson's body. Both from sexual intercourse."

"Jesus!" Jack replied. "Do you know whose?"

"No," he replied, "but we know it's not Kaliostri's. When you got him locked up he had to give swabs in the Scrubs. This is confidential because we're supposed to take new tests before we use them in evidence but I can tell you he's eliminated from both. So it's someone else, someone without a record or someone whose record pre-dates PACE." Jack was devastated. He'd practically bet his sanity on this hunch and here it was, shattered. Lowther continued: "there doesn't seem to be any motive for him either. Okay, he may have had a connection with both girls but it was tenuous in relation to Karen. Josephine Jackson had already reported that she was being stalked by a crazy fan. You pointed out yourself that she had a lot of security."

"What about Tom's evidence?" Jack reminded him. "Okay, Kaliostri may not have had sex with either girl recently but it's all a bit too much of a coincidence, isn't it?"

"Aye, well, that's Tom for you," Lowther responded dismissively, "two fruits don't always make a cake. Anyway," I don't know why you've got this obsession about this rock musician character, but the point is if the evidence doesn't stack up there's nothing I can do about it. You've given me nothing. He's too prominent a person to just go and arrest."

"You arrested me," Jack reminded him.

"Aye, well you're a lawyer. Grounds for suspicion on its own and you didn't have a cast-iron alibi." It would have been impossible to tell from his expression that he was joking.

"I still think he's involved. There's just too many roads, all leading to Rome. The fact that he has an alibi, even a strong alibi, doesn't entirely rule out the possibility that he was in the country. Why don't you make some enquiries of Immigration?" Jack suggested.

"What!" Lowther exploded, "Me put my career on the line by involving the Home Office in your madcap hunches! On your bike!"

"Hunches?" Jack replied, equally offended. "A few hours spent trying to prove that Kaliostri might have been in the country rather than just accepting he wasn't might pay a dividend."

Lowther squirmed. He didn't like being told his job but he realised there was method in Jack's madness. "I'll see what I can do," he said tersely.

Jack had done some research of his own into Max Kaliostri and the discoveries were unexpected. For the past five years he'd shunned publicity. There were no recent public photographs. He appeared on stage so hideously made up that it was impossible to distinguish his features. He gave no live interviews and lived the life of a recluse, moving between several homes in the United States, the Far East and the Indian subcontinent. Something about him couldn't be pinned down, as if he was the area left when all the empty space had been eliminated. From time to time he made a visit back to his roots but his movements were always shrouded in secrecy. He sustained himself by live appearances in massive venues throughout the world, the crowds never getting close to the stage. An album every year was greeted by sycophantic critics as a stupendous work of art. His music was woven with a sort of weird magic, marrying the divine and the diabolic in visual and aural imagery which captured the mood of the times.

Despite his reluctance to follow up a red herring, Lowther's investigation struck gold: a sequence of similar names turned up on the Frankfurt-Heathrow flight, the Copenhagen flight, one from Paris, and the Amsterdam flight. When Lowther read out the names they made sense to Jack: Luther, Saul, Zecarus, Apollonio, Marjury, Mathers, Crowley, Messien. "That's quite an entourage," the lawyer said. "There's a couple Kaliostri could be masquerading as. Crowley, the Silver Star, and Mathers' Golden Dawn. Luther, Saul. Apollonio could be Apollyon, Messien–Messiah, pretty obvious."

"Oh yeah, really obvious," Lowther replied sarcastically. These unusual names cropped up again and again on all the manifests. It sounded like a bunch of satanic characters travelling mob-handed. The dates tied up as well. These people could have been in this country at the time of the murders, assuming there wasn't a similar manifest showing their departure. The police hadn't checked that yet. Lowther wasn't prepared to give anything more than a cautious nod towards Jack's theory but he was now treating these people as potential suspects. If there was no evidence of departure he could pick them up, ask a few questions and he might get enough circumstantial evidence to charge some. It was a start anyway. The problem was the lack of hard evidence. "Well," he said, "they must have a motive for using false names."

"Tax avoidance, they'll say, if push comes to shove," Jack replied. "They probably can't admit they're in this country. And it's probably true. If they're found to be here there's probably a big assessment comes plummeting out of the sky." Lowther chuckled. "A pretty strong motive for lying." However, he'd saved the best until last because he added, "you weren't entirely wrong about Kaliostri either. He's on the FBI list of drug dealers. They have him earmarked as a crazy freak, he thinks he has an evangelical role to play in the world. Drugs are a way of controlling his disciples."

When Lowther finally came back with more information, he acted at first as if Jack had ruined an otherwise idyllic life, when of course he was just annoyed that the lawyers had been proved right yet again. Jack smiled inwardly but let it pass without comment. That sort of attitude is in the policeman's mentality and they probably pass it down to their offspring so that there are an awful lot of sad bastards running round who can't quite make police officers but equally can't get attitude out of their genes either. Another thing about them is, wind them up and they can't find the stop button. Lowther had done some digging. What he'd come up with about Karen was sensational stuff, although at first he wasn't prepared to give it much credence because the dead woman had been known to take hard drugs. Nonetheless he wondered what Jack would make of it. They sat in Jack's office. Lowther handed him a statement taken by one of his WDC's from a Social Worker at a womens' refuge in which Karen had spent some time. The Social Worker had related to the police woman a tale, which, she claimed, Karen had told her before she died. The statement was useless as evidence. It was second hand hearsay and it seemed deranged. Even Karen, as original narrator, couldn't really say whether she had been dreaming or not.

Karen had told the informant about her relationship with the cult. She knew what they were but they treated her well, introducing her to a life of luxury which she'd never dreamed possible. What's more they'd told her it could be hers for time everlasting. She described her days as being spent in a dream, forever out of her skull through alcohol and drugs, filming scenes for a movie her mentors were making. The story seemed to be the ravings of a drug addict until she got to the crunch. One night when she was staying with the cult she went into the bathroom for a shower. She felt uneasy but she wasn't sure why. What she would give to be rich and free? That's what she had been promised by the cult. She understood this needed a sacrifice from her. She didn't fully appreciate what but afterwards the world would be hers. She stood in front of the mirror, took off her robe and walked towards the shower closet. The bathroom door wasn't locked; she didn't see the handle turning. Entering the shower, her back to the cabinet door, she turned on the water and closed her eyes as it engulfed her. When she opened them again the shower door was open. Her legs went from under her. A white-faced ghoul stood over her. He wore a black coat, which, when opened, spread like wings. He advanced like a cat and smothered her scream. She felt a momentary pain as a hypodermic entered her hip then the ghoul lifted her bodily out of the shower. Her senses began to slip as he unbolted the door. Outside another man stood. He was shorter than the first but powerfully built. As she stared at him, his features appeared to distort. He looked like a wolf. He took her from the other man and carried her to the bedroom where she was flung on the bed like a sack of potatoes. She was used by one of her assailants. Suddenly she was being dressed. Pullover, jeans, shoes on her feet. A voice said, "we're going for a ride in the country." She felt she was in the clutches of a nightmare from which she would surely awaken. Led downstairs like a drunk, staggering from wall to wall, supported on her consorts' arms, she felt the cold night air, the cold black leather of a big vehicle. The city came on a stream of fantasy. Past the barracks to the urban motorway, the green steel girders of the Tyne Bridge, the river winding like a silk worm to the sea, all in the weirdest silence. She must have slipped away for a while because they were suddenly on the motorway. Outside it was pitch black. She couldn't see any stars. Soon there were no headlights. The car purred to a halt. She was bundled roughly out, still slipping in and out of consciousness. She woke up, aware of a door being opened somewhere. It seemed large and heavy. It creaked loudly in the darkness. She was pulled to her feet and across a courtyard. The door was open and light flooded out. Hoisted up on the shoulders of hooded figures she was brought into a vast stone hall and carried up an aisle between rows of pews. Silent figures sat, their backs to her. At the top of the aisle she was forced to her knees on a dais covered in a stretch fabric. She turned round to face the giant figure of Christ crucified. She hadn't seen a statue quite like it before. She was forced to lie on the dais beneath the statue's nailed legs. A cloaked man who stood on a plinth in the shadow of the statue began to chant something strange. Silent figures rose from the pews. "Light issues from darkness," the hooded man said. From the folds of the cloak his hand appeared and held light. She tried to focus and saw the light was seven stars. "The first and last," he intoned, "alpha and omega!" The crowd of spectators repeated his words. More sleight of hand followed and this time he held a key. "The key of mysteries is in his hands." Once again the crowd echoed the words. "He opens the great abyss of central fire." He reached out with one hand and a river of fire ran down the hall as the crowd repeated the lesson. "The great serpent awaits the wakening of the ages." The fire became a huge snake which emerged from the Cross. Karen watched out of saucer like eyes as it writhed and wriggled towards her. A black man separated himself from the crowd and held out a golden tray. On it was a beating human heart. Then something else happened. The hooded man screamed at two others, the ones who'd abducted her. The hooded man accused them of defiling the ritual. The taller one hung his head but the other was defiant. Everything began to shift away as her senses reeled. The onlookers stood over her staring, their eyes getting bigger as they started to fade. She couldn't let them disappear. She called out; they carried on receding; she called again; they were gone. In a void she lay thinking. Then, there was nothing. She awoke afterwards. She didn't know exactly what had happened. She understood that the ceremony had been interrupted and that she couldn't now fulfil her role. She had an abject sense of failure.

Jack put the document down. "It looks like the ravings of a looney to me," the Superintendent prompted, "and that's the way the WDC interpreted it too."

"Naturally," Jack replied, "it's the first conclusion any sane, rational person would jump to. But you have to take into account Karen's background and history as well as the way she died. The problem is I fear that she was central to the ritual somehow and they now need someone else."

Lowther looked quizzical, still not convinced but trusting Jack sufficiently to row along for the moment. "So, where do they go from here?" he asked. Jack held up his hands and shrugged. They were both silent for a long time. They didn't need to say anything more.

After Lowther had gone Jack made an effort to reach Rachel. She had friends who knew the Kaliostris and he wanted to give her a friendly warning. That was, of course, only half of the reason. He couldn't raise her; he hadn't seen her since that last fateful night when she'd said goodbye. She could get in touch if she wanted. She might be miles away in a foreign country but there was always the telephone. He decided to try her flatmates and see if he could get them to call her and give her a message that he needed to speak to her urgently. When he got round to Jesmond, the place was deserted. It just didn't look lived in. On a whim and fairly desperate now, he decided to put in a call to the Bandido's mobile. "Speak!" the voice on the other end commanded without identifying itself.

Jack nearly creased himself laughing but pulled himself together and started to sing, "Hey Joe? What you doin' with that gun in your hand?" Joe was even more mystified when Jack asked him, "hey, are you any good at breaking into other folks' houses?"

"Are you away with the mixer or something?" came the reply.

"That's exactly what I thought, so how about getting off your backside and coming up here to Jesmond and burgling this one for me?"

The big man arrived just like the U.S Cavalry. "Easy," he said as he surveyed the old-fashioned alarm. "Whose house is this anyway?"

"Wor lass's."

"Oh, this is a new kind of foreplay is it? The kind you educated classes enjoy?" Joe shinned up the ladders, did the business with the foam and then put a glass panel out downstairs. The alarm went off but with a funny whirring sound instead of the bell ringing loudly. "The neighbours in areas like this are worse than useless," Joe said scathingly as they crossed the threshold. "They're too busy minding their own business! What are we looking for?" Good question. The internal alarm was going off like a battleship's klaxon as they moved from room to room. They mounted the stairs to the attic bedroom and crept in. Jack recognised immediately some of Rachel's belongings on the bed. "Is she a heavy metal freak?" Joe asked, shining his torch on the walls.

Jack looked down the torch beam and his whole body chilled as if there had been a temperature change. "No," he said hoarsely. "She just follows one band." An agonised expression contorted his features. "Bitch!" he shouted and smashed his hand into the wall. "Sodding damn no good bitch!"

Joe looked at him in astonishment, unable to help so, in his usual way, he made light of it. "Wey, I understand what's meant by radgie gadgie now," he said, but one hand gripped his friend's shoulder. The reason for Jack's rage was that the wall was plastered with photographs, some of which were so rare that even the world wouldn't have seen them; some were even signed with promises of undying affection. The room was a shrine to the Devil's Disciple. Weak at the knees, Jack sat down on the bed. Joe, oblivious to his distress, wandered round saying, "no, can't see any loot here, bonny lad. What does she do with it, keep it under the mattress?" Then he looked at the ceiling and it was his turn to spring back in surprise. He tapped Jack's shoulder. The lawyer looked up morosely. "Video camera," Joe pointed, "we're on candid camera, sunshine!"

Even if it was a pointless exercise – if the camera was switched on they would have been identified long ago – they got out at the double and jumped into their vehicles. They made for Jack's home, expecting the imminent arrival of the Police. Jack's mind was in turmoil as he drove down the Coast Road. How could Rachel have treated him like that? He could see it all now. His very special girl was another cog in the machine of Kaliostri's revenge, just as Josephine had been. Thinking back bitterly to that first innocent meeting in a sunny Newcastle Square, it had been too good to be true. Beautiful young women don't just swoon into the arms of middle-aged, professional gentlemen. She was good all right; she should have been on the stage; she probably was. Other clues had been there too, now that he came to think about it. The Janet Gillingham connection for instance. He should have run a mile when he'd seen her in that photograph. Instead, he'd desperately wanted it to be true that this gorgeous girl, who could have had her pick of any number of young men, actually loved him. It was the propaganda, wasn't it? These things happened all the time in films and life imitates art. Why shouldn't it happen to him? Jesus, he cringed when he thought about it. Even when her behaviour had become erratic, long after she'd sucked him in, he'd hung in there, believing it could still work. "No fool like an old fool!" he said aloud to himself.

Back at the house, Joe said, "here, young un," – why Joe, who could give him ten or more years persisted in using such terms of endearment he had no idea – "I've been thinking, why does anyone have a video camera in a bedroom?"

"It's a bog standard intruder device," Jack responded.

"Aye, but not in the schlafzimmer – like that, did you? I'm bilingual me. Did a stint in Germany you know with the SAS. Used that word quite often. It goes well with fraulein." Despite his ill humour, Jack couldn't help but laugh as his big mate jollied him along. He had a point though. You usually found intruder devices in corridors or at points of entry, not hidden away in bedrooms. "She was fit too, that bird of yours. See some of them photos?" Joe was referring to photographs of Rachel in various states of undress, culminating in the altogether. Jack had been too devastated by the discovery of the treasury of Kaliostri memorabilia to take it all in. In other circumstances he might have reacted angrily to Joe's question but he didn't. "Yeah, she's super-fit, super-attractive. I should have known she was bound to break my heart. Anyway, you've hit a good point. Speculate, old son."

"Wey, the camera's there to keep an eye on the gannins on in the room, nowt else."

"Why would someone do that?"

"Yer bugger, Jack! Do I have to spell it out for you? If you've got a bird like that you don't want her shagging every gadgie in sight, do you? Whoever did that suffers from the green eyed monster and it's his way of telling her, stay out of other blokes' trousers pet, or else! Here, it wasn't you, was it?"

"Me?"

"Why aye! Divn't look so innocent, hinny! If she was my bit of petal, I'd have the Marines keeping her under surveillance!"

"Whoa!" Jack replied. "That's why she'd never take me there!"

"What? When she wanted a bit of the old pork sword, you mean, son?" Jack looked at his big mate scathingly as he stood there, a big grin on his face. "Wey, why not bonny lad? We all do it, y'nah! It's not just you. You haven't got the patent rights! It's all right, you can tell me. What's she like, then? A right royal un, I'd say."

"What kind of person keeps his girlfriend under video surveillance but lets her know it?" Jack asked, ignoring Joe's ribaldry.

"A control freak," Joe said.

"A Max Kaliostri," Jack replied.

"He can have just about any bird he wants, can't he? Anyway, for what it's worth, our lovely mugs have not been caught on the camera or the busies are even more laid back than normal so I'm gannin yem. Wor lass is in trouble. Them pics have got me well and truly worked up! You know where to get me, if you need any crimes committed!" Joe laughed out loud and tapped his mobile. Jack was left with food for thought after his mate left. Whichever way he looked at the conundrum he couldn't bring Rachel's actions within the bounds of tolerance until, of course, the yearning began again. He knew it would. She had got right under his skin. She had a wholesomeness about her, which, even now, made him find her association with Kaliostri incredible. Surely she couldn't be an accomplice in his depravity? But why not? Apparently, he had got her character wrong once. It was already dark when he got the phone call. An educated voice asked for him by name and, thinking it was police station emergency call out, he answered, "you're speaking to him."

The man on the other end of the phone laughed. "Well, well, Mr. Lauder," he said, "long time no see." The voice wasn't familiar but Jack had the distinct impression that it was disguised.

"Who are you?" he replied.

"Oh, I'm many things, among others your dark angel. Anyway, what I wanted to tell you was if you want to help your pretty little friend, Rachel, you'd be well advised to go to Weldon Priory tonight. Go alone. The first sign of the police or your large friend and the consequences are on your head."

"Why should I do that?" Jack retorted. "She doesn't give a stuff about me."

"Ah, but you've never played it that way, have you Jack? You've never let your own actions be governed by someone else's standards. You know you want to see her. You may be the only thing between her and damnation! Don't hang about now!" The caller rang off. Jesus, Jack thought, they had the psychological profile spot on. He hadn't recognised the voice but he knew the place. Kaliostri had, a short time before, changed address from a fashionable suburb of the city to an ancient manor house and priory out in the wilds of Wanney. The move had attracted a lot of publicity locally. Kaliostri's detractors decried the fact that he had been allowed to purchase a Grade 1 listed building, part of the public heritage, and the sycophants praised his commitment to the region, even though he spent nearly all his life in America as a tax exile. Jack hesitated but only for a moment. The plain inference of the call was that Rachel was in trouble. The cult's women didn't tend to survive into their dotage. He pondered making a call to Lowther, to the Border Bandido even, for back up. Ultimately, he went alone. Whoever they were would know if anyone else turned up. Whatever Rachel had done to him, he wasn't going to risk her life. He'd rather risk his own.

A few minutes later Jack was on the motorway. After driving north for an hour or so, he turned off the main road and down a wooded path towards lights glimmering in the distance. He killed the vehicle lights – no point in advertising his arrival – and the ground was steep enough for him to cut the engine. Freewheeling into a glade he parked up. He figured they'd expect him to drive straight in. The element of surprise might give him a slight edge. Crouching low Jack made his way down to the house. At first he thought that a peculiar sound was in his head but as he neared the ancient building he became certain that he could hear chanting. It seemed to be coming from inside the Priory, which stood in the grounds of the house. The sound made his scalp prickle and at first he couldn't quite place it. Then he realised that it reminded him of the siege at his home.

Weldon Priory was late mediaeval in construction but Jack's only interest in its architecture was to devise a way to get in. A large main door at the front was securely bolted when he tried it. He worked his way round the back. A door at the corner was locked. Jack looked up and at about half height was the slit of a mediaeval window. He began to shin up to it. It wasn't as hard as it looked. There were plenty of nooks and crannies for fingerholds. Jack's rock climbing experience came in handy and he made short work of the wall. He reached the window without breaking sweat and squeezed himself through. Making his way down spiralling stone stairs, the sound of chanting growing louder the further he penetrated into the building, he worked his way round to the hall and up some steps into a gallery overlooking the auditorium. Peering over the rails an astonishing sight met his eyes. Vast with ornate pillars stretching to the vaulted ceiling, the hall reached away to an altar with a statue of the crucified Christ of Karen's nightmare. "So she was telling the truth, then," Jack muttered to himself. In front of and facing the statue lay a stone plinth, on which was inscribed a double circle. The eerie Gregorian chant filled the hall but there was no one to be seen. Jack climbed over the rail and dropped like a cat to the stone floor. He stayed there in a crouch but nothing moved. Slowly, casting glances each way, he padded towards the circle and examined it. Outside the circle at the corners were stars in the form of pentagrams; the outer and inner rings of the circle contained indecipherable writing; within the inner ring at each prime point of the compass was another pentagram and in the centre a rectangle with each corner pointing to the prime points; at the end of each point was a cross. To the right, immediately inside the circle, were a number of instruments: two knives, one white-handled, one black, a hook, a sickle, a stylet, a needle, a wand, a lancet, a staff and four swords in descending order of size. Between this circle and the cross, another circle was inscribed. It was smaller and again was raised on a plinth but it seemed to be covered with a translucent fabric. A motif was inscribed between the inner and outer rings. Four objects adorned the corners between the two rings: a skull in the top right, the north east corner; horns beneath to the south; immediately west of these a dead black cat, and, above, in the north west corner, a dead bat. A triangle in the centre nearly touched north, east and west. It contained three circles at the end of a cross. Two crosses of St. George were below the circle with a cross of St. Andrew between them. "The Goetic circle of pacts," Jack whispered. He knew what that identification meant. The skull would be real, and if the ritual was being followed properly, the colourless fabric was likely to be the flayed skin of a human sacrifice. So where was Rachel? The thought occurred to him with the obvious but unwanted implication.

The tone of the chanting changed and Jack heard a screeching, as if some unearthly voice had taken up the song. The screeching became an awful cry, as if a terrible creature, which had been locked up for years, was trying to break out. He froze where he stood as the cry echoed round the hall. The auditorium was plunged into darkness. A brooding silence followed. Jack couldn't see a thing in front of his face. Gradually his eyes became accustomed to the gloom and he started back as the Christ figure reared above him. He plucked up sufficient courage to move across and touch its cold stone. As he did so a purple light began to swirl in the rafters a hundred feet above his head. The light spiralled down towards him. Soon he could make out faces – suffering faces, their mouths contorted in silent screams. They reminded him of souls lost in the vastness of space, or in the deepest recesses of hell. His scalp prickled unpleasantly as a moan, like a distant wind, started up. As the purple light dropped and began to weave about his head, the wind came closer. He listened hard; it was made up of disembodied voices.

"Rachel?" he called, "Rachel?" His voice started off frenetic activity. The faces, which had been slowly circling his head, now whipped around, taunting him. "Rachel!" they whispered in their agonised voices, "Rachel! Where is Rachel? Rachel, Rachel! Rachel doesn't want you!"

"Rachel!" This time it was a great shout from the top of the auditorium. He looked up and saw a man in a cloak.

"Kaliostri!" he cried and he began to make his way towards the man, who in turn marched in Jack's direction. They strode towards each other like two gunfighters heading for the O K Corral. Kaliostri's hair flowed behind him and his eyes flashed as he came. A disembodied voice shouted:

"Beware! Beware!

His flashing eyes, his floating hair.

Weave a circle round him thrice

And close your eyes with holy dread

For he on honeydew hath fed

And drunk the milk of paradise!"

Other voices whispered, "Rachel! Rachel! Rachel is gone! Rachel serves the one true God! Rachel has gone to her master!" Jack coiled himself as Kaliostri neared, determined to beat the living daylights out of the bastard. He threw the first blow. Where it should have smashed into Kaliostri, it met thin air. Jack staggered, off balance. A sniggering laugh came from high above. His heart leapt from its cage. Hands on hips, the ghoul of the scrapyard encounter stood on top of the balustrade. Their eyes met and a sneer creased the apparition's face. Jack screamed as it leapt in the air and then dropped like a slingshot towards him. He put up his hands. The blow on the crown of his head knocked his lights out. Before he passed out he saw the ghoulish apparition retreat back into the air, its limbs flailing as it shot upwards and bounced above him, jerking like a puppet. Jack passed out.

He came to some time later lying on the cold stone. The face of Christ looked down on him with a sympathetic expression. The figure was bathed in moonlight from a stained glass window and diamond, emerald, ruby and sapphire patterns played over it as if caught in a prismatic wind chime. Groggily Jack climbed to his feet, gazing about suspiciously. The Priory was empty. He wandered forlornly, calling Rachel's name. His voice echoed back at him. Once again, he had been well and truly suckered. The evidence was indisputable. Kaliostri was having another laugh at his expense, even to the extent of completing the quotation he had uttered to the Ethiopian girl at his wife's party. Even now he could be standing somewhere with the love of the chastised lawyer's life, howling with mirth at his misery. The galling thing was that he seemed to be untouchable; there was no evidence to implicate him in the sinister events which surrounded his entourage.

CHAPTER 3

A short time later Kaliostri disappeared from the European scene, cancelling a pre-arranged tour in the process. Pleading spiritual fatigue, he turned up in India. The days went by and, except for Jack's private heartache, life got back to a semblance of normality. As memories began to dim, it seemed that, perhaps nothing entirely outside the scope of rational explanation had happened. Of Rachel there was no news. Even though he had given her up as lost, assuming that she had been a willing accomplice in the musician's revenge, Jack fretted about her. Ultimately he swallowed his pride and asked Lowther to make discreet enquiries. It turned out she was in New York. "All right for some," Jack said.

"A story there?" the Superintendent asked cannily as they shared a rare pint one evening.

"Yes," Jack said, "I worried once that she would be the next victim of.....you know." He didn't mention Kaliostri. It was a sore point. The police still had no lead on the murders but they couldn't crack the musician's alibi. The trail had come to a dead end. "The main point," Jack added, "is the murders are over." Famous last words! The sting in the tail came a few weeks later in deep midwinter. Jack was at home one Sunday night reading the papers for a case due to start the next day in London. He planned to catch the 6 o'clock train. The telephone rang. The last thing he needed was an emergency call out but duty got the better of self-preservation and he picked up the receiver. It was the police and he groaned inwardly. "Mr. Lauder? Tyneside Divisional H.Q here." The next question blew him away. "Do you know a Rachel MacLean?"

When he had regained speech, his heart gripped by dread, he found he still cared! Despite what had happened he still cared! He stammered out the answer. "Yes, why? What's wrong? Has something happened to her?"

"No sir, well nothing dreadful. It's just that she was picked up by a patrol because she was acting suspiciously....."

"Suspiciously?" Jack replied, "what on earth do you mean?"

"Outside your house, sir. She was there for ages in the rain. Going up to the door, going away, returning. We had her under observation for an hour or so. We know you've had your troubles. Anyway, we brought her in because she couldn't explain herself very well and she's n.f.a. She's like a drowned rat. It's up to you. You can come down and get her if you want or we can turf her out. She's got enough money for a taxi but with nowhere to go...."

The desk sergeant didn't finish the sentence. "No, of course not," Jack said, "I'll come down and get her." Jack rang off and, without bothering about his coat, ran out to the car. A few minutes later he parked outside the station. The Sergeant came and directed the still bewildered lawyer through to one of the interview rooms. Rachel sat there, a cup of coffee in her hand. She looked at him out of tear-filled eyes. Her cheeks were streaked. She looked like a lonely, lost bird, wind-blown, dishevelled, orphaned by the storm. "I'll leave you two alone," the sergeant said with a gruff kindliness. "Just shout when you want to be out." He shut the door behind him. Rachel looked up and said, "bet this wasn't your idea of the venue for our next date?"

Despite the mixed emotions running through his head, he had to laugh. "What the hell are you doing?" he asked her.

Then he looked at the wall. He pointed at what looked like an eye. "If that red light goes on, we're being monitored," he warned. "So, what were you doing, hanging round my place? You and your friends planning another surprise for me, were you?" He couldn't resist the cynical jibe. A lot of water was still flowing under the bridge.

"I needed to talk to you," she said. "I know I've done you a terrible wrong. At first, I was just carried away by the joke –"

"The joke!" he exploded. "The frigging joke! Is that what you call it? I'm pouring my heart out to you and you're carrying every single syllable back to your lord and master, Mr. Tosspot Kaliostri! Is that your idea of a joke? Did he get off on you telling him what it was like with me when you were bonking away in his bed? Was it just him? Were you doing it with every wanker in that cult of his?" As if sensing the climate change inside the room the red light switched on. Jack noticed it out of the corner of his eye and visibly calmed down. The police were responsible for everyone in their station. It had been a mark of trust that the sergeant had left them alone. He couldn't abuse that.

"No, Jack, it was never as bad as that. Max, yes, I met him nearly four years ago now when I was fresh out of university. I didn't go with him for a long time but he gave me a job. Well, kind of a job. It didn't turn out the way it was supposed."

"Tell me about it," Jack responded bitterly. He had to know. What did she know of Kaliostri's depravity? He looked at the light again. Not here, he thought, not here. His voice softened. "Where are you staying?" he added. "The police have you down as no fixed abode."

"They're right," she replied. "That's about it now. Alone again." She looked so pathetic that Jack couldn't help but take pity on her.

"You can stay with me," he said. Only her eyes thanked him. She collected her meagre belongings from the desk sergeant and signed the form for her release. "Don't go wandering round the streets late at night," he said to her gruffly, "whatever arguments you've had, they're not worth pneumonia." Jack smiled. The sergeant was one of the old school.

There weren't many of them left. "And you," he said to Jack, "don't give that lassie a hard time!"

Jack put up his hands in acknowledgment of the admonishment and the two of them were out in the rain. They said nothing in the car or as he led her into his front room. Pouring her a malt whisky, he said, "I'll make a pot of tea." She was coming down with something. Her face was flushed and she dabbed her nose repeatedly. She mumbled her thanks as he took her coat. When he returned she managed a brave smile. He waited for her. Dying to ask a couple of things, he nonetheless realised now wasn't the moment. Eventually Rachel spoke. "I had to come and see you," she said. "I've done a terrible thing. I owe you an explanation."

"Or two," he smiled and waited.

"Yeah, but I couldn't do it, you know? I didn't dare face you. I kept on walking up to your door, lifting my hand to the bell and then I'd just freeze!"

Jack sat in silent contemplation for a few moments. He desperately wanted to learn the answer to many riddles but he had the feeling that the steps he took now would dictate the rest of his life. "You never had anything to fear from me," he said. "I wouldn't have been angry for long." He couldn't help but notice her beautiful eyelashes as she sat with head bowed, looking into the fire. He shook his head. "You are so gorgeous," he said gently. The floodgates opened. Suddenly he was holding her and it didn't matter. He was suddenly the comforter. "Hush!" he said, "you don't have to say anything. If it hurts, wait until it's easier."

She smiled wanly through the tears. "Could you really accept that?" she asked.

"Rachel, I'd wait years if it meant you would spend them with me." He could hardly believe he was saying it but he meant it. He still wanted her that badly. "I'm not a child," he added. "Young people can't let things lie. It just burns them up. I'm not like that." He meant that too. Some things are best left unsaid. Only the most possessive people enquire into every detail of their partners' lives and drive themselves mad with each enforced revelation. "That's not good enough, Jack," Rachel replied. "You're being over generous again. I've warned you about that." She wagged a finger at him. She looked radiant suddenly but perhaps it was the high colour of an imminent fever.

"You see," Jack said, "welcome back to the land of the living."

"Okay," she said, "truce." She held up crossed fingers. "I've got to do this thing. It's a kind of catharsis. I wish I too could let it lie but I can't. But you're right, not now. You really don't mind if I stay here tonight?" She shivered as she looked towards the window.

"Hey," Jack said, "I'd be disappointed if you stayed anywhere else." Then he held up a hand. "And it's not about that," he said. "The spare bed's made up."

She looked at him, visibly recovering her confidence. "Is it not a little bit about that?" she asked.

Jack Lauder, 40-year-old trial lawyer, blushed. "Well...a little," he responded.

"Good," she replied, "I'd have been disappointed if it wasn't. So okay, I'll tell you Rachel's story tomorrow." He had totally forgotten in the euphoria of her homecoming. "What is it?" she asked, suddenly concerned.

"I've got to go to London tomorrow. First thing. I can't get out of it."

"Don't worry," Rachel replied brightly, "I'll come with you."

When Jack woke at four in the morning, his head ached and the last thing he wanted to do was forsake the warm and fragrant woman by his side. But he had no choice. It was the Bank Manager again, waiting for no lover. He didn't have the heart to disturb Rachel. She looked so relaxed and he remembered his fear that she was coming down with some ailment or other. It would be better for her to rest so he left her a note. He had the feeling that when he got back they'd have plenty of time to talk about things. If last night was anything to go by, they might even get to the subject of the future. Surely this one too couldn't be another of those Scottish summits? It was still dark as he left the house. It had snowed overnight and everything had a fine dusting of white. This winter was particularly cold. A gale from the northwest had blown across the country for weeks. The cab was already waiting as Jack double-checked the security. He'd had the locks changed, security devices fitted, taken just about every precaution he could think of since the intrusions.

The house was secluded. Built in three storeys with large meandering cellars and attics, its layout had changed little since the French Revolutionary wars. Rachel said it was one of those houses it took years to find your way round. The changing light meant this corridor or that room never seemed the same today as yesterday. As befitted a house of such antiquity, this one had a history of ghosts. A number of apparitions had been seen, particularly on the upper floors. The testimony from previous occupiers went back well beyond living memory. Things like that didn't faze Rachel. There was more to fear from the living than the dead. That evening, around eight o'clock, as soon as he got back to the hotel after his conference, Jack rang her. "You should have woken me," she scolded him.

"No," he said, "it was better to let you sleep. I'll be out of this thing before lunch tomorrow. I can't wait to see you."

"Hurry," she replied. Eventually, they said goodbye. He remembered just before he put the phone down that he had forgotten to tell her that he was likely to get released by the Judge in time to get the one o'clock flight. The train was too slow. "Rachel, Rachel!" He found himself talking to the phone but, even though she'd put down the receiver, there was a clicking. Then he heard another sound, like a snicker of laughter. "Rachel! Rachel!" he shouted again. The phone was dead. He tried to ring her back but the line was engaged. The operator said there was a fault. Frightened, he rang the police and asked them to send someone round to the house. "It's an emergency!" he told the desk Sergeant. Rachel was unaware the line had gone dead until a policeman called at the house and told her Jack had phoned. "Bless him!" was her reaction.

"Are you all right, ma'am?" the constable enquired.

"Yes," she said, "I'm fine."

"Would you like me to come in and check the house?" he persisted.

"I'm sure it's not necessary," she replied with a big smile.

The policeman seemed disappointed. The assignment was slightly out of the ordinary on this beat. "Very well ma'am." He nodded and got back in his Panda.

Rachel had already had a bright idea. It was going to be difficult to look Jack straight in the face when she revealed her part in his troubles, so she decided to write it down. That way she could make herself scarce while he decided her fate. She switched on the computer and, waiting for the programme to come up on the screen. When it did she began to write:

My dear Jack,
I hope you will forgive me for being so cowardly as to tell you the truth in this way. I feel that if I don't write it down

I will never come clean.

The truth is Max Kaliostri and I were lovers. I was the woman he was seeing when his wife consulted you about a divorce. I know about your fling with Josie, another of Max's ex's, and that he set that up too. He is a control freak and he can't stand the idea of anyone besting him. He's obsessed with you. Getting locked up was no joke for him. It left him really shaken and feeling vulnerable. He hates any sign of human weakness in himself because he thinks he's some kind of superman. Not only that but what you did to him made the FBI raid his house in America and what they got cost him a fortune. He couldn't go back for months until he'd bribed enough people to take the heat off.

I met him when I was twenty and he rushed me off my feet. I was out of work. I just loved the way he could change his appearance at will and become a totally different person. He was fascinating. He gave me jobs in band videos. He introduced me to his contacts and the work flooded in. I was going to be famous, I thought, but I see now the routine wasn't that much different from the casting couch. I fell for it hook, line and sinker. I worshipped Max. Our meeting (yours and mine that is) was a set up from the beginning. I was supposed to seduce you (which wasn't very hard as it turned out!). I know you'll think me a slut and wonder what kind of woman even stays with a man who hires her body out to another like that. I don't feel very good about myself, I can tell you, and I realize what a fool I was. You don't see it, though, when you're in the middle of it. I thought I was very cool and modern. God, I was out of my brains on coke most days. I want you to know that when Max asked me to help him he explained how you'd stitched him up, got him jailed and made sure he got a really hard time inside. He said you had contacts there who abused him and tortured him. He made it sound horrific. He said you'd blackmailed him and he had to give in or he'd be locked up for a long time. He said it wasn't the first time, he knew of someone else you got sent down because you didn't like them. I didn't know you then and he made you sound like a monster. So I agreed to help. At first it was easy going, harmless stuff and, of course, Max couldn't do anything wrong.

It began to get to me when you proved to be an entirely different person from the one I'd been led to expect. That's when I started to behave oddly. I was ripped apart by guilt. Things started to get worse when Max became more and more weird. He's always had some very unusual powers. He did things you just couldn't explain by rational means. Once when we were in Heidelberg he pulled a trick in a crowded Square. In front of hundreds of onlookers he just levitated, lifted himself off the ground. I swear there was a space between his feet and the pavement and there was nothing there, above or below, to help him. It made everyone gasp with amazement. I was used to him being brilliant at sleight-of-hand but I'd never seen anything like that. At the same time he was becoming more and more religious, except, as you know, the god he worshipped was not a benevolent one. Things done once in a spirit of jest or parody began to take on a sinister edge. Hangers-on and drinking buddies became disciples and they seemed to take it seriously too. Scary things started to happen. The videos began to plumb the depths of mysticism and the role-playing became sinister. After Max bought the Priory, the rites became more and more satanic. Then he brought in this other man. His bodyguard he called him. I never met him but Janet did and she said he was a heavy, heavy dude. She said he looked like the undead. Max called him the vampire and he kept him away from me on purpose. "I don't want him to see you," he told me. It was like he knew this sinister guy was dangerous around women. Some time later he was joined by another man who was even more dangerous. Max called him the wolf. He'd known him before and written "the Wolf's Cry" about him.

I got out about then. I was in really deep. I'd fallen in love with you and something like that couldn't be kept from Max. He was devastated and I just had to split. I knew I'd brought terrible things down on your head and I felt it would all end if I disappeared. I knew that, if I was with you, it would never end…."

Rachel heard footsteps. Someone was walking heavily across the top floor landing! That floor was of polished ships' timbers and the sound of footsteps was unmistakable. She listened hard, tiptoeing across the room to prise open the door. The footsteps stopped. The hair on her scalp prickled. She imagined a person poised, one foot in front of the other. She called upstairs. No reply. Then again came the same sound, echoing through the ceiling above the noise of the television. Walking out more boldly, she stood beneath the stairs but was met by the same brooding silence. The shadows in the old house seemed to stare at her, waiting for her to do something. An electric tension crackled in the air. She stood looking up into the darkness then she turned on the landing light. Nothing stirred. She went into the kitchen and made a cup of tea. Looking out of the window she stiffened. A white face disappeared quickly. She shook herself and said, "get a grip on yourself woman!" She took her cup back into the drawing room and settled once again to her epistle. She heard a bang. Terrified now she stood up and opened the door. A scratching sound came from upstairs. She followed it right up to the attic. Her heart beating, she stood outside the door. Eventually she plucked up the courage to push the door open. The rooms of the attic were connected by a passage beneath the rafters. The electric lights were dim. She walked down the passage, looking in each of the rooms. There was a cupboard door in the end attic and with a pounding heart she opened it. She found nothing. Bewildered, she started to retrace her steps. Switching off the lights, she went into the bedroom, taking care to lock the door. She removed her clothes hastily and put on a nightdress. She left the light on by the bed and read awhile, but each time there was any sound in the house, a creak, the wind in the chimney, she jumped in fear. Eventually she turned off the light and lay awake listening. Reassured by the silence, she fell into a deep sleep. She didn't know what time it was when she awoke but she knew what had awoken her. Something lay in bed with her. It brushed lightly against her nightdress, coarse, hairy. Paralysed by panic, it took several moments to pluck up the courage to reach out for it. She felt something and her whole body jumped. There was a sniggering sound in the darkness. She pulled away, screaming as it touched her. It gripped her by the hip, pulling her towards it. She reached up for the light but couldn't find it. She threw back the bedclothes and the thing sat up. It grasped her and grunted. She screamed and pushed it away. Terrified, she leapt out of bed. She ran across the room and, tugging at the lock, flung open the door. In front of her stood a tall figure, ghoulish, so white its face seemed bloodless, its thin red lips curling in a mirthless grin through rotten green teeth. She staggered back, and was grabbed from behind by something, which roared like an animal. The ghoul's hand came towards her, deliberately, slowly, and she felt a terrible thud. Her knees buckled and she fell to the floor.

☾

Reassured by the police that everything was all right, Jack

arrived home the next day on the lunch time flight only to find the house deserted. The computer was on in the drawing room and, cancelling the screensaver, Jack saw the unfinished note. Studying it without any change of expression, he smiled at the thought that Rachel had probably gone out, frightened to be there when he read it. She had nothing to worry about. Nothing in it surprised him. He hadn't known the details but he'd guessed enough and the sort of thing which might make other men senseless with rage reminded him merely of his own failings. Evil is a thing men do, sweetheart, he wanted to tell her, not an intangible thing with a life of its own. It can be seductive but ultimately it is the resort of those too afraid to live in the light.

Interested solely in having Rachel back he wasn't concerned any longer about the confession. Why, though, would she run away if it wasn't complete? For the first time he was worried. His worst fears were confirmed when he found an envelope on the bedside cabinet. Tearing it open with trembling hands he read:

> Jack, I'm sorry but I couldn't go through with it. I've left, this time for good. It's better this way, believe me. I'm sorry. I'm really sorry.

He suddenly realised he didn't know her handwriting. He'd never received anything handwritten from her. That made him wonder why she had left this note but not even printed out the unfinished confession on the computer. Beside himself with grief, he studied the letter for an indication of where she'd gone. She'd written it on the back of a piece of used paper, which had the name *Goldsmiths* on it. So keen had she been to get away, she hadn't even bothered to get a clean sheet! Even so he was worried and that made him telephone the police and tell the story. "She only arrived back the day before yesterday," he said.

"What was her demeanour like?" the Desk Sergeant asked.

"Well, she was obviously concerned because we had a lot of bridges to build. We were going to start today."

"Sounds likes she's bottled it, sir, don't you think? Sometimes people just can't face up to things."

"Yes," Jack agreed, "but the note just doesn't ring true. It's not the kind of thing she'd say. All she had to say was, I've changed my mind, I thought we could get over it but we can't." God, it suddenly occurred to him that he was pouring his heart out to a police officer. The Sergeant was also pretty unhelpful. The note spoke volumes as far as he was concerned. He took Rachel's description but his lack of enthusiasm gave Jack no confidence that he would circulate the information. It was a story as old as time itself. Someone's partner had left him and she'd turn up sooner or later with her lover somewhere. The Sergeant had more important things to dwell on and Jack's protestations cut no ice. He wondered if he should divulge the events of the previous months, but it would get him nowhere. The policeman would say the events weren't connected and he had a point. Why should anyone want to harm Rachel and then forge a note just to mislead Jack? It didn't add up. "We'll keep our eyes open," the officer promised, "and if we hear anything we'll let you know."

Physically and mentally drained Jack didn't go into work. He drank a few whiskies and then, feeling no better, went to bed. He lay awake feeling incredibly lonely, like someone just bereaved, and then fatigue took over and he fell into a fitful sleep.

PART SIX

CHAPTER 1

Jack had taken a lot on his plate this last year. Not only the run in with Kaliostri but also the grisly discoveries of the two murders had taken their toll. Now his beloved Rachel had reaffirmed her status as a serial leaver. It was no wonder he went into a decline. Within days he was drinking over the top, his hair was unkempt, his face unshaven and he had a wild look in his eyes. His home had become a mausoleum. With no family the earth was again an orphanage. He soon began to run a fever.

Thinking that he could walk off whatever was afflicting him, he left the car at home and took a taxi into town. He walked towards the quay. At the bottom of Howard Street next to the Stag Line building he looked from the viewing platform up the river towards Smiths Docks where they were building another North Sea oilrig. The evening sun was on the water like a carpet of fire near the bend in the river. Finally, he set off down Tanner's Bank towards the Fish Quay where he wandered aimlessly around the fish shops. He bought some fresh Dublin Bay prawns for dinner and then began the long walk along the harbour wall towards Tynemouth Priory. On the hill towards the barbican, his feet became more and more leaden and he started to think this wasn't the best time for sightseeing. The night revellers were starting to gather in Tynemouth Front Street so he could get a taxi home without too much of a wait. He struggled into the Priory wondering how he was going to turn this round.

He had to take responsibility for his own actions. Everyone has. He was trying to work out if the failure to do so explained everything that went wrong in a person's life. Maybe he had only himself to blame for losing Rachel. He sat down in the chapel in front of the rood screen and thought about her. He concentrated entirely on her, not on himself.

Where was she? Could he see her? No, he couldn't. He tried then to envisage his mother from the old photographs among the pathetic belongings, which had taken the journey through life with him and he couldn't see her either. Had he become so self-centred that he could no longer visualise anyone other than himself? Jack had never felt this close to despair before. There had been times back in the lonely years when he had found himself just having to trudge on – like a mountaineer already in oxygen debt, already in the death zone, his whole body dying as he walked, only the lure of the summit beckoning him on. He began to appreciate that he was being too hard on himself, that the fever, whatever it was, had been fuelled by heartbreak and a renewed sense of that hopelessness, which he had thought might be banished forever by Rachel's return. With this realisation came a blurring of his vision, as if the organism had simply, at that moment, decided to pack in, and he staggered to the taxi rank on Front Street where he blurted out his address to a driver who looked at him pityingly for being pissed this early in the day and drove him home. Jack was generous with the tip. "That your car?" the driver asked as he turned his taxi round. He pointed at the Mercedes in the drive.

"Yes," Jack replied through a foggy haze. "Why?" He turned to look at it and then saw what the driver was pointing at. Placed squarely on the bonnet was a white item. Jack stared at it, unable to focus. "It looks like a sheep's skull," he said to the taxi driver, who was staring out of his window.

"Nah," the man said, "I was brought up on the country and that a goat's skull if ever I saw one. You got some kids round here playing tricks on you, mate!" Jack nodded, his head rattling with the movement. "Yeah," he said. "There's a bunch up the parkway who're never out the garden."

"Aye, that'll be it then," the driver said. Jack felt as if his feet wouldn't obey him as he walked across the drive. He took the dried out skull from the bonnet, waved at the taxi driver as he honked his horn, and examined it, turning it over and over in his hands. He couldn't think straight but one thing he was sure of. Whatever he'd said to the taxi driver, the kids up the road hadn't put the skull on his car. Someone else had but who? He went into his house, looked in the hall mirror and didn't like what he saw. "Where are you going Jack?" The path through life, once clearly defined, had now entered into a mazy sequence of traps and pitfalls. Not fussed about eating and determined not to drink, life was on a real downer. There was nothing for it except bed. The skull would have to wait. "Eliminate the impossible and what you have left is the truth," he told himself as he crawled up the stairs. Rachel! With the thought of her every other consideration was blown away. He sighed and, getting under the covers, fell into a deep sleep but awoke about an hour later in a cold sweat. It was only seven o'clock. He took his own temperature and was horrified to see it had risen substantially. He telephoned the doctor's number and spoke to a young woman who told him she'd call the doctor's pager.

He must have passed out because the doctor was in Jack's bedroom before he realised he'd arrived. Jack was privileged. His own doctor, Richard Yates, knowing his patient's history had taken the trouble to call personally. He opened his black bag. "How did you get in?" Jack asked.

"Door was open," Richard replied. "I knocked but there was no answer. I hope you don't mind."

"No," Jack replied, "I just can't believe I was so careless."

"You're ill. It can make you forget things. It's not sensible round here, though, to leave your door open. I'll lock it on the way out."

"Thanks," Jack replied weakly.

The two professionals had known each other a long time and, if not exactly the closest of friends, they were more than passing acquaintances. "What have you been doing with yourself?" Richard felt his patient's forehead. "I've never seen you look so rough! You look like an aging hippy!"

"I don't know," Jack groaned. "I've been thinking about so many odd things of late."

Richard grew more and more wide-eyed as Jack recounted the tale of the last few months. It culminated with Rachel's exit a couple of days previously.

Richard nodded his head when he heard this. "You've been running a fever, and it seems to me this obsession with religion and magic may have resulted from an overworked imagination. All this stuff is important, Jack. We can do with a lesson from the alternative medical practitioners in reliance on case history."

"You believe in that, then, do you? Alternative medicine?"

"More things in heaven and earth, Horatio!" Richard grinned.

Jack lay back. He was in good hands. He knew he could confide in this guy without risking ridicule. "It is difficult to know where the truth lies. Fact and fiction may have become a touch intertwined."

"You've genuinely had a brush with witchcraft? Just hold there." Richard put the thermometer in Jack's mouth. He prepared a hypodermic syringe. Jack looked up at him. "Do you know anything about that kind of thing then?"

He shrugged the question off. "It's a field of study in which I have an interest," he said. "The effect of religious archetypes on the mind can be stunning – as the research of Jung has demonstrated. I'm going to give you something to bring your temperature down quickly." He held up the syringe. "Your mind's been playing tricks on you, you've really got to do something about that." He put the syringe against Jack's arm and pushed it slightly. Jack felt the pain. "I'm not surprised though. I read about those murders in the newspaper and it's a strange case, all right," Richard added. He compressed the handle. Amazing, isn't it, how the most ordinary lives can be intertwined with extraordinary events?" Jack winced. Richard wasn't the greatest with a needle. He seemed to think it important, however, and continued about his own experiences. "I had a similar case once before. I used to work in Brixton. Only difference was the villains there were doing it for videos, you know, filming it?"

"Snuff videos!" Jack replied. "Whoa!" Jack started to get up but he was pushed firmly back down. He had no strength in his limbs. Even adrenaline couldn't lift him. "Oh no!" Jack mouthed, "how could I have missed that?" Richard withdrew the syringe and waited for him to drift away. Then he did the hospital corners bit and tucked him in carefully. Making sure everything was in order, he left. He was careful to lock the door on the way out. "I've given him a sedative," he told Jack's friends, who greeted him at the bottom of the stairs and enquired of the patient's well being. "He'll be out for the count until tomorrow morning."

In his delirious state, Jack saw the other two enter, the pantomime trolls, both vaguely familiar. The door was open, he thought. I didn't leave it open. "Pity it's all too late!" a male voice said. If he could reach back through the fog-bound banks of his mind, he would remember who these two were and the key to all these strange events would be in his grasp. The tall one came towards him, reminding Jack, as the cold fog moved slowly in, of a creature from folk law, a Long Lankin, someone you warned kids never to go near. His cruel, thin face with its bloodless lips and its bleak, shark eyes grew all the more grotesque as he leaned over the stricken lawyer, mouthing something. He struggled to hear. "Don't worry, Lauder, your woman's ours. She squeals like a puppy every time we give it that." He made a fist and grinned through rotten, green teeth. Surely this was a nightmare? These ugly bastards couldn't really exist. The Feds would arrest them just for looking like that, if they walked round loose. Maybe this was the world one-removed, the place you went to as a sort of clearing-house when you died, before they worked out where to slot you in for your next existence. Like a sort of orphanage, where you were put in the hands of awful, horrible people, who were free to do with you as they pleased. It was kind of a test for later, an early induction to the grim fact that life is tough. Listlessly, Jack watched the gruesome duo go out of the door, their vile mouths saying the silent good-byes. "It wouldn't be fair to end it like this. We've left you clues, Jack, we've left you clues!" the smaller one said. He couldn't help but think as he watched them, you'll regret this. You should have finished the job. But it might have been wishful thinking.

Suddenly they were gone and, summoning the last vestiges of his strength he got up and, grabbing one of his silk ties, made himself a tourniquet, which he wrapped round the arm Richard had injected. Whatever he had put in wouldn't have got fully into Jack's system because the illness had lowered his blood pressure. He tightened the tie round his upper arm and then he cut the knot of blood vessels with a razor blade. The blood began seeping out and then the sedative kicked in. Delirium – that intoxicating state in which mortal men catch a glimpse of an existence beyond the ecstasy of the animals – allowed him to glimpse horrors normally concealed behind the curtain of individuation. The gruesome part was that the horror was real. Two steps from the pit, about to topple in, the images could no longer be dismissed as hallucinations. Voices in the distance called his name as if to emphasise that you cannot cheat your destiny – you are always living on borrowed time; the voices were as sweet and deadly as sirens'; the beat of the wings was the dark angel's passover; a misshapen man limped towards his supine body, carrying a severed head. Behind him followed another who dragged the lifeless body of a woman. "Rachel!"

CHAPTER 2

Jack awoke with a start in a hospital bed. He had seen a vision from the past, a face previously seen only in photographs – that of Tony Cooper, the scrap dealer from Tyneside murdered that chill night in Langhorn forest and, as the verdict said, the victim of Henry Herron. In Jack's half-sedated dream Rachel had been dragged through a wood by two shadowy figures. Now fully awake, Jack felt much better but he couldn't remember how he'd got here. Although his immediate memory ended just after the moment when the doctor had injected him with a drug to ease his fever, he could recall vaguely a visit from two others. They had left him clues. To what? To Rachel's disappearance? He thought about the letter again, less convinced now that it was her signature. A good try, but was it hers? He got out of bed, a little unsteady on his feet until the feeling came back into his legs. Crossing to the window, he was astonished to see, silhouetted against the winter sky, the enormous figure of the Angel of the North, a gigantic sculpture hewn out of ship's metal. Ramrod straight, it towered over the landscape, its face staring southwards down the Great North Road. This symbol of the strength, the resolution and ingenuity of the North made the blood pump in his heart and his fists and teeth clench with determination. He strode down the corridor until he came to a room where a nurse sat at a desk writing up records. She looked at him in surprise. "Where are my clothes?" he asked.

"You can't just leave," she said, "one of the doctors will have to see you."

"Okay, okay, call one of them, but where are my clothes?"

"Go back," she said, "I'll bring them to you."

Jack saw a public phone at the end of the ward. "Can you lend me some coins for the phone?" he asked. He had remembered something he wanted to tell Lowther, something the doctor had made him think of. The nurse shook her head as if in irritation at the fact that the National Health Service can't help people who don't want to be helped but nonetheless produced some coins. Jack went to the phone and called Lowther.

"You up and about, eh?" the policeman asked jovially. "My God, Jack, you've had us all worried!"

"You'll have to give me chapter and verse some other time," Jack replied, "I can't remember a thing. That's not why I rang you, though."

"Which is?"

Jack told the Superintendent of his conversation with Richard before he had passed out. Now Lowther listened. "Snuff videos?" he said. "That's an angle I hadn't thought of. That would figure. There's fortunes in the international snuff trade. Millions."

"Do me a favour," Jack replied, "Kaliostri's bound to have some connection with a recording studio, one that does videos too. There might even be one locally. See if you can find it. There could be a connection with the murders!"

Lowther chuckled. "You won't rest till you see him hanged, will you? What has that man done to you?"

"He's just an evil bastard. Trust me!"

"I will, Jack. You've still got some credit with me. Even if you did send me on a wild goose chase with that information about murders at the bloody cathedral! I hope this is better quality stuff?"

Jack knew the Chief Superintendent sufficiently to leave well alone. He went away to do some digging whilst Jack returned to the ward to await his exit visa. Before the doctor came to see him he had another, even more welcome, visitor: Hans Heidemann Q.C, his strident voice, honed to perfection by many years of addressing deaf, if not daft, judges, strode down the ward, a bundle of energy, despite his advancing years. "My dear chap!" he boomed, "I came as soon as I heard." Even though Jack and Hans had become great friends over the years, the friendship revolved around work and seldom passed over to social occasions, so the idea that the Q.C might take a personal interest in his professional client's welfare had never previously occurred to him. "I didn't realise you were up here," Jack said.

"No, that's right. I was doing a case up here. I was round for dinner two nights ago at Simon Parker's house and he told me of your accident." Hans winked as if he appreciated that there would be more to the story.

"Oh, yes, talk of the town am I?" Jack replied with a nervous laugh.

"Not in an unkind way, dear boy. Everyone is very concerned about you."

"Not Parker! He hates my guts. He'd be the first to cheer if I went down!"

"You underestimate the respect so many have for you, Jack, and the affection. People don't always express it in the same way you know!"

Jack grimaced at the friendly ticking off. "Well, if you're right," he said, "Judge Parker is a bigger man than I gave him credit for, that's for certain."

"I can assure you he is," Hans replied with a friendly, if puzzled, look on his face, "but what makes you say that?"

Jack laughed nervously. "Do me a favour, Hans!" he exclaimed. "The things that guy's been through!"

"Oh," Hans replied, suddenly all ears at the thought of some juicy titbit he'd never previously suspected, "tell me more. It's not more of that stuff with Shona MacDonald, I trust? It's old hat now, even if he'll never quite get over that affair becoming public. He's gone as far as he's likely to, I'm afraid." Hans chuckled.

Jack looked at him perplexed. How could he be so callous as to think his news was mere gossip about something so minor? "Well, you know, about his daughter?"

"Jessie or Ruth?"

"Jessica of course. I know it's all very hush hush but I have it on good authority that it's something to do with the Devil's Disciple." He watched the barrister's face for a reaction.

"Ah, yes, that awful bunch that Parker can't stand. Yes, she's been in India with him and his coterie, hasn't she? What's his name?"

Hans didn't know. He didn't know! "Kaliostri, I assume that's who you mean," Jack said.

"Quite, that's the blackguard! Well, so what did you hear about Jessie?"

"That she was killed of course, in India!"

Hans looked genuinely shocked. "My dear fellow," he exclaimed, "you know, I heard that rumour too. The circuit was abuzz with it at one stage."

It was Jack's turn to look surprised. "Rumour?" he repeated.

"Yes," Hans replied, "It's utter balderdash! Pure drivel! I don't know where on earth it came from but I can tell you that Jessie's very much alive and kicking. She was home when I was there two days ago. I talked to her for an hour or so and I know she's got aspirations to the stage but she don't make a very good corpse! Delightful girl, really, don't you know? Just keeps bad company. Father doesn't approve of her lifestyle of course, but that's the younger generation for you." Hans looked at Jack's thunderstruck face. "You ought to take better care of yourself, dear boy, you look as if you're on the verge of a heart attack!"

Jack looked at his old friend open-mouthed. "You're telling me that Jessica Parker is not dead?" he asked slowly as if measuring every syllable.

"Well, not two days ago she wasn't," Hans replied, "and I haven't heard of anything drastic happening in the meantime."

"So it was all misinformation," a flabbergasted Jack replied. "Hans, you have to do me a favour!"

"Of course, dear boy, what is it?" The Queen's Counsel replied, genuinely concerned.

"Take me now to see Jessica, I must speak with her."

Hans looked slightly doubtful. It never helps the career path of any barrister, even one so senior as Hans, to jeopardise his relationship with a high-ranking Judge but, seeing the distress of his solicitor friend, he replied, "of course, Jack, of course!" On the drive over to Gosforth, Jack, lost in his own thoughts, proved to be a taciturn companion. "You don't mind if I don't take you in, do you?" Hans asked as he stopped outside the Judge's palatial mansion.

"Of course not," Jack replied, "and I shan't mention your involvement at all, trust me."

The barrister looked grateful for that reassurance and added, "I hope you find what you're looking for, dear boy."

After waving goodbye to his friend Jack walked up to the front door of the house and rang the doorbell. He wasn't entirely certain what he'd say if the Judge or his wife answered. He needn't have worried. It was the lady herself. Jessica recognised him immediately and put a hand over her mouth. "Oh my God!" she said as if she knew exactly why he was there.

"Can I have a moment of your time?" he asked her politely.

"I suppose so," she replied with none of the exuberance, which had marked their first meeting.

Jack followed the young woman into the drawing room and said, "look, I'm not here to cause you any trouble. It's just that....well, I don't quite know how to say this, but I heard you were dead."

"I know," she said, blowing away any pretence at inscrutability. She sat down, her dark eyes revealing her embarrassment. Jack said, "I'm not here to accuse or blame, I just want the truth. For my own peace of mind."

"Well, you can see the truth," Jessica said. "We were all part of an elaborate hoax. Max loves these weird and wonderful mind games, particularly if the victim is someone who should be able to take care of himself." She couldn't resist a little dig. "However did you get to be a lawyer, Jack? You're as naïve as a newborn baby!" Jack shook his head in disbelief that this slip of a girl was talking to him like this. It wasn't the first time the accusation had been made but he had always been content with his sense of optimism, his confidence in goodness and the rewards of a generous disposition. Was that so bad? Apparently, it was; it had made a fool of him. Jessica continued to speak. "We were astonished it took you so long to find out the truth. You were set up that night at the party. That was him, the old guy. He's brilliant at disguises." She seemed to have repented of it all and wanted to talk about it. "Max gets his own back on everyone sooner or later. I went along with this like a fool and he had a dual agenda. He wanted my parents to hear about it and get worried. They were out of their minds for a couple of weeks until I got in touch. It was a way of getting back at my father. It didn't stop there either. Max even sent pictures of us in flagrante to my home. You can imagine the furore that caused! No one crosses him, I mean no one. You he seemed to earmark for some pretty special treatment. His venom was greater in your case than it was with the usual minions, as he likes to refer to them. He really had it in for you. Maybe because your backgrounds aren't much different, maybe you didn't give him enough face, maybe you were just too self-assured and capable." Jack smiled, listening to adjectives worlds removed from the truth. "Or maybe," Jessica continued, "it was like pulling the wings off an insect. He fancied torturing someone and you just happened to be there. It was meant to be part of a series of actions to drive you out of your brains. Each time you thought you'd solved the conundrum, he'd do something else. You know what I mean?" Jack nodded but made no comment, just letting her run. "Well, he figured you'd find out this was a sick joke, you'd just ask one of your pals. When you asked Kirby Potts, he creased himself. He and Potts realised you'd fallen for it, so they kept up the pretence until it didn't matter anymore. The truth is they never expected to get this mileage out of it. Max just never figured you wouldn't have the gumption to talk to someone in the know, so the story just perpetuated itself. He found that the funniest bit of all. He'd figured he'd have to keep using his ingenuity to think up things to drive you nuts but he didn't. You did it all yourself. It became a bit of a game in itself after a while. Just sowing in another seed to keep the pretence up, to see how long he could spin it out."

"No doubt everyone had a good laugh," Jack replied with as much dignity as he could muster in the circumstances. He could scarcely say that he had never entertained the idea that people could be so cruel because he had seen enough examples in his professional life. Perhaps this was the reward for egocentricity. Did he suffer from such a lack of concern for the fate of others that he could be so easily fooled? A few discreet questions, if he had been inquisitive enough, might have prevented a lot of heartache. Even so he didn't overdo the self-flagellation. There was a more important question.

"What about the murders then? Not you, okay, but Josephine Jackson and Karen Spencer?" he asked.

Jessica's eyes shot towards the ceiling. "Whoa!" Jessica exclaimed. "That wasn't in the script! I was out of there, Jack! Things did come on top; it all got very heavy when these new dudes turned up."

"New dudes?" Jack's forensic training kicked in again and he remembered a similar remark in Rachel's letter.

Jessica wasn't however being drawn. For some reason, fear, self-protection, she didn't want to go there. "I know nothing, see nothing, hear nothing, say nothing. That's my motto now."

After that, there was no point in saying anything more. Jessica was distressed enough as it was. At the door, however, a thought struck him and he added, "who else was in on it?" He didn't mention Rachel. In a way he didn't want to know.

Jessica shrugged. "Everyone I guess. Even that policeman."

"Freer?"

"Sorry," she replied, "I'm truly sorry. It got so out of hand." In a remark the irony of which made him shrug, she added, "I guess I never thought someone like you would care about what happened to me."

After that, he wasn't sure how he got back home. He seemed to wander round for ages until eventually he took the Metro and then walked a mile or so to his house. The walk centered his mind. He still needed to know what had become of Rachel. When he got in the house he retrieved the note she had left. Pencilled on the back was the name which he had thought previously had nothing to do with the message. *Goldsmiths*. Maybe it was correct, he had been left a clue. He racked his brains to think where he had seen that name before, then it occurred to him. It was the name of the solicitor who'd written the letter to Pardoe about Henry Herron's property in Northumberland. He drove down the office to get Henry's files and found a contact number among the papers. As luck would have it Goldsmith was in. He sounded a timid man and he explained, as they talked, that basically he was a conveyancing solicitor and seldom left the office. He remembered the case, because he'd never previously bought a property for a person in prison. He laughed dryly as he said it. Jack asked him if he recalled where the property was. He couldn't remember precisely. "Is there somewhere called Goat Head or Goat Fell?" he asked. He didn't know the North Country at all well. He was a Midlands man himself and always had been, although he understood the fishing in Northumberland to be second to none. He remembered that Pardoe had collected the deeds on his release from Long Lartin – that's where Mr. Goldsmith's practice was, Leicestershire. This had all happened within the last eighteen months, although he couldn't remember precisely when.

Jack toyed with the idea of ringing the police, but it wouldn't do any good. Pardoe perhaps wanted to be found. He had allocated to himself the lofty title of Henry Herron's spiritual heir. Presumably he was fulfilling some obligation to Henry. Why else should he leave clues? Jack decided to try the Council at Newton St. Abbs, where Henry had died, and see if they had any information. When he described his role in the administration of Henry's estate, the council officer seemed suddenly to forget about the Data Protection Act, which had previously been his stock response to every question, and told the lawyer that the council house given as the address at which the former bandit had died had been let to one John Pardoe. Surprise, surprise! Pardoe was playing mind games as the result of some pact he'd made with Henry prior to his death. Incapable of accepting responsibility, if he could put blame on others, Henry's illness had aggravated his desire for revenge. An illness like that takes over when the spirit flags. Perhaps it is always there, with a form of intelligence all of its own, waiting for the moment when the shields are down. Pardoe couldn't have anything against Jack so it had to be something to do with Henry. Jack got out Henry's journal, which he had previously neglected. It was a bundle of looseleaf papers, some typed, some handwritten in the criminal's neat but idiosyncratic style, with little illustrations here and there to highlight the text: smiling faces; a hangman's rope; little plans: the prison script, the way they communicate with each other without the screws understanding. After his discovery that it was a jumble of assorted memories, he had never pored through it but now he thumbed through a few pages until he came to a telling sentence: 'The only way to hit smug twats like Jack L is to fuck up their lives like they've fucked up mine.' Another entry read 'The bastard took my family and my life from me. I'll pay him back in kind.'

"Damn it!" Jack cursed. He was paying the penalty for his own laziness in not checking out this document earlier. The more he read through it the more he saw that Henry had seeded it in the most obscure places with spiteful little references to his legal team's, particularly Jack's, efforts in the trial. The prisoner's bitterness at his own impending demise had obviously spilled over into rancour against the man whom, for whatever misguided reason, he presumed to be responsible for his incarceration. His dying wish was to communicate that bitterness. Jack had not obliged him; he had largely ignored the manuscript. Indeed, if he had read it earlier he might well have destroyed it.

Jack then spotted something else he might have noticed earlier if he had paid more attention. There were several references to Langhorn forest, even though there was no mention of the Cooper murder. Henry had been obsessed with the place. Circumstantial evidence at the trial had highlighted that. The surmise that Pardoe's cottage was somewhere in Langhorn forest was confirmed when he found an actual reference in the journal to a place called Herron Cottage. It was a long shot but it could be the same place. The Herrons were an infamous family of border reivers. Jack had a reference book somewhere on the old border families. When he got home he went up to the attic and hunted for it. In it he found a reference to the Herrons, which read as follows:

> A North-Northumbrian family with many branches. The most infamous is the so-called 'Bastard Herron' known by that sobriquet because of his legendary bloodthirstiness which was renowned even among the ruthless Border folk. He inherited vast tracts of land by Langhorn and Goat Head. He had a great house built there which was long ago razed to the ground. Much of this holding is now National Park land but there are places still in private ownership. There are still places in the area which bear the family name.

"Goat Head," Jack breathed and suddenly it did not seem such a long shot: it was in the borders, somewhere near Langhorn. He resolved to make his way there at first light, snoop around and ask some questions. In the middle of these thoughts a telephone call from Lowther interrupted him. "Jack," the Superintendent said, "I owe you one. Get over to the Pandora's Box Recording Studios on Eighth Avenue, Team Valley, right away."

CHAPTER 3

When Jack arrived he found the place heaving with cops and SoCOs. Silently Lowther led him round. The place had been wrecked but dozens of pornographic videos lay on the floor. Graphic stills on the dust jackets betrayed their content. Jack noted that many had the Christ figure he had seen at Weldon as a central artefact. "I told you," Jack said, "he's obsessed with the Antichrist!"

"Depraved bastards!" Lowther said. "It never ceases to astonish me how methodical these sickos are. This place is owned by an offshore company. We're enquiring into the owners now but it's not hard to guess who they'll turn out to be. It's serious this though Jack. You can see everyone's done a runner." He leaned across to the lawyer and whispered conspiratorially: "this is confidential, right?" Jack nodded. "They got a tip off we were coming," he added. "Would you believe from Barry Freer?" Lowther was so angry at the betrayal, it was etching lines in his forehead. "He's been a pal of Kaliostri's for years," he replied bitterly. "On the take, feeding him information. Kaliostri was a big source of information for him. You know what Barry was like? Larger than life! He was always getting the goods on some choice villains. Interpol used him as their main contact up here. I never could figure out how he got all the secret information. Now you can guess why. It's confidential what's on the Register, but think of a name and double it!"

"Kaliostri?"

Lowther motioned upwards with both hands.

"The two of them? Husband and wife?"

"My lips are sealed," the policeman replied. "You never heard it here. But seriously, Jack, sometimes these coppers running snouts forget they're coppers. They cross over. Barry did. Big time. He was panicking. No wonder he was anxious to pin that murder on you! I began to suspect him then. I wondered why he should be so desperate to get a collar."

They both lapsed into contemplative silence, wondering what might have been if they'd known some things a deal earlier. Jack picked up one of the video boxes. The scene on the cover seemed familiar but he couldn't place why. "One more thing you ought to know," Lowther said as Jack was beginning to leave.

"Yeah?"

"We did a check on Lorenza Kaliostri. She comes from a rough background. Down your way in fact. The Spring Garden. Father was a real drunk. The mother did time for him. She killed him with a shard of glass from a mirror. Stabbed him in the back. Punctured the lung."

"You live and learn" Jack said, "probably explains why the daughter's such a hard bitch."

"Yes, but that's not the best of it," Lowther added. "Her brother's a convicted murderer. He's dead now. I put him away myself. You were on that case"

Jack stared at Lowther, his nerve ends jangling. "She's not a Herron?" he exclaimed.

The effect on Jack was electric. He gave Lowther a look, which made the policeman move towards him protectively.

"Jack, what is it?" he asked. "You look as if you've seen a ghost!"

"It's Rachel," Jack replied. "I think they've got her."

"What are you talking about?" Lowther questioned. "I know your lass left you, but what do you mean, they've got her?"

Words failed Jack. Too used to being scoffed at, the

proposition he was about to explain seemed suddenly as ridiculous as any other he had espoused recently. He held out his hands as if in surrender, a bewildered look on his face, then stumbled out of the door. Lowther shouted to him to hang on but Jack ignored the plea. He had planned setting off for the Borders at first light but now he went down the cellar and grabbed the rucksack in which he kept his winter gear. He hadn't used it for ages. The bag smelled musty and damp but he knew the equipment – crampons and boots – would be serviceable. The binoculars would be handy too. He grabbed a winter ski jacket and salopettes. The snow was thick up Langhorn way. Just as he was leaving he turned to check all electrical implements were switched off. His eye was drawn to an item he'd left on the hall table. It was the video he'd brought back from the recording studio. Although he was desperate to get away, instinct made him tarry momentarily to fit the cartridge into the machine. After a few moments the video came on and a blond hooker strutted down the Bigg Market, past the Cathedral. A man in the shadows watched her and then, stubbing out his cigarette with his foot, followed her. They stopped in St. Nicholas' Churchyard where, after a few moments' silent negotiation, she knelt and began to perform. Strange creatures began to emerge from the mist hanging over the graves. Having seen, at Rachel's friend's house, the television programme in which the news had broken of the hooker's death in St. Nicholas's churchyard, he knew this was the same incident. As he watched, a large figure pulled out a sword. Grinning horribly, it grasped the hair of the woman. The camera turned to the head held in the ghoul's hand. Jack went cold. He had met Tropical Tom's other half a couple of times. The 'victim' in the video was Karen Spencer. Snuff videos, that's how she had made her pin money. Only real life had caught up on the fantasy. Jack watched the video through and had his second shock when

Josephine Jackson came into it. He recognised the point at which he had interrupted Janet Gillingham's viewing and understood now her expression of surprise. It had been at the fact that he had thought it was a news programme. But she hadn't let on. She had realised it might be something Kaliostri could use, just like he'd used the hoax about Jessica's death.

On his way to the borders, his mind in turmoil, Jack toyed with involving the police but he still didn't know what he had stumbled on. His brain tried to make sense of it: so the Cathedral murder was a snuff video; Janet Gillingham had known that; perhaps Rachel had known it too; they both must have known that Jessica's death was a fake; the Kaliostris were definitely behind it all.

"Jesus!" he said aloud, "what a mug I've been!" That was the big problem with involving the police: what if Rachel's reappearance and disappearance was just another charade? Against that, however, was the most striking fact of all: the two 'stars' of the video were both dead. Karen must have died first; that's who Josephine was talking about when she'd said, suddenly there's a girl dead and I'm scared. He'd thought she meant Jessica but it was Karen she was referring to. In a bizarre way they had both enacted their own fate – life had imitated art.

If something heavy was going down, the one person Jack could have done with on this crusade was the Border Bandido but he couldn't raise him on the mobile. He was probably tucked up snugly in bed with his latest flame, while Jack fought the forces of evil single-handed. He could hear his big pal saying, "well one of us has to save the world, bonny lad!" He settled for leaving a message on the answer phone. It was a bit complicated and he wondered if Joe would understand it, assuming he ever got it.

Jack checked into an inn near Langhorn, hoping to get a lead. The proprietor was friendly enough but didn't know of any cottages up at Goat Head. Workers from the Forestry

Commission estate regularly drank in the bar and the proprietor reckoned that if anyone knew the place it would be them. "Mind," he added as the lawyer's face lit up, "they're a taciturn bunch not much given to passing the time of day. You shouldn't question them too closely or they'll clam up." With that warning in mind Jack retired to his room, overlooking the bleak, snow clad hills of the roof of England. In spite of his impatience, he was struck by how beautiful they were in the winter. You could see all their contours. Things had changed little since the days when the wild horsemen rode these passes on their marauding errands. After eating in the hotel, he went into the bar. It was empty but he'd not been there long when in came a grisly looking man in his mid-fifties wearing a Forestry Commission tunic. He ordered a pint of lager. Jack left him a few moments then spoke to him after he'd savoured the first of his pint. "Cold night," he said.

The man looked at Jack and nodded. "Aye, there's more snow on the way. It's been canny bad, this winter like. The ground's like iron."

"Have you worked on the estate long?"

"Thirty years," the woodsman answered in a broad Northumbrian drawl, the 'i' like an 'o' and the 'r' rolling deliciously. Jack held up his pint glass for a refill and offered the workman one. "Aye," he replied, "reckon I will. Thanks a lot." Jack ordered a pint of lager and a Guinness. "Devil's brew, that stuff," the man said.

"Well I've been drinking it twenty years so I'm not going to stop now. I'm having a whisky chaser," Jack said, "can I tempt you?"

The woodsman looked again as if not quite sure about his new friend, but the offer was too appealing. "Aye," he said, "don't mind if I dee."

Jack ordered two Glenfiddichs, much to the man's approval. "Wey, I didn't know you meant a malt! One of them birds would have done." He indicated the Famous Grouse bottle. He squinted at the liquid against the light. Jack was at a bit of a loss as to how to draw the conversation round to the subject but human intercourse is a peculiar thing: the victim seems sometimes to be as attracted to the predator as the predator is to its prey and, as if by some kind of serendipity, which owes nothing to cause and effect, quite unexpectedly, the victim came up with the crucial clue. "Aye," he said as if reminiscing, "there's not much about the forest I don't know."

"Is that right?" Jack paused so it wouldn't appear contrived. "I remember there was a murder here some years ago. Do you remember that?"

"Do I not!" the woodsman said. "I was on the team that sorched for the body. Never found it. He was a scrap dealer from doon your way."

"Yes. That's right. It was a queer business."

"They got the morderer though."

"Yes. Well a man was convicted of the crime." Jack almost bit his tongue. Was he showing too much knowledge? However, the woodsman was interested in the subject and he rambled on without any prompting.

"Aye, It was the chap who used to rent the old Herron place for holidays."

Jack's heart skipped a beat. That detail hadn't surfaced at the trial. "Where is the Herron place?"

"Up on Goat Fell. You can only get at it from the south. The hintend's the Black Goat Wall."

Jack had a surge of *déjà vu*. Of course! He should have known. The Black Goat Wall! Memories of himself as a young man tugged at him. "Of course!" Jack said, "the Billy Goat's Beard!" His face must have been animated with excitement. It was many years since he'd climbed the frozen ice of the Beard – before he'd done his impersonation of Humpty Dumpty.

The woodsman sipped his whisky. "It's reckoned to be haunted you know, that Herron place. It always was. He were the only one who went there, but he was one of them, wasn't he?"

"Henry Herron?"

"Aye. That's the villain." His eyes clouded over. "Aye, there's been a few scares there since it was empty."

Jack's blood was chilling in his veins. "Is there anyone there now?"

"It's funny you should ask. I've seen smoke rising. Probably travellers. Them Herrons was a travelling family. Nae one's been up there. You can't get near without being seen."

Jack was a poor companion after that. His mind was elsewhere. He'd stumbled on the key to the puzzle. It had started out as a long shot, but now it seemed likely that John Pardoe was living in the old Herron place. He considered involving the police now, but the Kaliostri connection dissuaded him. He'd been wrong too many times. This was either another hoax or Pardoe didn't want Rachel, he wanted Jack. If so, he had an edge because the villain didn't know Jack wasn't a million miles away.

CHAPTER 4

Despite the weather closing in, he didn't wait for the next day. If the cottage was difficult to get to without being seen, the dark would improve his chances. The route took him down the forestry path until the ice-filled ruts were impassable. He parked up in a glade, just out of sight of the road and walked along the path until he heard the sound of machinery. Round the next bend a massive digger shifted tree trunks and rubble off the path. He skirted it, passing like a wraith through the trees, not wanting to alert anyone to his presence. As he came level, the vehicle wheezed to a halt and its driver opened the cab and climbed down, his working day finished. It wasn't long to the spring equinox so it would be light for a while yet. Jack stood for a moment watching the yellow beast pant mechanically in a strange parody of a creature of flesh and blood until the workman had passed out of sight. Only then did he resume his stride. The path petered out and went across a row of fields, the lower of which had played host to a convention of moles. Beyond, the ground began to rise. The cottage wasn't visible – it was two miles up that path, the perfect hideaway. Resolving to keep away from the path he forged on in the teeth of a gale. At the next false summit he took a look round to get his bearings and was astonished to see, some five hundred feet or so below, the car park he'd used all those years ago, when he'd first inspected the site of the Langhorn murder. He hadn't realised then this house was so close to the spot. It was incredible that the police had missed such a telling piece of circumstantial evidence. He wondered if the purchase of the cottage had been Pardoe's idea, or whether Henry himself had insisted on it. Perhaps it had been his intention to die here rather than in Newton St. Abbs, but the reaper acknowledges no man.

From this stronghold, capable of being guarded against a small army, the occupants of the cottage had an eagle's view of the approaches from miles around. Lawless for many a century, known in ancient times as the Debatable Lands, these parts had been warred over by factions from north and south of the border from before the Roman occupation. The ground had the hollowness of peat as Jack tramped uphill. As he climbed higher, the blizzard increased in intensity. He bent his back and forced his shoulders into it, watching for a first sight of the house. He saw it as he crested a hillock, lit up like a beacon. An anti-intruder system of that sophistication was enough to arouse suspicion by itself. Crouching down, he examined the floodlit yard with deepening interest. A four-wheel drive, canvas-topped pick-up was parked by a dry stone wall. Two men appeared at the door of the building. One of them waved to the other and started up the vehicle, then drove from sight behind a rise. The other man stood in the doorway alongside two large dogs, a Rotweiler and an Alsatian. The man carried a shotgun over his shoulder and was looking straight at Jack's position. He turned away and patrolled up and down the yard a few times, the shotgun cocked over his shoulder, then he went inside, leaving the dogs to continue the patrol. They would prevent anyone from getting within striking distance of the cottage. Land to Jack's right dropped away down a steep bank to the edge of the cliff known as the Black Goat Wall. Without any exact plan, he began to move down the hill, initially crouched, keeping out of sight of the house, until he struck the cliff. He hesitated. He still bore the scars of his last visit to this crag. Shrugging off the fear, he rounded the buttress and climbed down, the familiar feeling of the smooth, volcanic rock bringing a smile to his face. It was okay. The scars were physical, not mental. A tent was pitched on the plateau immediately beneath the face. There was nothing strange in that. This had been a favourite place for winter climbing for generations. Approaching the campsite he shouted but the occupants must have gone down to the village for a night out. Gazing discerningly at their equipment, stacked tidily on the ground, an idea occurred to him. It was a crazy idea but if it worked it would upset all the odds. The men in the cottage assumed that no one could approach from three accessible sides without their knowing. They had discounted any approach up the Beard. Jack's mobile rang and he answered it, speaking quietly as if there might be eavesdroppers about. "Joe!" he said when he recognised the voice.

"What are you up to now?" the Bandido replied. "Is housebreaking not enough?"

"Joe, listen to me," he said. "I'm in the borders at a place called Langhorn. There's a waterfall there called the Billy Goat's Beard. At the top of the falls there's a cottage called Herron Cottage. I'd like you to get there as quick as you can."

"Yer bugger, what for?"

"I don't know. I've got a hunch they're holding Rachel here."

"Who is?" came the astonished reply.

"Someone who was a friend of Henry Herron."

"Wey," Joe replied dismissively, "I thought you were in the shit for a minute. You'll be needing nae help then!"

"Don't underestimate them," Jack said, "they've got guns."

"Tooled up, are they? Two can play at that game, bonny lad. You wait for me there. How long will it take to drive up?"

It would take the Bandido two or three hours to get to the cottage. "I'll go and recce it. Be careful when you approach it. They have a great view of all sides except one."

"Which one's that?"

"The Billy Goat's Beard. I'm going up it. Don't worry! I've done it before."

"And you've fallen on yer arse before, bonny lad," the Bandido reminded him gravely. "You take the proverbial biscuit you do, marra. I'll be there as soon as."

It is a recognised principle in climbing circles that necessity may excuse theft. The emergency must be genuine. With an alpine 100 metre rope, two slings for belay points, a couple of Friends, two nuts for insertion in cracks, ice axes in addition to his own step-in crampons, Jack was well enough equipped to tackle the Eigerwand. Armed to the teeth in climbing terms, he traversed to a point above the first pitch, gritted his teeth, unslung the crampons and took out the axes. He uncoiled the rope, intending to use it for self-belaying the dangerous pitches. Placing the two slings across his chest like bandoliers, he suspended pro from his harness, tied the rope in a bowline and, the slings of both axes semi-tightened around his wrists, began to compose himself. Feeling the fear, he moved through it. He was going to do it anyway. Not for himself. He didn't need this test. He had walked away from a passion because, like a moth attracted to the flame, it had singed him and he had understood. Then it was a plaything, a toy. Now it had a purpose. He had two hundred feet to climb and, if, in contemplation, it had seemed a daunting proposition, as soon as he began to move, the familiarity encouraged him; the adrenaline began to rise; the psychosomatic pain in his knee disappeared.

At first the route was well banked up with snow. The avalanche risk from the large cornice at the summit reduced by the cold, the first difficult pitch was the dogleg, fully fifty feet of sheer ice shining blue in colour. The purchase was good but he had a blind funk about half way up, realising he'd been too blasé. He dug in, making headway slowly but surely, front-pointing, axe penetration no more than a fraction of an inch in places. The small platform at the dogleg provided momentary respite; the snow felt securer as it bunched up under his feet. He worked upwards, axes and crampons sinking in firmly under his weight, over a number of minor but technically difficult ice steps. The second big pitch, near the top, was forty feet of ice slab with a bulge at two-thirds height. Protection was possible on the wall to the right but the pitch couldn't be climbed without going over the bulge, a fearsome prospect. He must have done it last time on autopilot. Opting to self-belay, he looked up to a point where a rocky spike would take a sling. He resolved to make that his first belay point. Measuring out a length of rope, he tied a figure of eight on the bight and attached it to a karabiner. A Friend fitted snugly into a crack in the wall and he tied in the end of the rope so he could climb to the extent of the sectioned-off bight. He began gingerly, aware that a fall from the highest point would be near enough a hundred-footer, assuming of course the protection held. It was hard work but he was getting there, taking as few chances as possible, adrenaline largely compensating for lack of condition. When he began to congratulate himself disaster struck. He was below the bulge and couldn't go round it. He couldn't remember this point from the previous ascent but that wasn't unusual. An ice climb depends so much on the conditions that it's seldom the same twice. His upper body leant out over the bulge at an acute angle to the face. He had to keep moving; gravity would otherwise take him down. Striking again with the right axe he teetered on the left toehold. A good thirty feet above the protection, on the centre of the bulge, fatally, he hesitated, lost momentum, his wrist catching the top lip of the bulge as he struck with the axe. The tip didn't bite properly and he brought his right leg up without purchase. With no time to scramble for a toehold in that moment of perfect equilibrium he struck with the right leg. If the hold had been firm he would have been secure but his foot met verglased rock. A shower of sparks and he was off, the foot slipping down. Horror-stricken he sailed through the air. The jerk as the rope came taut was followed by a cracking noise as the spike broke. The next second would determine his fate. His weight came on the chock. It held, the elasticity of the rope taking some of the shock out of the fall. Sighing with relief, he was scarcely in an enviable position. Thirty feet below his protection, having fallen at least sixty, he had no prussiks or jumars to get back up. As so often happens, in the moment of despair his plight worsened. Reaching in his pocket for his over-gloves the ice got through to his fingers, he forgot he had stashed his mobile phone there. As he pulled out the gloves he dislodged the phone and it fell down the hill, making a distinctive clunk as it hit the wall below and then spun off into oblivion. "Damn!" he shouted into the wind. The phone had been his only means of bringing in back up. What was he to do now? Go down? Admit defeat? He looked up at the chock. It seemed firm enough. Something told him it would hold. Penduluming across the ice wall to the left-hand side he managed to grab hold of a projection of rock, using the tension of the rope and his left foot on the wall to make a yard upwards, then a second yard. He was six feet nearer his protection as he hit the right wall. Repeating the process several times, suddenly he could reach up and grab the krab. Not good practice but it would have to do. He transferred himself to the wall again and grasped his axes, hanging from the slings on his wrists. He now had only one point of pro below him. Back to his previous best position he reached up to the bulge again. This time, altering the sequence of moves, a narrow gunnel provided better purchase for his left foot. He got in a good axe point and, praying, pulled up on it. He brought the left foot over the bulge and kicked it home. Glory be! He could stand on it and now, with the top of the bulge, the angle eased. Jack dug a tunnel in the summit cornice and struggled through. The Goat's Horn towered up in front. Panting heavily he was able to look round it. He ducked back down. No more than ten feet in front of him stood a man with a shotgun over his shoulder. Beyond him, running in the field, were the dogs. Turned away from Jack so that the lawyer could see only part of his left profile, the man faced south. He then turned towards Jack and looked momentarily in the direction of the wall. That one look was enough. Jack's heart skipped a beat as he recognised Henry Herron.

CHAPTER 5

Rachel awoke with a gagging sensation. The nightmare had been of terrifying beasts and men with reptile tongues. She had a vague recollection of seeing strange people moving around her. Now, wide-awake for the first time, she found herself stretched out on a cot in an old cottage. The interior stone walls were unplastered; mortar had been daubed into the joints between the stones; a fireplace and chimney with a wooden mantelpiece stood at one end of a single room, a wood fire kindled in it. The chimney hadn't been cleaned for some time and acrid smoke from burning logs caught her throat; not much light came in through the narrow windows; a smoke-darkened, pine ceiling stretched out above her. The room was overdone with furniture of poor quality: to her right was a junkyard armchair on wooden legs; a settee of similar provenance; another chair, a rocker, with spindles to prevent the incursion of mice. With a start she remembered the ghoul, who had been her last waking memory. She tried to get up and discovered she was tied down; on her back, wearing a skirt and blouse, she could not recollect having changed from her nightclothes. The sound of the door made her turn. A large man entered, carrying a shotgun, his face pitted with marks like smallpox, possibly the result of malnutrition. His nose was squashed flat and he wore a cap, which couldn't disguise the fact that he was balding. The hair that stuck out beneath the sides of the cap was ginger. She stared at him. The grin widened. "Ah," he doffed his cap and, in an educated voice, totally the opposite of what she had expected, said, "how does our sister duchess bear herself? You've been out cold for four days and nights!"

"Who are you?"

He gazed at her quizzically, a twinkle in his eye. "Guess my name, is it? And before you ask it's not Rumpelstiltskin."

He smiled momentarily, his voice changing to a regional accent. "I could think of better games to play, mind!" He came over to her and ran his hand over her belly. "You thought about that, have you, who put your clothes on? I might have had me leg over already, you never know!" She shuddered in revulsion. "What's the matter? Can't control yourself? Want me that much, do you? Don't you lassies play hard to get any more? Don't you fret now. I like my meat fresh, not hung." He winked. "I'll oblige you when I'm good and ready, just because I'm a gentleman. I can't stand to see a lassie begging."

"Don't be revolting!" she cried.

"Revolting, is it? Know nowt about things like that, don't you? You don't fool me, pet. Your other lovers might be gentle with you, but I took one look at that," with which he paused momentarily to slap her bottom just above the thigh, "and I said she likes a bit of rough and tumble. Besides, I've got inside information. You're said to be very enthusiastic and from the videos I've seen….." He left it hanging there and winked. It was enough for Rachel to realise he knew Max. The man interrupted her thoughts. "Not that I'm a sex offender, mind. No need to be." He changed accent again and affected the educated voice. "Ladies faint in my presence. Virgins long to be deflowered. Housewives plead for passionate embraces." The flashing grin came. "Nae problem, pet. Yous'll be taken care of." He sat down and took an apple out of a dish, which he began to peel with the aid of a knife from a sheath in his belt. "And you know," he added through a mouthful of the fruit, "the quality and the conviction of your performance may ultimately determine another issue."

Rachel struggled to a half-sitting position, her stomach muscles screaming at her to lie down. "What's that?" she asked suspiciously.

The man grinned at her again. Carefully, he peeled another sliver of apple. "The moment of a mutual friend's death. Note I do not say if. I say when," he said and his eyes took on a faraway look as if he was contemplating pleasures beyond the ken of normal men and women, "and he'll be the judge. He'll be sitting right there, dear lady. I'll be able to tell whether it's a convincing performance on your part by the number of tears rolling down his cheeks." He smiled his smile, which flashed on and then off again, giving it a peculiar menace. Rachel remembered suddenly something Jack had told her about a former client. She racked her brains to remember the details of the conversation. "Oh aye," the man went on almost as if she wasn't there, "meanwhile of course I'll be giving it six nowt up there!" His hand traced across her groin. Her whole body convulsed in shock. "I'll be letting 'em fly! Swim on boys! Course, you won't have been on your pill for a while will you?" He seemed to be thinking about this. Looking slyly at her horrified expression, he graced her with the same flashing grin. "Hey, come on hen, there's many a woman would be happy to be chosen to maintain the Herron line! And why not? I'm not proud!" He must have noticed the look in her eyes. "Wey yer bugger, man!" he exclaimed. He put two fingers to his head as if in a mock execution. "I've gone and given me name away. No more spinning straw into gold for you bonny lass. I'll have to take the bairn." He laughed and rumbustiously rubbed her tummy again.

"Aren't you supposed to be dead?" she exclaimed.

"Ha, ha, yes, clever that, wasn't it? I had a good friend who died that I might live. With a new identity, so to speak. Very Christian that, don't you think?"

"Why me?" she asked, "what do you want with me?"

Henry's eyebrows shot up as he stared appreciatively at her body. "Oh, I dare say, I could find a use for you. I'm not too choosey."

"It's Jack, isn't it?" she replied. "You want revenge on him, because you think he did you wrong?"

"Think?" Henry exclaimed. "Twelve frigging years on the block, he cost me! He left me to rot. Twelve years in hell. I was tortured. I spent twelve years in solitary. I lay there in the cold at night dripping wet where they'd turned the power hose on me, no frigging clothes, no blankets. They spat in my food. They pissed in it. They beat the soles of my feet with a stick. They broke my fingers. They kicked me in the balls. Anywhere the bruises wouldn't show!" He was building up to fever pitch now. "He frigging put me there! He had the evidence that the witness was a put up job and he suppressed it."

"Jack wouldn't do something like that."

"He was in the pollis's pocket, man!" Henry exclaimed. "How else could the tape go missing?" Rachel returned his stare and shook her head. She couldn't answer but she knew instinctively that she was right about Jack. Henry smiled craftily again. "But it's not as simple as that, bonny lass. There's more than one agenda here. You see, they all think that Henry Herron is just a workiticket, as thick as pig shit." Changing again to his educated voice, he added, "but I have an I.Q of 159! What I have done is bring about a situation of winner takes all. Three agendas, all dovetailing with the skill of a master craftsman. There is the agenda of Jack the Lad! Then there is the agenda of the wonga, the spondulicks." He pointed at Rachel and gave the flash lamp grin again. She said nothing and let him go on. "Yous've upset some people, bonny lass. One in particular asked me to take care of the business."

"Are we talking something to do with Max?" she asked.

"You're quick. Mind, I can see why he got carried away. It gets between a man and his brains, does that! Course, there's a little localised problem." Henry started to muse again and Rachel waited in trepidation for him to explain further. "It's their lass, you see. The lovely Lorenza. Well, Lorraine she used to be back on the Ridges, but that's nae name for a pop star's tart, is it? The problem is, she's not quite so enamoured of the idea of you warming Max's bed."

"No problem, we're agreed on that one, I can definitely confirm it's all over" Rachel replied.

"Oooh! All not perfect in the garden of love and sensual delights, is it not? Which brings me very conveniently back to my first agenda because you are my payback on the sheister! I'll make the motherfucker eat shit!" He shouted with such venom and came down so close to her with his acrid breath that she cowered back on the bed. He stood glowering over her for a few moments and then grinned again in the same horrible fashion. "You know what it is, it's funny that Maxy thought he was in control. He jumped at it like a shot when I told him my plan to get my own back on Jack the lad. He even came to believe it was his own idea and I must admit he put in a canny couple of embellishments I'd have had difficulty inventing. He wasn't ready for it when it came on top though. Not so frigging evil when the pollises started sniffing about. A' reet when he thought he was untouchable!"

Rachel gazed at him wide-eyed, conscious that it was essential to maintain this dialogue and try and get this madman's confidence. "What's the third agenda?" she asked, trembling.

"Oh, now that's between me and the gatepost," Henry replied. "Revenge, as they say, is a dish best served cold. That one's for me to know and yous to worry about," he teased.

"No, I'll tell you what it is, I'll give yous a little clue. See if you can guess! I'm a believer in the Godfather's philosophy, me."

"What do you mean?" she asked. "Look, you can untie me, can't you? My circulation's being cut off here!"

Henry appeared to think about this for a moment and

then decided she was no risk. Just for good measure he unsheathed his huntsman's knife and drew the flat of the blade slowly across her naked thigh, his tongue between his lips as he watched it. "Just indulging in a bit foreplay!" he told her then he began undoing her bonds. He talked as he worked. "I smelle a Lawyere in the wynde!" he said, "with apologies to Geoff the Chauce and all that." He grinned at her again, the semaphore grin. "Well I've not made it too easy but he's gannin canny. He's already found old gobshite's address."

"Who on earth is old gobshite?"

"My benefactor," he replied. "One Mr. Pardoe. He waved his hands in the air like a Black American preacher. "He gave his blood for the cause. Ha, ha!" Becoming serious again he continued. "By now he'll be running his bollocks off round the county, trying to find out where you are, suspecting someone's kidnapped you. Of course he's also got a suspicion that you've just run away. I like to confuse people. The poor bugger hasn't got a clue who he's dealing with. He thinks it's the bunch of wankers I'm perpetually surrounded by! He'll be here. Tomorrow, the day after tops. You mark my words! We that outlive this day and come safe home will stand a-tiptoe when this day is named!" Rachel's wrists and ankles burned as the blood began to flow again. She looked up in fear as he traced a hand down her silky skin. "Dee us a favour, divn't try and escape, bonny lass." He smiled. "Gorgeous," he added, "you can always tell a well-brought up lass. I'd like to keep you with me. Twelve years maybe. Divn't fret! You'd like it. Six nowt every night. You'd be clammin' for it after t' first time!"

He felt in one of the many pockets of his hunting coat and brought out a flask-shaped bottle of whisky. He swigged back a draught.

Rachel looked at him artfully. "Well, come on, let's have a wee dram?"

Henry handed the bottle over and watched her carefully

as she drank. She took a good swig and his eyes opened in amazement as she carried on glugging it down. Then she paused, wiping the bottle as she handed it back. "Never come across a lassie who could knock it back like that. Wor lass couldn't."

"Sassenach!"

"Aye. Sodding cow and all. Pissed off with the ticket man, didn't she! Gan on, say I'm sorry about that," he mimicked her in a silly voice.

She shrugged. "Might have been a good looking fellow, might have had hidden talents."

Henry found that funny then sat a moment measuring her words. "Aye." He stood up. "Us Herrons own this land." He went to the door. "You stay there, I'm gannin to feed the dogs."

"Can I come with you?"

"Aye, all right, but you'll need your ganzie and I've tellt ye, if you try and escape, I'll set the dogs on you. I divn't give a stuff that you're a bonny lassie. You got that?"

"I got it."

"Good. You'll do for me, hen." He handed her an old jacket. "Put them socks and boots on," he added gruffly. She was astonished at the sudden kindness in his voice and reached out for his arm as they stepped out into the Siberian wind. The gesture was not instinctive but coolly calculated to create a bond between her and her gaoler which would make it more difficult for him to injure her. It appeared to have had the desired effect. "It's been a long winter, this year," Henry mumbled. The dogs came over and sniffed Rachel. Henry opened the door of the ramshackle barn. The front was full of sacks of dog food. He shone his torch. The back was piled high with gear of all descriptions. Boxes of televisions, cartons of cigarettes and other goods. He stepped across and opened one carton. He took out another bottle of whisky.

Rachel looked at him open-mouthed. "I know what you're thinking," he said. He winked at her. "It's all hoisty, right?"

"Aren't you afraid of getting caught in possession of all this?"

"Nah!" He tapped his nose. "I keep it clean. No one bothers me. Any road up, I can produce a receipt for everything I get, show I paid good money for it. Let them prove it's chordy. Not my problem." He started to ladle food into two bowls; the dogs stood expectantly; the one with a tail, the Alsatian, wagged it happily; neither made a move until Henry pointed to the bowls. Rachel stood outside the barn and took the bottle from him again. He put his arm round her. She stiffened. "Howway!" he said, "be nice to me and I'll be nice to you. We're gannin to know each other for a while." He winked at her. She smiled nervously. "The dogs sleep in there," he said gruffly. "And in case you've got any ideas, I leave the door open." Down the hill headlights showed. He turned round, craning his eyes into the darkness. "Just on time," he said, "the rich member of the family." Rachel cursed inwardly. Engrossed in getting to the situation where she could handle him, she hadn't counted on company. A new player in the game could change all the moves she had carefully constructed in the last half-hour. She shivered involuntarily.

CHAPTER 6

Jack stayed hidden behind the rocks. Those dogs, out of control, were certain killers. They were enormous. The Rotweiler was as heavy as a man. With them and their master gone, he plucked up sufficient courage to dodge, bent double, across the field to the wall. He wished he had the mobile. This would be the moment to bring in the police helicopter. At least Joe was on the way or so he hoped. Once safely ensconced behind the wall, he had a view of the front of the house. Beyond it stood a barn with the door open. He saw a flash of eyes in the darkness and realised that was the dogs' kennel. He crouched in the freezing cold for several minutes. Darkness, aided by the odd blizzard whenever the wind changed direction, had taken over completely. Then the sound of the front door told him something was happening. Henry Herron came into view, walking out towards the barn, a rifle slung over his shoulder. The two dogs came out to meet him. Beside him, in an ill-fitting greatcoat and hunter's cap, walked the unmistakable figure of a woman. Jack knew instinctively, from the way she walked, it was Rachel. She wasn't under any restraint. What was more, she and Herron passed a bottle between them and both drank from it. His heart skipped a beat. The dogs appeared friendly, even fawning, towards her. Wild fancies went through his head. He couldn't think rationally. On the verge of standing up and demanding to know what was going on, the sight of the dogs dissuaded him, together with the nagging thought that, despite the lyrics of *Black Jack Davy* running through his head, he had never looked upon a less likely Lothario than the aging Henry Herron. The couple disappeared into the barn and they emerged a few minutes later. Again they passed the bottle. Henry stepped across to Rachel and put his arm round her. She didn't seem to object. This idyllic scene was interrupted by headlamps down the hill. Jack watched in morbid fascination as the dogs went ballistic. The pick-up truck he'd seen earlier from his reconnoitre point pulled up and its two occupants stepped out. One of them petted the dogs then returned Henry's wave. After a few choice and ribald remarks, Jack recognised the apparition of the office staircase and scrap yard. His face as pale as albumen, he was tall and spare with cruel, thin lips. He was totally bald on top but his side hair was tied back in a piratical queue. The only prop missing was the theatrical make up. The other newcomer was obviously female, but well buttoned up against the cold. Rachel looked suddenly less assured. The foursome disappeared into the cottage. He couldn't catch the snatches of conversation because of the wind. The dogs slunk back into the barn for shelter, first of all checking their immediate surroundings for intruders. One of them went up to the vehicle and put its paws up on the sill looking in the window.

☾

Inside the cottage the ghastly looking newcomer spread-eagled himself on the settee while the other went straight to the stove, held both hands out to the warmth then turned to Rachel. "Here we are then," Henry said jovially, "Robin Hood, Little John and Maid Marion here. Well, lassie, meet Mrs. Lorenza Kaliostri and the one and only Blacklock Spiers!" He said the latter name in the manner of the announcement of Billy Spiers from the Beatles' Sergeant Pepper's album.

"You're letting hor wark roond loose?" Spiers asked Henry incredulously.

"Aye. She's all right. She's a pussycat. Wants to join our merry band!"

Henry's colleague looked at Rachel lecherously. "Charm the bords off the trees, you could Henry. You had its kit off yet?"

Lorenza took off her hood. She looked at Rachel coolly. "You little tart!" she said icily.

Blacklock Spiers went through to the kitchen where he could be heard rummaging about in the cupboard. Lorenza looked at Henry and whispered, "do you realise what he's cost us?" The direction of her glance made it clear she referred to Blacklock.

"All in good time, all in good time," Henry replied affably. Rachel had a flash of insight. The third agenda! But why? "Your man would be up here like a bat out of hell if he knew she was here," Henry added, obviously enjoying torturing Lorenza.

Blacklock Spiers came back into the room. He had the cruellest face Rachel had ever seen. She eyed it with revulsion. As white as a sheet, ghoul-like, with mad, staring eyes, Spiers' lips were like bloodless rubber bands; they moved perpetually as he mumbled incoherently. Rachel shook involuntarily with horror at the thought of this fiend laying hands on her. Her covert glances had not, however, gone unnoticed. Spiers fixed her with a baleful glare. "You got a problem, you fucking slapper?" Suddenly he leapt forward like a cat. He grabbed Rachel's arm and twisted it behind her back. He forced her to her knees. Henry licked his lips. It didn't suit his purpose to see everything break down into chaos at this point.

He moved quickly on Spiers, who snickered again, a sound like a snake rustling through the undergrowth. He pointed a finger at his colleague and flung Rachel's arm away. She sprawled on the floor. Lorenza looked at him with loathing. "Don't you think you've caused enough trouble already?"

This had all the hallmarks of an earlier unfinished conversation because Spiers seemed to catch her drift immediately. "I only smacked that lass once. She had it coming, she did. She had a face like a smacked arse. Fucking prick tease!"

"You stupid bastard!" Lorenza shouted. "You ripped her apart! And the other one! What was the excuse that time?"

Spiers' face took on a twisted look. "Wash your mouth out!" he yelled and he leapt across the room, only to be halted by Henry's iron frame.

"Ha'd your horses, hinny," Henry said calmly. "That's my flesh and blood you're talking to!"

"I nah Henry but she's making out I'm off me trolley. Them was accidents."

"Wey aye, man," Henry agreed soothingly. "Shut it," he added, turning to his sister.

"Fine, let me out of here," Lorenza said coldly, "but, before I forget, there's two tickets for the States." She handed an envelope to her delighted brother.

Henry screeched with laughter. "Told you son," he said to Spiers, "it's the Big Apple for us."

"Yee how," Spiers shouted in reply and cavorted round the room, slapping his rump in imitation of a rodeo star.

Lorenza's eyes fluttered up to heaven. "I don't know why you bother with him," she whispered bitterly.

"I have my reasons, an agenda of my own. I wasn't able to have one of those in the past, was I? Where would your man be, though, without people like Blacklock here?"

Lorenza smiled a cold smile. "Headbangers are ten a penny." She thrust her chin out at Rachel. "You'd look good with some acid in your pretty little face!" She stood there, hyperventilating. "Take care of this one Henry." Henry looked nonplussed. He was used to just ordinary sadism. He couldn't fathom the ways of women. "Anyway," Lorenza went on, "run me back down the hill. I've got a plane to catch. He is not to know about this. It must look like an accident. Nice meeting you, dear!" She waved at Rachel sarcastically and gave Blacklock a look of contempt. Sweeping dramatically towards the door, she opened it as a flash of lightning cracked the sky apart. She shrieked and held up both arms like a lightning conductor. Henry nodded to Spiers to accompany her.

"Ah! I just got 'ere," he whined.

"Piss off," Henry said, "no way am I leaving you alone with her!" He indicated Rachel with his thumb. Grumpily, the lanky ghoul grabbed his shotgun and headed off behind Lorenza.

When they had gone, Rachel tried to resume where she'd left off. "It's him you're keeping close, isn't it? He's the one who grassed you up. So Max gave him a job because he's just the kind of psychopath he liked to play at being. It backfired though, didn't it? He's the one who's gone out of control. He's blown everything. Max was just playing games and it all got out of hand!"

"Nae flies on you, hen!" Henry sighed as he polished furiously the barrel of his gun. He handed Rachel the whisky again. "You see," he replied, "people like Maxy are truly evil because they never do their own dirty work. He's no DIY expert, he's got nae toolbox. Instead he's got a satchel full of artisans, people who do the dirty work for him. When he has a use for one he just opens the bag.... and since Blacklock became his right hand man the corpses are gannin' doon faster than a whore's drawers! It was a joke at first, until he did that telly lass and the other bit from Whitley. Have you ever heard of crime passionelle?" He laughed and shook his head. "They'd have been a' reet if they'd just submitted. I divn't nah what it is with these lassies. Putting their lives on the line like that. It's not as if they're virgins." The familiar grin came on and off. "Max put that in his head. You can be whoever you want, he told him. You can be Dracula. The stupid twat took him at his word." He sat looking at her for a few moments and then he added, "he always had a temper, did Blackie. Could go right off it. Mate of ours was a scrapman. He was a good fence was Tony Cooper but he didn't always play it straight. Once when he didn't weigh us off for a load of smokes from a heist, Blackie boy went to try a bit gentle persuasion. One thing led to another and the scrapman parted company with his noodle. I nah. I went doon for it. Ah well, revenge as I said is a dish best served cold."

So that's how it happened, Rachel thought. Jack would have loved that information. It didn't change anything but at least he wouldn't have to blame himself any more that Henry, for whatever weird ethical reason in that criminal circle of his, hadn't spoken up earlier. "You can only play the hand you're dealt," she replied.

Henry's nod of acknowledgment suggested that he thought she was referring to him rather than to Jack.

☽

Jack watched the two newcomers drive away. He gave them a few minutes to get clear. Just when he was plucking up courage to make a move, he saw the lights of the vehicle coming back up the hill and his heart sank. The driver brought the vehicle past the cottage door and parked it close to the wall. Bent double against the blizzard, he ran to the cottage. It occurred to Jack that he might have left the keys in the vehicle. He crossed the gap to the passenger door, opened it and peered in. The key wasn't in the ignition. He was disappointed and about to close the door again, when his attention was caught by something in the well behind the seats. Reaching over he found a gun. His heart was suddenly pounding. Bringing the weapon back to his hiding place, he checked it out. It was a sawn-off, pump action shotgun. There was no sign of the dogs so he risked going through the hole in the wall, up the narrow passage between it and the house and listened at the back door.

☾

Blacklock Spiers reappeared in the doorway, stamping the snow off his boots. Henry looked at him like something the cat had dragged in but it seemed to pass over his gargoyle head. He was actually cheerful. "It's blowing up a corker out there," he said, pointing over his shoulder at the storm. "It's so frigging loud them dogs didn't hear t' van."

Henry poured out two tumblers of whisky until they were both over half full. This time he ignored Rachel and gave one to Blacklock, who downed it without it touching the sides. He handed the glass to Henry for a refill. "Wey yer bugger," Henry said good-naturedly. They must have gone through three or four glasses like that and both looked flushed. They became raucous and started to reminisce, first about street fights and then past sexual conquests, screeching with laughter when anything took them as particularly funny. "Fancy a game of cards?" Henry said at length. He took a pack of cards from the wooden mantelpiece. "Brag?" he asked.

"Poker," Spiers replied.

"Suit yourself." Henry cast a wicked glance at Rachel. "Just keep yourself still, hen. You'll see plenty of action soon."

"Ye-ee-es!" Blacklock gloated. He leaned over Rachel and grabbed her backside in a shovel-like hand. "I fancy the tradesman's entrance, me. I've seen a few blues of yous, whore!" The men played a couple of hands, a few coins changing places in front of them, then Blacklock said, "what about making it more interesting?"

Henry poured out a couple more glasses. "What? Upping the ante?"

Blacklock looked at Rachel. "Strip poker?" he leered.

"Fancy a private viewing, do you?" Henry stood up and reached over to Rachel, taking her arm roughly. "Get over here!" he ordered. Shaking, she obeyed. Any gentlemanly tendencies Henry might have shown in private would not be repeated in this company. With one movement of his hand Blacklock ripped her blouse open. "Look at them!" he enthused. He pulled Rachel roughly towards him, groping her thigh, and tried to kiss her. She struggled. "No," she yelled. She tried unsuccessfully to keep the tremor out of her voice and looked entreatingly at Henry, who ignored her. Suddenly, she was hit across the legs from behind and she fell to the carpet. "Get your fat backside on the floor you cow or I'll hev ye where you fucking stand," Blacklock shouted.

"I bet you've not seen fanny like that for a while," Henry said nonchalantly. Blacklock was breathing heavily. "Come on," Henry said, "deal her in."

Shaking with fear, Rachel composed herself. She concentrated. They played a number of hands and at the end of each one of the men had to remove an item of clothing. "Bollocks to it!" Blacklock shouted on the fourth occasion. "This is fucking ridiculous!"

"What's wrong with you?" Henry chuckled good-naturedly.

"When's she gannin to take summick off? She's cheating, hor!"

"She's not cheating. She's just better than you!"

"I'm tekkin nae more of this!" Blacklock stood up and started to unzip his jeans. Rachel looked on horrified.

"Howway!" Henry said. "You haven't won yet. That's what's wrong with you, bonny lad, you never play by the rules. It's not the first time I've told you."

"Nae tart is taking the piss out of me," Blacklock whinged

on, "if you cannot see what she's doing that's your look out. If you ask me, she needs one thing." He strutted up and down, beside himself with rage.

Rachel thought, it's now or never. "He's not taking you to New York, you know," she chipped in.

Blacklock looked at her askance. So did Henry. "What d' yous mean?" Blacklock asked suspiciously.

"He's not taking you anywhere, you tosspot," Rachel shouted fierily. "He's done time for you once. You've been useful to him, but you don't seriously think that a man with an I.Q of 159 is going to spend a minute longer with you than necessary, do you? He's going to have you for getting him sent away!"

She had obviously hit a nerve and the effect was immediate. Blacklock jumped up as if he'd had an electric shock. "Shite! You'd better not fuck with me, Herron!" Realising the mind game was up, Henry nutted him. Blacklock shot over the sofa backwards and ended up in a crumpled heap on his back, his gangly legs still hanging over the rear of the chair. Rachel seized the moment to head for the door. Henry, catching her movement out of the corner of his eye, lurched after her but as he passed the sofa, Blacklock, back on his feet, stuck two fingers in his eyes. "Bastard!" Henry shouted as he reeled backwards. Blacklock followed up with his boots, kicking Henry in the groin. "Right," Henry yelled, "it's been coming for a bit. Yous've got twelve years to pay for now young 'un." They drew blood from each other and lurched sideways over a table, smashing it like matchwood. With his ear to the back door, Jack could hear raised voices. Something was brewing. He listened closely. There were thumps and crashes then the noise died down. Rachel reached the front door, hoping the dogs hadn't been aroused by the commotion. The two crooks hammered away at each other on the floor; they hadn't noticed Rachel had gone. Outside the icy wind buffeted her just as Jack moved round the front. To his astonishment a figure appeared round the corner. He immediately dove back behind the wall. The game was up. A blizzard still blew from the north and he couldn't see the intruder properly, but this might be the chance he was waiting for, an opportunity to divide their forces. With the firearm he had half a chance. Rachel reached the hole in the wall and stumbled through it just as a figure reared up in front of her. She was astonished to see Jack. He had leapt up to make the challenge, then realised it was Rachel. Drawing her to him, the surprise turned to delight. She hugged him and he removed his large jacket and put it round her shoulders. A commotion at the house told them they had no time to lose. Questions could wait. Jack started to lead her up the hill. "Quick," he said, "come on." She fitted her arms into the jacket as they ran. "Come on, come on!" Jack shouted, close to panic. A flash came from behind and a shot echoed out over the fell. "Come on!" he shrieked. "I'm coming," she panted. Another shot rang out but they were lost in the blizzard. They reached the rocks and he hugged her. "How...?" she started but he hushed her with a finger.

He took the rope from the belay at the top of the crag and said, "come on, it's the only way down." He fashioned a makeshift harness from the two slings. "I'll have to lower you," he said. "You won't need your hands. When you get down, just unclip the karabiner like this," – he demonstrated with his free hand – "and let the rope out. Leave the knot in. Whatever you do don't untie the knot in the end of the rope." She was looking at him a little bemused but repeated what he'd said until she had it by rote. "What about you?"

"I'll ab off, don't worry about me." Jack put his pack on her back. "There are things in there you may need," he said. Then he handed her the gun and added, "carry this for me. It may come in handy." He didn't say in case he didn't get down.

He clipped the Sticht plate into the krab on his belt and said, "go on then!" She looked terrified as she stood on the lip of The Beard. "Just walk off," he said, "I've got you." She smiled bravely and stepped back into the abyss, one hand clutching the shotgun. He had no time to lower her slowly and she descended into the bottomless pit at a rate of knots. A growl told Jack he'd been rumbled. He turned round and saw the Rottie there. It glared at him menacingly, its eyes rolling. It snarled. The bottom of the climb was well banked up and Jack could see from the mark on the rope it was past the half-way point so he let it go quickly. Rachel would land in the snow and she would be down safe and sound.

Henry Herron appeared over the top of the crag. He looked at Jack and, momentarily, he didn't recognise him. Then the look on his face became one of astonishment as his brain tried to compute. Eventually, he smiled that old familiar smile. "Wey yer bugger, Jack," he said, "that was a soon louse. I did not expect you that sharp. Where's that lass of yours?" He looked round as if he'd just noticed she wasn't there. "Come out, bonny lass!" Jack smiled grimly. Henry had seriously underestimated him. He sensed also the dog's fear of the slippery rocks. Slowly, with deliberate movements, he pulled in the rope until it felt slack. He hoped against hope she hadn't fallen heavily. Surreptitiously he took from his pocket the figure-of-eight descender and hooked the rope into it. The movement wasn't quick enough to escape Henry's attention. Craning his eyes into the darkness, he said, "looka, Jack!" He had obviously spotted the rope. "Howay Samson," he added. In the face of a command, the dog didn't disobey. It leapt over the first rocks. Jack already had the figure-of-eight clipped into the karabiner on his belt. He hoped Rachel had obeyed him and just slipped out of the krab. That lower knot might be the only thing between him and a thousand broken bones, provided it didn't rip through the pro. The dog threaded its way carefully down the rocks until it was about six feet above him. Jack looked up and saw it primed to pounce. He felt slack on the rope. "Kill, Samson!" the command came. The dog crouched to spring and Jack did the same. An owl shrieked up on the hill. "Hear it, Jack!

It is a knell
that summons thee to heaven,
or to hell."

Henry laughed. The dog sprang. It hurtled towards Jack. Simultaneously, he leapt backwards. Man and dog fell together in a bizarre dance in space. The dog's fangs inches from his throat, Jack held the trailing rope behind him. The dog didn't appreciate the danger. The rope snagged as the knot stuck in the krab, pulling Jack up with a jerk. The dog's teeth ripped his side as it hit him. It howled as it hurtled into space. Jack dangled there in the darkness. He looked down into the abyss, confident the dog couldn't survive a fall like that. It was bound to hit the rock band at the halfway point. He looked up and saw Henry's face staring frantically into the gloom. Spinning on the rope, he pendulumed into the wall and struck with the axe. Its point held him against the rock. He got hold of the bottom of the rope and flicked it, trying to free it. A roar of rage from above alerted him to Henry, lying over the top of the chasm, cursing for all he was worth. Henry tugged at the rope, trying to rip it out of its socket, but he couldn't make it budge. With horror Jack saw the villain had a knife. He grinned at Jack. "Do not go gentle into that dark night!" he yelled. The rope was like piano wire. The blade's touch would fragment it into a thousand strands. Jack kicked for the cliff again and struck with the axe, finding purchase for his crampons at the same time. The knife touched the rope and it exploded. He felt a momentary shudder as he lost support from above, but the toe-hold and one axe point saved him. Groping for his other axe, he started to kick down the ice wall. Above, Henry pointed his rifle and let off a couple of barrels, but the bulges in the ice prevented a direct hit. However, an ominous crackling told Jack the shots had started an avalanche. He could see momentarily the fear on Henry's face as he thought he was about to be swept over. He scrambled back into the darkness as the top of the crag came roaring down, just as Jack passed the rock band. To his right he glimpsed the shattered body of the Rotweiler, then the avalanche struck. He tried to clutch on to the rock face, but the weight was too much and it plucked him off. Managing somehow to keep his head he swam to the top of the moving snow only to hit a thicker band. He was buffeted up in the air and then, descending again, this time the wrong way round, he tried desperately to right himself and swim upwards so that when the avalanche came to rest he would be as close to the surface as possible. He came to a halt, tried to move upwards, but couldn't make headway against the compressed snow. On the verge of suffocation he thought only of one thing. "Go, Rachel!" he tried to shout but his lungs filled with snow.

CHAPTER 7

Rachel saw the whole mountain pile on top of Jack. For a moment, she was going to lie down and give up then she heard a ghostly cry on the wind and picked herself off the ground. Treading gingerly across the snow-covered scree, a fantastic figure against the bleak, black and white landscape, picked out by the odd flash of ghostly electricity, she was conscious that a broken ankle now would mean game over. She had the uncanny feeling that she wasn't alone. Several times she looked back, imagining footsteps clambering over the glittering boulders. After about half an hour she emerged on to the fringes of the forest. She could hear the sound of a motor vehicle, working its way down the track. If she could hole up somewhere until morning she'd have a chance but she'd have to stay off the main drag. She looked at the sky. It had started to snow again. Staggering across the floor of the forest, her feet crunched the frosted bark.

She must have walked for the best part of an hour and she was in trouble. Rescued from one ordeal, she'd stumbled into another. The one man who had done anything to help her was dead. Fatigue showed on her face. She needed rest. Through the swirling snow she saw a light in the darkness and headed towards it. A circle of large, erect stones glowed eerily in the dark. Striking a match from the emergency pack in Jack's coat, she had a snapshot of the place. It looked like a miniature Stonehenge. In the dying flame she saw a cave undercut into a cliff. The recess was about ten feet in height, full of fallen leaves, enough to act as a cushion. At the entrance she constructed a makeshift fire of leaves and twigs and other forest debris, dry enough to kindle. She gathered branches from the fringes of the clearing and built them behind the fireplace so its light wouldn't be obvious. Hastily constructing the firewood into a pyramid, adding more branches, she lit it. The glow from the flames cast fantastic shadows but Rachel's face softened in the firelight, the pain leaving it. The flames crackled cheerfully and she moved closer, holding out her hands for warmth. Pulling Jack's coat tight round her, she felt suddenly as if he was there, enveloping her in his arms. She saw his smile and heard his warning. *Don't drop your guard*! She glanced round warily and moved out of the firelight into the stone circle, gathering as many branches as she could to keep the fire healthy. She kept the rifle with her. When she'd gathered enough fuel, she sat down and thought of Jack. She tried to think of him positively but each time she saw those tons of snow and ice sliding down the mountain and broke into tears. She carried the gun on her lap and her spirits improved a little. She looked at the fantastic shapes of the standing stones. The neatness of their placement suggested they were no natural phenomena. Crying herself to sleep, fingers on her shoulder made her sit up shaking. There was nothing there. The fire had died down but life in the embers made her prod at it, feeding it branches, pushing them down over the glowing ashes. She bent down and blew gently to kindle a flame. Satisfied with her efforts, she stood up and glanced out into the circle. Her body stiffened in shock. Animal eyes reflected the flame then disappeared. An owl hooted, flitting in eerie silence across the clearing. Out in the wood, twigs cracked. The thunder rumbled as the storm circled. Bent double Rachel moved to the edge of the clearing. Her hair stood on end as electricity cracked in the atmosphere. Suddenly, the Alsatian roared through the undergrowth. She turned to run but it hit her, its teeth bared. The impact made her drop the gun. She reached up for the beast's neck, but its teeth clamped on her wrist and tore the flesh as she tried to pull free. It bit her all over the body as she grabbed hold of its fur. She flung it round against the rock. It yelped and readied itself for another attack. She picked up the gun as it jumped for her throat. The dog was dead when it hit her. Calmly she began to reload, aware the shots had blown her cover. Her fingers felt as if they had been stitched together in the cold. She looked up suddenly as she heard a sound in the bushes and then recoiled in shock as Blacklock Spiers appeared. Flecks of saliva at the corners of his mouth set off the madness in his eyes. Hurriedly she fed in the cartridge but the ghoulish figure was fast. Before she could retrain the weapon he had devoured the space and flung himself at her. His blood-curdling scream rooted her to the spot and his heavy body crashed into hers, knocking her to the ground. "Heh, heh!" he chortled in a wheezy voice, "so you thought you'd lost me, did yous?" The lanky man had his hand across her mouth to stop her screaming. She could smell his stale sweat, see the cut-throat razor clasped between bony fingers. Lecherous hands started to reach for her clothes and his knees forced her thighs apart. Chuckling merrily he talked in his sibilant whine. "You can scream if you want. I like to hear lasses scream. Gan on. Nae one will hear yous. You know what I'm gannin to dee, divn't yous? How long do yous think yous'll survive after I've had me way? I don't mind if yous're alive or dead. I'll dee it anyway." Rachel braced herself for the pain as the ghoul unbuckled his belt and slipped down his trousers. "Very cold it is, brass monkeys weather, but not for long, soon it's gannin to be very warm, ha, ha!" He hovered over her. Just as he was about to thrust, his head shot back. At first Rachel couldn't see why and then, as Spiers was heaved, screaming and struggling, from her prone body, she saw that Henry had sneaked up and grabbed him by the queue.

He grinned at Rachel. "Ill met by moonlight, my proud Titania!"

"Gerroff us Henry!" Spiers yelled.

"Get off you. No way, young un, no way at all! In fact, this is where I settle a few scores. Like who did the crime and who did the time! He's buried here, isn't he? Wor Tony. We had a deal, didn't we? Whatever happened neither of us would grass on t' other. Like all gentlemen's agreements, they're nae good if there's only one gentleman!" He winked at Rachel as if she was a co-conspirator.

"Henry, that's history," Blacklock wailed.

"History, I nah, son, like twelve years of my life fucking history!"

"Henry, I never made any statement. It was Barry Freer, he paid off the witnesses!"

"I didn't hear you giving evidence at the trial, hinny. No, must have missed that. Funny, I was concentrating hard."

"I couldn't Henry, yous nah that. They'd have put in me form if I'd said the lad was a liar!"

"You know what it is," Henry went on, "I had a lot of time to think about this and I came to the conclusion that you and Freer did a deal. You got a manslaughter, out in 6 months and I was weighed off, because you didn't speak up." He looked down at Rachel confidingly. "One nil to yous, pet. I kept this workiticket close. I told Mick to get him on the team. I didn't plan it quite like this but Jack changed the rules a bit. Where is he, by the way? Took flight has he, leaving you here? Well, that's not very chivalrous, is it? Funny what can happen to bonny lassies in these hills, these here Herron hills! Jack! Jack! Where is he lassie? Not trying to sneak up on us are you, Jack? None of your dirty lawyer tricks, mind!" Henry yanked

Blacklock's head further back and a large hunting knife in his right hand touched the screaming ghoul's throat. "A'reet when you're handing it out, hinny, battering some screaming lassie? Not much at the sharp end, are you?" Blacklock's screams went up another decibel as the knife drew blood, just a thin thread at first. Confident, Henry released Blacklock and kicked him all round the clearing, Blacklock knelt, shouting and bawling, pleading with Henry to show mercy. Henry gazed at him and appeared to relent. "Aye, all right, then, bonny lad," he said, "I can see you've learned your lesson, you'll never be arguing with your dad again, will you?" Blacklock swore he would do anything Henry wanted: give himself up; admit the Cooper murder; clear the Herron name. This seemed to make Henry's attitude soften. Then, as the whimpering thug lifted his face from the floor, Henry heaved his head back by the pony tail and slashed deep and long across the carotid arteries. The effect on Blacklock was electric. He bounced up into the air like an unco-ordinated puppet, a shocked expression on his face. Then he fell over on his back and lay still. Cursing loudly, Henry kicked the rag doll of a body with an almost superhuman frenzy. "Ye-e-e-es!" he shouted. His teeth clenched in exultation, he turned towards Rachel with a mad expression. Still flat on her back, Rachel fired the shotgun. The shot flung Henry backwards and he lay winded for a moment. Then, to the young woman's horror, he clambered unsteadily to his feet. She pointed the gun again but, before she could pull the trigger, he pointed at her and said, "fucking Amazon, you, pet!" With that he staggered off into the forest. Rachel retreated to her cave. He could only come from one direction. Hailstones rattled on the standing stones like a celestial vibraphone; lightning ripped the sky apart; thunder rolled out towards the sea. Rachel couldn't afford to sleep. She had one cartridge left.

CHAPTER 8

Towards morning the snow stopped. Plucking up the courage to peep out of the cave, Rachel's eyes took in the carnage of the stone circle. She crept towards the place where Henry had disappeared and smiled thinly at the trail of blood leading into the forest. Surely he couldn't have survived that? Even so she walked cautiously in the direction of a glow in the east. It grew in intensity as she approached and it wasn't the sunrise. That's a fire, she thought. She moved towards it with greater purpose, the gun slung over her shoulder, keeping one eye open all the time. A fire might mean the emergency services and rescue. The first thing to do was get them to dig out Jack's body. She came to the top of a rise and looked down at where the lightning had struck. Two or three hundred pines must have been alight in the clearing and on the track a yellow giant of a machine had frozen in the act of uprooting trees in its great steel claw before being abandoned by its driver. Its paint was blistering in the heat. She looked back along the road and saw skid marks. They deepened as she neared, stretching at least fifty yards. Curiosity getting the better, she walked over to inspect the seat of the fire. Peering over the dyke at the edge of the road, she realised what had happened. In the dene stood the battered, burnt-out hulk of a Mercedes sports car. She picked her way down until she could see, in the driver's seat, impaled on the jagged end of a branch held in the steel claw of the earthmover, the body of a woman. The long, jet-black hair was a giveaway. "I hope they make sure you're buried with that through your heart," she muttered unkindly.

The voice from behind took her by surprise. "I knew you'd survive," it said, "I'd have given odds on it."

☾

Jack thought exactly the same. "I knew you would survive," he told her. "I'd have given odds on those guys going up against you."

"How did you get out of that avalanche?" she asked. It was more matter-of-fact than seemed appropriate but wasn't that always Rachel's way, to take him down a peg or two when he took himself too seriously?

"Ah, now there's a little trick," he replied, " a technique but you need some luck!" A troubled silence indicated a problem. It had to be addressed. "I was thinking," he said.

"That explains the strange noise."

"About a couple of things that happened. I mean, Jessica Parker for instance. It was you who told me she was dead."

"Ye-es."

"How must you have loathed me to go to that kind of trouble!"

"Not loathed you, Jack. We were both victims of mind games."

"Everyone wanted me to think Max was a killer. He knew, sooner or later I'd make a prize idiot of myself. I nearly did. If Lowther hadn't been so sceptical…" Jack waited for a reaction. There was none. "Is it just me or is that really evil? I mean, would words like betrayal be out of context?"

She bit her lip momentarily and then she replied. "What do you want to do, Jack? Leave the stone where it is or roll it back?"

Jack realised he was alone. Ah, yes. Roll back the stone. Unearth the contents of the cave; uncover the well; discover that everyone is a mine of contradictions. Jack dragged in air and a throatful of snow. On the verge of suffocating, he realised it didn't matter what had gone before. There was no right or wrong Rachel. If only he could speak to her he wouldn't waste his time with recrimination. He'd tell her he wasn't looking for an angel; everyone makes mistakes. There is nothing in human relations, no evil, no viciousness, no meanness of spirit, no act of treachery, which cannot be forgiven if it is approached in the spirit of love. Jack wanted to tell her, *I love you and nothing else matters.* The hardest of history's lessons is one taught by Christ and the Buddha: that revenge is not the way of redemption. But then, totally helpless, pinned under tons of snow, the air in the pocket all but exhausted, Jack knew he was kidding himself. Some fences can't be mended – the livestock has already been rustled; some bridges can't be built – the flood has breached the banks. He thought of the men and women who had terrorized him as a child. They were adults, possessed, he had then believed, of special powers. That wasn't true. They were pathetic creatures, frightened of the light of day; he could crush their bones between thumb and forefinger. Evil isn't a supernatural force; it is the product of human fear long before it is fear's creator; it is a tawdry and cheap thing peddled by those who have lost their souls and live in darkness; it is the way of the fear of oblivion. Dignity is the quality it fears most and those who have it evil cannot buy.

The defining moments of his life stretched away like stones across a river: the death of his parents; his treatment by those intended to care for him; his resulting love of solitude and the high mountains. Then there was his near-death experience. Since then he had felt diminished. He had had one foot in the grave. A wind not unlike cold, clammy, human breath touched his cheek and made his hair stand on end. He heard the whispered chant of the bringer of death. It is nearly time, he thought, and despite all the sadness of things not done, words not spoken, of the diffidence that had faltered, he knew all roads reach here. Since his accident he had lived on borrowed time. From the closing of that day he had been no more than a cipher, a shade out of Hades. Was it because his time had been borrowed that he had faded more and more each day? Or was it simply the way of life that, with every knock and each small compromise, once bright things pale into shadows? Suddenly Jack wanted desperately to survive.

☾

Rachel turned towards the voice. Max sat in the cab of the earthmover. Something about his posture, his body language, made her uneasy. She had grown over time to detest someone whom she had once believed the love of her life. Under no illusions that he was deranged, she watched as, with cat-like grace, he leapt from the vehicle. "Yes, quality always shines through," he said, a sickly smile suffusing his features. "And here I was expecting trouble! I came here to obtain your release from my crazy brother-in-law and you walk into my arms! Henry must be losing it. I don't know, though, you can't choose family, can you? I bet there is more trouble caused through families than anything else in the world. Why, the history of Europe is just one big family squabble!" He tutted as if he found it all too tiresome for words. "Still, as long as you're all right, my dear?" he added brightly. "You'll have noticed that the impediment to our long-term happiness has been mysteriously removed. Well, the Lord does work in mysterious ways!" A wide sweep of his arm took in the body impaled in the car. It evoked no pity in either of them but for wholly different reasons.

Rachel took courage in both hands. "Don't get the wrong idea. I'm not returning to you, Max."

"Not returning to me?" Max pulled a face. "And after I put together a king's ransom to placate the black sheep? Of course, my dearest Lorenza was working with him to cheat me! Can you credit that? I should have got rid of her when I could!" He spread his coat like a raven's wings and preened himself. "Justice has been done," he gloated, "at least to one of them."

"I don't know what happened to you, Max," Rachel replied, "but, take it from me, I'm free of you now. You disgust me." She turned her back and began to walk away but Kaliostri ran after her and grabbed her arm. He put a finger to her lips and she recoiled as she tasted something unpleasantly acid. "You're not going with him!" he said quietly. "I can't allow that."

Her face looked suddenly drained but she forced herself to look Kaliostri in the eye, forgetting that was a mistake. "If you mean Jack, he is dead," she said. "He died in an avalanche."

"Ah!" Kaliostri held both arms up to the sky as if in supplication. "I knew," he said, "I felt it!" He began to chant rhythmically. Nervously Rachel cast a glance over his shoulder. Something had caught her eye but whatever it was had gone. "Now look at me, Rachel," Max continued, "you know you want to, come on, look me in the eyes and tell me you don't want to come with me." Rachel averted her eyes, uncertain of her ability to resist the musician's snake-like charm. He began to move around her, spreading his cloak in a hypnotic dance. She could hear music as he circled her, never taking his gaze from her face. Moving his arms, he danced slowly. He hung there a moment. There it was again. Someone stood over near the earthmover smoking a cigarette. She saw its glow in the dark as the person inhaled. "Who's that?" she asked.

"Oh come on, come on, baby! You can't distract me!"

The smoker disappeared. "You need a minder, even to deal

with me?" she asked scornfully but even as she spoke she felt her senses swim. She gritted her teeth; she'd fallen for it, one of Max's tricks – drugs or hypnosis or both. She could still taste the acid. Awareness heightened, from some distance she heard the beat of heavy wings. A bird fluttered through the trees, its dark wings crashing through the spruce fronds. A moment later she screamed as it brushed her face. Another followed and another. She began to run. Raucous cries and swirling shadows pursued her flight through bushes glistening with frost. Max shouted gleefully and began to caper and cavort as if he had lost his senses.

The Bandido, racing his four-wheeled truck up the forest road, saw a young woman run across in front of him, pursued by demons only she could see. "Funny place, this, but don't I know her?" he asked himself. He turned and looked backwards as she ran into the forest and didn't see the man emerge behind her in hot pursuit. Bang! The vehicle smacked into Max Kaliostri. He went up in the air and over the bonnet, slamming up against the windscreen, his mouth wide open, a bewildered expression on his face. Joe stopped the vehicle and got out. "Bloody hell!" he said. He looked up just as the Boulmer rescue helicopter appeared, chopping the air in thick swathes as it descended. Frantically, Joe waved it down. He was on the horns of a dilemma. There was an injured man on the ground but the lass could be the clue to finding Jack. He made a decision and ran off into the forest.

Exhausted, Rachel stopped. Still for a moment, she detected a scurrying noise. Turning, she started in fright. On the bush in front of her a spider had spun a fine, frosted filigree of web. It covered the foliage, filling every nook and cranny. The scurrying noise was the spider crawling along the wire. An insect, caught in the web, screamed with a human voice. Her head told her this couldn't be happening but she couldn't take her eyes off the creature as the beast bore down on it. The insect had her face; it looked towards her in an agony of fear. "Oh my God!" Rachel screamed as she felt the black, long-legged hairiness envelop her. Henry Herron materialized from the bush.

"Thrice the brindled cat did mew,
thrice and once the hedge-pig whined,
Harper cries, 'tis time, 'tis time!"

His tunic was bloodstained at the shoulder but the shot had caught him flush in the chest. Rachel's hand trembled. What value now the remaining cartridge if the last, from point blank range, had done so little damage? Even so she trained the weapon. Henry leered, seeming to invite it. He stood still, his chest thrust forward in conceit.

A voice behind Rachel made them both jump. "Wey, Henry, they never let a dipstick like you out! And now you're gannin' round molesting young lassies! I don't know." Overcoming his initial shock, Henry recognized the Bandido immediately. "It's none of your business, Joe," he growled in reply but his body tensed as if for action. He didn't fool himself. He was no match for this formidable opponent but he had a trick or two up his sleeve. "Wey, I'm not too sure about that, bonny lad," the Bandido responded as if he was calmly arguing some logic in court. "A good marra of mine came here to find this lassie and here she is with you. You may know him? Pretty unorthodox brief, name of Jack Lauder?"

Rachel didn't know who her saviour was but she had her wits sufficiently about her to speak up now. "This guy was trying to kill Jack. He took me prisoner to lure him into a trap. Jack saved me. He went down in an avalanche." She turned to Herron. "You killed him!" she accused.

"Oh dear," Joe added with a quiet menace in his voice, "I'm a great believer in the bible me, hen. Eye for an eye and all that! It's not that easy to get a good brief these days, y' nah!"

"Moi?" Henry, conscious of the Bandido's legendary

prowess, played the innocent. "Wey not likely. I just wanted a bit crack with me former brief, that's all." Saying that he started to turn away, surreptitiously removing the handgun tucked in his belt. The Bandido, with an instinct for danger, was already diving to his right. Two shots rang out: Henry's missed; Rachel's took his head off his shoulders. Heavy-winged birds flew screeching into the air; somewhere a pack of dogs yelped. In the silent aftershock, Joe scrambled to his feet. He turned the decapitated villain with his toe, revealing a Kevlar jacket. Rachel nodded knowingly. "I thought I couldn't have missed the first time!" she exclaimed as she saw the reason for Henry's apparent invulnerability.

"Where did you learn to shoot like that bonny lass?" Joe asked in admiration.

"I'm a Highlander," Rachel replied, "I could get my own breakfast before I was five."

The Bandido threw back his head and laughed. "Jack was a lucky lad when he found you, pet." Then a frown appeared on his face and he concentrated. "An avalanche, you say?" Joe looked thoughtful. "You know, I did some climbing in the SAS. You need some nerve for that game. Forget about that three points of contact stuff."

Rachel looked at him expectantly as he paused. "So?" she replied. "What's your point?"

"It might be a few years back but he's very experienced, that old bugger," Joe replied. "He's been in more landslides than a tip wagon. Are you any good at geography, hen? Can you find your way back there?"

"No problem," she replied, irrationally filled with hope.

When they got back to Joe's vehicle Kaliostri was nowhere to be seen. However, paramedics were trying to prise Lorenza from the tree; the helicopter's propeller circled slowly as it stood waiting. "What happened to the gadgie who was here?" Joe asked the paramedics. He looked at the dead woman. "Nasty that," he added. The chief of the paramedics looked at him uncomprehendingly. "What gadgie?"

"The bloke I hit, the one who ran out of the bushes. He was there, on the ground."

The paramedic looked mystified. "I didn't see anyone," he replied. "There was another chopper on the ground before us. You can see for yourself. There's only this one and she's beyond help."

Shaking his head, Joe bundled Rachel into the passenger seat and drove off. "I ran a bloke over," he told her. "It was his fault like. But he's disappeared."

"Max!" She shivered. "He always escapes. He stirs everything up and when it comes on top he's out of there. He'll turn up, like a bad penny."

Joe looked at her silently. "Aye, well he'll have a headache for a while, that's for sure," he replied gruffly.

The vehicle sped across country until they came to the frozen waterfall of the Beard. Pulling to a halt beneath the avalanche spoil, they noticed two lads up the hill digging in the snow beneath a needle of rock. "Bullseye," Joe said, "I think this is it, bonny lass." Joe took a spade out of the boot and marched up the scree, Rachel close behind. "What yous deein' lads?" Joe shouted.

"Someone nicked our climbing gear," one of them said. "We've found some of it."

"That's nae tea leaf, marra, that's Jack the lad," Joe replied. "He went down in the avalanche. Dig bonny lads, dig for your lives!" He began to set the example. "Jack!" he called, shovelling furiously. One of the lads threw Rachel a spade and she set to with equal fury, the effects of the drug wearing off at last. "No one could survive that," the other lad groaned, downing tools momentarily to mop his forehead. Tons of snow and spoil disappeared over the Bandido's shoulder as he grafted like a navvy. "You just keep digging, son," he replied with sufficient menace to make the youth rush to retrieve the implement.

☾

It was strange watching all this from the top of the needle, the sunrise giving warmth to the rock. It felt so comfortable Jack didn't want to move. Voices meandered up like lazy smoke. He wondered momentarily if he had passed to the other world and was privileged now to watch the toil of humanity below. Should he tell them about the chimney where the rock face met the spoil or just sit like the Buddha and smile? The arcs of the spades, glinting in the sunlight, were almost hypnotic. Soon he would call them to a halt and watch the expression in Rachel's eyes.